GIO

GIO

(5th Street #2)

By Elizabeth Reyes

Danielle,

wishing you all the best!

Elizabeth Reyes

GIO

Elizabeth Reyes
Copyright © 2012
All Rights Reserved.

Dedicated to D. You are the closest I've ever had to a sister. Your love and support has gotten me through some of the worst times in my life. You are truly the most selfless and giving person I've ever met. I love you SO much!

PROLOGUE

The bloody mouthpiece flying through the air in slow motion as Trinidad's lifeless body hit the floor was just one of the things from that day that would forever be seared into Giovanni Bravo's memory. The screaming was the other. The ref jumped in front of Gio as if he'd even think of still going after Trinidad.

Trinidad lay there completely out and within minutes it was chaos. He wasn't breathing. The buzzing in Gio's ears got louder as the medics jumped into the ring and began trying resuscitation. People in the audience stood in motionless silence, most holding their hands to their mouths looking as stunned as Gio felt. He froze where he stood not even noticing that Abel and Jack stood by his side.

They started CPR on Trinidad, pounding forcefully on his chest. That's when the screaming started. The paramedics placed him on a stretcher continuing to pound on his chest. Trinidad's pregnant wife's screams grew louder as a few people struggled to hold her back.

"You okay?" Jack asked, looking very concerned.

Gio glanced at him for a moment nodding but his eyes went back to the stretcher now being rushed out of the stadium. "He's not responding," he heard himself say.

"He'll be okay," Abel said, placing his hand on Gio's shoulder. "He just went down pretty hard."

Trinidad was pronounced dead before he ever

reached the hospital. Dead at only twenty-two—and Gio had killed him.

CHAPTER 1

The broadcaster on the small television in Gio's garage, stood outside the cemetery where services for Trinidad had been held. The light from the television screen was the only thing that illuminated the otherwise dark garage. Gio wasn't even listening anymore. He'd stopped listening hours ago but still, he sat there on his Raiders beanbag, like he had for days, staring at the screen.

The knock at the door was soft and he didn't bother responding. Someone opened it anyway and walked in. Gio's eyes never left the screen that now panned out, showing the mourners entering their cars as the recording of the broadcast of the services played on. Trinidad had been buried days ago. Gio had already watched this footage repeatedly. Just like the first time, he felt numb each time he watched it again but he couldn't tear himself away from the television.

"Hey."

Without looking away from the screen, Gio lifted his chin. It was the only response he showed to hearing his best friend Noah's voice.

"Roni made zucchini bread. She wanted me to bring you some."

"Cool. Tell her I said thanks."

Noah took a step forward pulling the string above Gio's head to turn the lights on and turned off the television. "You gotta stop this, G. Your mom's worried. She asked me to come over and talk to you. I was going to anyway. Everyone's worried, man."

"About what?" Gio said, staring at the floor and tossing the remote aside. "I'm not the one who's dead."

"So what? Because his life is over, yours is, too?" Noah sat down on an ice chest near Gio. "What happened sucks, Gio, but he knew the risks when he stepped into that ring. Hell, we all do. It's a tragic thing but you can't blame yourself."

Gio finally turned to face Noah. "What do you mean I can't blame myself? Who else is there to blame? I'm the one that took the shot at him. I ended that guy's life."

"Boxing ended his life! You just happened to be the opponent in the ring with him at the time. If it hadn't been you it would've been the next fighter he faced. He had a pre-existing condition for Christ's sakes. If anyone is to blame, it's whoever cleared him to fight. He should've never been in there in the first place."

Gio stood up, hands at his waist and paced. "What's gonna happen to his wife?"

"That's not your problem, G. I know it sounds shitty but—"

"You're damn right it sounds shitty!" Gio stopped and glared at Noah. "She's pregnant. What's wrong with you?" As long as he lived, those agonized screams would haunt him.

"Look." Noah lifted his hand. "All I'm saying is she has a family. She'll be taken care of. You shouldn't burden yourself worrying about that right now. You should worry about this." Noah pointed at Gio's forehead. "You're my friend—*my* family. And I'm worried about you right now. Worried about what's going on in that head."

The door opened. Gio's other friend Abel and his younger brother Hector walked in. "We all are," Abel said. "You need to get your ass back in the ring. Sitting around in this cave isn't gonna do you any good."

Gio collapsed back into his beanbag. "Maybe I don't wanna get back in the ring."

They all stared at him but Noah spoke first. "You're just saying that now but—"

"No. I've been thinking about it. Maybe I don't wanna risk it. What happened to Trinidad can happen to any of us. Maybe I don't wanna take that risk anymore."

"But this is what you—" Noah stopped talking when Abel touched his arm.

"So you train," Abel said. "You're a hell of a trainer. You know those two you've been training have 'up and coming' written all over them. You said it yourself."

Gio glanced at Abel but said nothing and then stared at the floor again. He hadn't even stepped foot in 5th Street since that horrific night.

"They've been asking about you," Hector added. "Just today at school. Nate asked if I knew when you were coming back."

Both of the guys Gio was training were still in high school. Juniors like Hector but both had massive potential.

He couldn't believe he'd actually said it out loud. That he didn't want to get back in the ring. But it was true—for now anyway. Maybe some day he'd get back in it but for now, he didn't even want to think about it. Not for himself. But Abel was right. He did love training. He'd even thought about asking Jack, the owner of 5th Street, what he thought about him starting up a beginner's class for some of the younger kids in the neighborhood.

He turned back to Noah, who still held the zucchini

bread wrapped in plastic wrap, glad that his friends had gotten his mind off Trinidad even it was for only a few minutes. "Give me that."

"Is that Roni's zucchini bread?" Hector asked.

Noah nodded, handing it to Gio as Hector's jaw dropped open. "Relax, she made a whole bunch. I didn't know you guys were gonna be here or I would've brought you some, too."

"What?" Hector's eyebrows pinched. "He's gonna eat that whole loaf by himself?"

"Damn right," Gio said with a smirk. None of them had ever even had zucchini bread until Noah's girl made some for Christmas last year and they all loved it.

"I gotta go," Abel said, making his way to the door but stopped before walking out. "So will we see you at the gym tomorrow?" Gio shrugged. "I swear to God, G. If I have to come get you and drag your ass out of here I will."

Gio frowned, tearing a piece of the zucchini bread off and handing it to Hector who was still staring at it. "That's it. The rest is mine."

"Don't act like you didn't hear me," Abel raised his voice.

"I heard you." Gio took a bite of the bread.

"All right. 'Cause I've had it with this shit." He pointed around the garage. "Your mom gave me the go ahead to kick your ass if I have to."

For the first time in weeks Gio laughed. "Like you could."

"You're lucky I'm in a hurry or I just might right now." Abel opened the door. "I'll see you guys at the gym."

Gio didn't doubt for even a second that Abel would

come and drag him down to 5th Street if he didn't show up soon. Considering the fact that Abel outweighed him by at least thirty pounds, Gio didn't doubt Abel could whip his ass if he really wanted. In fact, he knew this was coming. The guys had given him a few weeks to wallow in his guilt, but he knew it was just a matter of time before they came and demanded he snap out of it. None of them were the coddling type either. Just like Noah walked in there telling him it sucked, but to move on already and Abel threatening to kick his ass, Gio had expected no less from them.

Noah and Hector hung around a while longer. They told him about some of the things happening around the gym in the last two weeks since he'd been a no show. The most interesting of all was that Felix Sanchez, an old neighborhood buddy of theirs and only alumnus of 5th Street in over forty years who'd made a name for himself in the boxing world, had contacted Jack saying he'd be by for a visit soon.

Not only had Felix made a name for himself, he was now the WBC welterweight champ of the *world*. He'd clinched the title just last year by knocking out the former champ. It was a huge upset but it was well deserved. Gio and the guys were all proud of him but none more so than Gio. Felix and Gio had been the closest when he still lived in the neighborhood. Felix always said he'd never forget where he came from and to this day he'd kept his promise. He even donated money to help Jack get new equipment in the gym.

"He asked about you," Noah said with a lift of an eyebrow.

"Yeah?" Gio knew with all the media attention Trinidad's untimely death had incited, Felix had to have heard about it. "What did he say?"

"Like the rest of us. He was worried about you."

Gio walked out with them when they said they had to go and went inside his house. Since the fight where Trinidad lost his life, Gio had spent the better part of every day in the garage. His mother and sisters came in often to bring him food and sit with him. He'd come in the house late in the evening only to brush his teeth and go to bed. He was sure his mother would be glad to see him in the house before eight tonight.

*

The media vans in the parking lot of 5th Street were the first clue. The line to get in was the second. Felix was in town. Gio made his way through the crowd to the front door of the gym. One of Felix's *big* bodyguards and driver, Tony, recognized Gio as he walked up to where he stood guarding the front door.

"Hey," he said with a big smile and a hearty chuckle, shaking Gio's hand then clapping his back. "How we doing, G? Long time no see!"

"I'm good. How've you been?"

Of course, his first day back would be a madhouse. It'd been almost a week since Noah, Abel and Hector's visit to see him. Noah had texted him to tell him he was holding Abel back, telling him to give Gio more time but he warned he didn't know how much longer he could hold him back. It was time. He had to face it. Trinidad's death, while tragic, was *not* his fault. It would haunt him for years, if not forever, and he was still sticking to his decision of not getting back in the ring.

After chatting with Tony for a bit, he went inside. It was mayhem. Camera crews were everywhere. Photographers taking pictures not only of Felix and his entourage, but of some of the regular guys training.

Felix stood by the ring smiling as a reporter interviewed him in front of a television camera. As usual, there was a girl in his crowd and as usual, she was all glammed up like all the girls he ever brought with him. He brought a different one in every time he came. Gio peered at her for a second to see if he recognized her from anywhere. The last couple of times he was here both girls he'd brought were small time celebs. One was the previous year's runner-up of American Idol and the second one played a supporting role in one of the hotter sitcoms on TV.

This girl didn't look familiar at all but he knew that didn't mean anything. Gio hadn't recognized or heard of the first two girls either. Noah and Abel walked up to him halfway to the locker room. They seemed more excited to see him than having Felix at the gym.

"Hey, you're finally back." They both greeted him with the usual guy shake and patted him on the shoulder. "And not a moment too soon," Abel added with a smirk.

"No shit." Noah laughed. "He ain't lying. He just finished telling me this morning if you weren't back by tomorrow he was coming to get you."

Gio chuckled. "Well, then I'm glad I did."

It felt a little weird being back and having Felix's circus there made it feel even weirder. He turned to where Felix was being interviewed. The girl he'd brought held a phone to her ear and covered her other ear with her hand. "She anyone we should know?"

Gio had felt a little stupid the last time he'd been introduced to Felix's flavor of the week and he had no idea who she was. He wanted to prevent that happening again.

"I dunno," Abel said with a frown. "Somehow it got leaked that he'd be here today. The camera crews have been here all morning. He just arrived about an hour ago. He was mobbed as soon as he walked in. We barely had a chance to talk to him."

"I don't recognize her from anywhere." Noah tilted his head sideways.

Gio gave up trying to figure it out and headed to the locker room to put his things away. He hadn't been in there very long when he heard a commotion and then loud voices coming toward him. Felix and Abel walked to him. Felix had a big smile on his face. "Hey, my man! How's it going?"

"I'm doing all right." Gio reached out his hand to shake Felix's but Felix pulled him in for a man hug.

Felix pulled back to face him and the smile slowly collapsed. "I heard about what happened, man . But you know what? This shit happens in boxing. They say you're really beating yourself up about it. You can't do that, G. It's not your fault and hey, it might even happen again."

"No, it won't," Gio said turning back to his locker. "Not to me anyway. Because I'm not fighting anymore."

Felix glanced back at Abel who shrugged, leaning against a row of lockers. "What do you mean you're not fighting anymore? You can't give up because of this one thing. Gio, it wasn't your fault."

"I know." Gio stuffed his bag in the locker. "But I'm done."

"Dude, so what are you gonna do now?"

"I'm gonna train. There is some real good talent coming in here lately who I think have a lot of potential. I'll focus on getting them ready."

Felix's eyes opened wide then he smiled. "Fuck that. If you're gonna train, come train with me. I need a good sparring partner and you were one of my best."

Gio stared at him for a moment not sure if he was serious. "With you?"

"Yeah, it'd be perfect. This fight is coming up in a few months so I'm headed up to Big Bear to train there. You can come with me. It's only a couple of hours from here so if you ever need to come back home for whatever you can just drive back."

Gio and Abel exchanged glances. "Are you serious?"

"Hell, yeah," Felix laughed. "This will be awesome. You'll be well compensated, too. Because even though we'll do the whole snowboarding and partying with all the snow bunnies up there, I'm putting your ass to work. This guy I'm fighting is supposed to be the best thing outta the Philippines since Pacquiao. I got my work cut out for me."

"Yeah, you do," Abel agreed then turned to Gio. "Some time away might do you some good, too. Who knows? Sparring with Felix might get you itching to get back in the ring."

Gio wasn't sure about that but he was right about one thing. The time away *would* probably do him some good. "When are you headed up?"

Felix smiled. "Next week. I'll be up there for two months straight. 'Course there's gonna be times I'll have to leave. Since I'll be in California, my agents lined up some stuff for me to promote the fight. Television appearances, morning radio shows, shit like that, but I'll only be gone for two, maybe three days tops when I do that stuff. You can stay up there and ski or go snowboarding while I'm gone." He winked with a smirk. "I'll make sure you have company."

Gio chuckled, knowing exactly what he meant. "Speaking of, who's this chick with you today? Anyone I should know about before I make an ass of myself like I did last time?"

"Nah, she's a jazz singer but she's small potatoes. I met her in Vegas after one of my fights. She does have her own show out there but nothing you'd know about."

"So, she your new chick? " Abel asked.

Felix laughed. "C'mon brother, you know me. Life's too short to settle on just one chick. Although there is one who seriously has me considering it."

"No way," Gio said, closing his locker. He'd heard rumors about Felix and a girl from Big Bear but just like all the other rumors he'd heard about Felix, Gio hadn't thought anything of it.

"Hey," Felix said, lifting his hands in front of him. "Stranger things have happened. So what do you say? You in?"

"I'll give it some thought and let you know in a couple of days. I gotta talk to Jack, too. This is my first day back and already I gotta tell him I may be leaving for two months."

"I doubt he'll have a problem with it," Abel said "He'll probably agree you could use the time away."

Gio frowned. "Still, I gotta run it past him first." Gio had to admit the more he thought about it, the more he agreed with Abel that getting away might do him some good.

As it turned out not only was Abel right about Jack agreeing that Gio could use the time away, he insisted Gio did. That evening Jack took Gio aside. "I'm getting old. Too old to be managing this place. The busier it gets, the harder it gets for me."

"That's what me and the guys are here for. You know you can count on us for anything."

"Oh, I know that," Jack said coming around to sit at his old desk. "I already have Hector doing the bills and payroll for me."

"Hector?" Gio asked, confused. The kid was still in high school.

"Yeah, that boy is smart as a whip. I showed him the other day how I do all the back end stuff around here and within minutes he had it all going on the computer—said I could do it all faster and more efficiently that way. He's working on getting everything in there now."

Gio remembered Abel telling them how his little brother had always been smart and talented that way. He said if the kid ever stopped messing around, he might actually do something with that talent.

"Anyway, so Felix is talking about remodeling this place and putting some big bucks into it. He really wants to give back."

Gio's eyes opened wide. "That would be awesome!"

Jack turned to Gio. "That's why I need you to go and get yourself all better. This place is gonna be all of yours soon and I need you to be here one-hundred percent, both physically and emotionally. But there's something else I wanted to run by you." Gio nodded, waiting silently for Jack to go on. "Your name is already on the title of 5th Street. I added you years ago."

Gio's eyes opened wide. Jack had made comments in the past about how someday he'd pass 5th Street on to him but he had no idea he was already on the title.

"I wanna add Noah, Abel and Hector's names too, but I wanted to make sure you were okay with that."

Gio couldn't believe Jack would even have to ask. "Of course it's okay. They put in just as much work around here as I do. But Jack, I don't... I don't know what to say."

"Just say you'll always work as hard as you do now to keep this place running smoothly. This place is my life and I'm trusting you boys with it." Jack stood. Gio walked over to him and hugged him.

"You have my word."

Jack smiled. "I knew I would, son. Just do me a favor. Don't tell them anything yet. I wanna get their names on the title first. And keep to yourself the fact that your name was the only one I added at first." He pressed his lips together. "You were just the first one I got close to. But now I love you all the same. They don't need to know about that."

Gio promised not to say anything and with that their guy talk was over and Jack left him with a lot to think about. Gio always knew in his heart that someday he and the guys would be running things. Jack, who had no family of his own, always treated them like family and he'd been a father figure to all of them. For the first time in weeks, Gio felt excited again.

CHAPTER 2

Nana and her mother stared at Bianca as she got off the phone. She hadn't been able to wipe the silly smile off her face fast enough.

"Was that who I think it was?" Nana asked.

Bianca gave in, nodding. Ever since the past summer, she'd been seeing *the* Felix Sanchez, current welterweight boxing champion of the world. She didn't know a thing about boxing but everyone, especially in her neighborhood, knew about Felix. She'd gone to high school with him and he became the local hero when he started winning fight after fight. Then he'd won the championship over a year ago. He was now known worldwide and *she* was dating him.

Although she admitted him being famous and insanely rich was part of the intrigue, she'd actually had a crush on the guy way back in high school. She hadn't seen him in person since she graduated, but last summer when she came up to Big Bear after her grandfather's death she ran into him. She'd been surprised he remembered her. One thing led to another and they began seeing each other.

A first she had her doubts about it working out. She even reasoned that it would be okay if it didn't. She knew he lived a busy life that was much different from her small town life in Big Bear.

Another reason for her doubts was his fame. Boxers weren't usually the target of the stalkarazzis but because of Felix's age and looks—the fact that he'd been linked with quite a few young Hollywood A-listers, *and* because his upcoming fight was so highly anticipated, he'd now become just as much of a target as a movie star.

Bianca had never been one to follow the tabloids but ever since she'd gotten involved with Felix she couldn't help but get sucked into them. Especially when they talked about him being seen with a new girl — this after he'd assured her their relationship was an exclusive one.

She'd been doing her best not to buy into the hype and made up drama, which Felix said, was *all* it was. One particular incident last year was when she saw a photo of him and Shana Thompson, the current women's figure skating champion, said to be the front-runner in this year's Olympics. It was the week he'd had a photo shoot for Sports Illustrated's Hottest Young Athletes layout. They were caught in a compromising pose where they apparently were on a date sitting in a very cozy restaurant booth in New York. In one of the photos it appeared as if they were about to kiss. It made Bianca crazy. They'd only been intimate for a few weeks when the photo surfaced and she'd lost it.

Days after letting him have it and telling him she was done with him, the same photo resurfaced only this time Shana's boyfriend and Felix's publicist Andy were also there. The other photo had been doctored. They took the most damning picture of them when they'd leaned in to say something to each other and cropped everything and everyone else out. Just like Felix explained, it wasn't just a restaurant it was also a blues club and the music was really loud. She felt terrible, especially because Felix had tried in vain to explain to her that that's what the paparazzi did to sell stories and word was beginning to get out about his mystery Big Bear girlfriend.

Neither her grandmother nor her mother were crazy about her dating a celebrity, especially one known to be such a womanizer, so of course they were concerned when they saw how upset all the tabloid stories made Bianca. But once the truth was out about the photo they actually convinced her to call Felix and apologize. They also made her promise she'd stop reading the stupid tabloids. More than anything they hated to see her hurt and her mother said it was a better idea if she just followed her heart instead of the gossip. From that day forward, she vowed to never read any of the tabloids. Though there were times she'd slip and give into the temptation. But it had been a while since that happened.

"So he'll be up here for two whole months?" Nana asked with a coy little smile.

"Yes." Bianca clutched the phone in her hand, feeling like a silly schoolgirl. The time she got to spend with Felix always felt so short. Knowing he'd be up here for two whole months and his saying he wanted to spend as much time with her as possible made her insides go wild. She eagerly filled them in on how long Felix would be there and when he'd arrive. Then she remembered. "But don't worry, I won't cut my time away at the shop."

Nana waved her hand at her. "We can more than handle it if you want to take some time off."

In addition to Bianca and her mother she had two cousins who also worked at her grandmother's rental shop. During the winter, they rented everything from snowboards and skis to sleds. Then in the summer, they rented all the water sport stuff — rafts, fishing gear, kayaks and they sold bait all year along with a ton of souvenirs. They weren't insanely busy but business was steady year round with summer and winter being their busiest seasons.

With it being the middle of winter and more heavy storms expected, business would be booming from now through the end of ski season. Just last night they'd gotten eight inches of fresh powder. "No. I'll put in my regular hours as usual. I'll have plenty of time to spend with him before and after my shifts."

Bianca could hardly wait. Felix had just called her to tell her he'd be up next week. He was in Los Angeles today but wouldn't be able to make it up because he had to fly back to Vegas, then Chicago to take care of some final business before he *moved* to Big Bear for the next couple of months. She loved the way that sounded. She hadn't seen him in weeks and now she'd have him all to herself for two whole months.

This was by far the hardest part of their relationship. The amount of time they had to be apart from one another. Sure he'd set her up with a webcam so they could have live chats via the internet but it just wasn't the same. When he was gone, she missed him so much. Even though he offered to bring her along many times, she could never leave her mother for too long.

He'd taken her to Miami, New York and even Puerto Rico but she'd always go for just a few days. The longest she'd vacationed with him was the trip to New York for a week around the holidays. She'd mentioned that she'd always wanted to see New York during the holidays and he made the arrangements immediately but she came home to be with her grandmother for Christmas. New York had been great but nothing beat Big Bear, especially during the winter. There was something so homey and quaint about the small town.

Gabe, one of the cousins who also worked at Nana's shop, walked in. "Oh, good you're here. I can leave now."

"Where are you off to?" Nana asked.

Bianca smiled. "To Toni's to get my hair cut."

Her mother quickly signed to her that she should be careful driving. The roads were still very slippery from the snow earlier. Bianca had to smile, even via sign language and without ever voicing her words like some deaf people did, her mother's worried anxiousness came across loud and clear. She signed back that she would and that she loved her and was off to Toni's.

Her hairdresser, Toni had quickly become one of Bianca's closest friends since she'd moved up here. At first, Bianca thought Toni was just good at making her feel comfortable because it was part of her job. Making conversation as she worked on her client's hair came with the job description but it turned out Toni was just cool—more than cool, she was *awesome*. When she found out Bianca was a newbie in town she took it upon herself to show her all the hot spots to shop, the best places to meet men and even taught her how to snowboard the more advanced slopes. Not that Bianca was a total beginner. She'd gone snowboarding plenty of times when she visited her grandparents in the past but she'd never attempted the more advanced slopes she now snowboarded, thanks to Toni.

When she walked into the small hair salon, Toni sat reading a magazine. The first thing Bianca noticed was that her hair color was different—again. Toni was a few years older than Bianca and a bit eccentric. The hair that was curly and blonde the last time Bianca had seen her just last week was now straight and dark brown with a couple of blue streaks. Her eyes lit up when she saw Bianca.

"Your hair?"

"You like it? Toni asked, flipping a strand of hair with her hand.

"It's different," Bianca said examining it as she got closer. "But yes I like it. How is it that every color and style looks good on you?"

"Because I wear the hair, honey. It doesn't wear me."

Bianca giggled. This was true. Toni could take any look and totally own it.

"So, is it time?" Toni asked.

Bianca nodded, feeling keyed up again. She'd known about him coming up to train for months now but he hadn't given her an exact date until today. "Yes. He called today; he'll be here this weekend."

Toni jumped out of her chair. "Well, let's get this going."

Bianca hadn't expected Toni to be busy—not on such a snowy day as today. So it wasn't surprising her little salon was empty.

"What's it going to be?" Toni asked as she wrapped the cape around her, tying it around her neck.

"I don't know, Toni. Just make me stunning."

"Girl, you're already stunning and you know it. There's a reason why that boy, who can have any girl he wants, keeps coming back here. He ain't blind."

Bianca winced taking in Toni's words. *Any girl he wants.* She stared at herself in the mirror. Never in her life had she been insecure about her looks. In fact, she'd been blessed with the Rubio family's beauty gene. Her father's sisters had actually won a few beauty pageants back in their day and everyone said Bianca was a Rubio through and through. From her long legs to her big expressive eyes, to her full lush lips, she'd always been a head turner. Yet, she hadn't really blossomed until after high school. Which is why she was surprised Felix remembered her.

But she couldn't help feeling a little intimidated knowing Felix was constantly around some of the most glamorous women in the world. She'd told herself from the very beginning when she decided to allow herself to become involved with Felix that she'd never been insecure before and she certainly wasn't going to start now.

"Just work your magic, Toni. I wanna look perfect for him when he gets here."

"I know exactly what to do." Toni smiled at her reflection in the mirror. "If this boy thought you were hot before, wait 'til he gets a load of what Magic Hands Toni has in store for him."

Bianca took a deep breath and smiled. It was almost scary how excited she felt about this.

*

Abel had offered to give Gio a ride to Big Bear since Felix told him driving his bike in the snow would be a sure death sentence. But Felix insisted on sending a car for him. Some of his other trainers and a driver were already at his *compound* getting things set up for his arrival. Gio wasn't sure what he meant by compound but he sure as hell was surprised when he got there. The property was secluded, and tucked away deep in the mountains. And there were several structures on the property. Everything was constructed of logs but it was luxury beyond anything Gio had ever witnessed.

He stood there for a good ten minutes; his still stunned eyes taking everything in. The spiral staircase that went up to the second floor was all made of logs as well. All the furnishings: the tables, lamps, even the full bar was either made of wood or boasted some kind of wooden accent. The chandeliers throughout were made of antlers. Deer or moose or maybe even elk since they were so huge.

Gio walked slowly through the cabin, glad no one was there with him yet because he was completely speechless. He stopped and looked into what appeared to be a theater room complete with a huge screen, theater seats and an old fashioned but shiny new popcorn maker.

Continuing with his tour, he walked into what was obviously the game room. A pool table was the centerpiece of the room with a party sized Jacuzzi in a corner. Then he saw it: a giant, wall-sized, salt water aquarium. "Whoa."

Gio had an idea of what something like that must cost from a reality show. It was about a family whose business was building these elaborate things for customers like Felix who could afford to have one custom made. As he approached it he noticed the underwater village of some sort. When he got close enough he knew this was definitely custom made to Felix's specifications. "What?" he laughed.

It wasn't a village. It was 5th Street. Not just the gym. The entire *barrio*. 5th Street was in the center, but the park where they used to play hoops and the liquor store they'd frequent was there. He didn't leave any detail out. He got it all, right down to the broken street lamps.

Ray, one of the other trainers and also former 5th Street alumnus, walked in and greeted him. He showed him to his room. Just like all the other rooms it was spectacular. Gio could hardly believe he'd be spending an entire two months here.

Since there was no snow in Los Angeles he'd seen no reason why he should wear his snow gear on the way up but now he was here, it was snowing and colder than shit outside. Gio changed into the snow pants, jacket and boots Felix had promised would be in the closet. He checked the drawers for a beanie and gloves and they were full of them. Just like Felix said. He'd hooked him up good.

He heard a car pull up and a car door close so he walked to the window to see if it was Felix. The driver walked around the car, opened the back door and a girl stepped out. "The hell?"

Gio couldn't see very well due to the window fogging up already and the snow still coming down pretty densely. From what he could see, she was glammed up just like all the other girls he ever saw around Felix. But why would she be here now? Felix said he wouldn't be up until later tonight. Then Gio remembered. *I'll make sure you have company.* "Ah hell."

He'd planned on checking out the rest of the compound. He'd gone straight in when they got here but he'd gotten a glimpse of the other cabins out there. Most importantly, he was anxious to check out the gym. If this main house was any indication he was sure everything in the gym would be state-of-the-art. If this was what he was thinking he'd now have to deal with the awkwardness of hired *entertainment* instead.

Gio waited in his room for a few minutes trying to think of how best to handle this. Even when Felix had mentioned making sure Gio had company he didn't think he was serious about hiring anyone for him. He'd heard some of Felix's crazy stories and he had a feeling they might get a few nights of fun with the *snow bunnies*, but he wasn't expecting something this soon.

He froze when he walked into the front room and saw one of the most breathtaking girls he'd ever laid eyes on. She'd just taken off her beanie and scarf. She stood by the door, her dark hair a bit undone, looking a bit startled herself.

Gio gulped, now not sure if he wanted this or not. He'd never been with a hired entertainment of *any* type and wasn't sure exactly how this worked.

"Hello," she said, speaking up first. "I'm Bianca. Felix's... um, girlfriend."

Gio let out a breath. Although he was a tiny bit disappointed she wasn't here for him he wasn't ready for the stress of having to figure out how to go about this. Felix had talked about some crazy shit he'd done now that he had access to so many women.

"Hi." He took a few steps, meeting her halfway and pulled off his beanie before reaching out his hand to shake hers. "I'm Gio. I'll be training with Felix."

Now that she was closer, she looked familiar and Gio cursed himself for never watching any of the celebrity gossip shows. He should have anticipated this—done his homework. As stunning as this girl was she had to be a model or celebrity of some kind.

Her eyes brightened suddenly bringing more emphasis to how big and nearly black they were. She *had* to be a celebrity. Only *they* had amazing perfect smiles like hers. Damn, how did Felix keep his cool being around women like this all the time?

"I remember you!" she said smiling.

Gio blinked cluelessly feeling a little panicked. Could it be possible that Felix had already brought her around and he didn't remember her? There was no way he wouldn't remember this girl but the name did ring a bell.

"You're Giovanni Bravo, Felix's friend from high school, right?"

Gio nodded, still having no idea who this gorgeous thing was and how the hell she knew him but the more he looked at her the more familiar she seemed.

"I'm Bianca Rubio from high school." She rolled her eyes. "Oh, I'm sure you don't remember me. You were the popular heartthrob and I was the tomboy softball player."

Suddenly it hit him and his mouth fell open. "Bianca?" Unbelievably, her big eyes got even bigger. "World History, Bianca?"

She laughed. "Oh my God, you actually remember?"

"Yeah, yeah." He looked her up and down remembering her hair was always in a tight ponytail. It was down now and went almost to her elbows—as dark and straight as he remembered. He took her in completely from top to bottom. "Wow, you look so different."

Did she *ever*. He thought she'd looked familiar but he would've never put two and two together. She looked *too* damn different now. In high school, she was just one of those girls that, save for those big eyes, went unnoticed for the most part. She was quiet, kept to herself. The one thing he remembered about her most was how hard it was for her to contain her laughter once she got going. It was absolutely contagious and the best part was he could tell it embarrassed her which always made him smile.

She sat next to him in World History class senior year and he often had to borrow her notes or paper or even a pencil. She'd always been so nice about it, too, rolling her eyes playfully but never refusing.

He also remembered feeling a little disappointed when she often had to leave early because she was on the softball team and had a game.

"I was surprised when Felix remembered me but I'm even more surprised *you* do."

"Why's that?"

She'd begun to remove the layers of clothes she wore. "Because you were so popular with the girls, how in the world would you remember all of them? Especially one you hardly knew."

Gio smirked. "Actually, you looked familiar to me I just couldn't place you. But you look so different now and I'd never seen you like this." He pointed at her hair and then down the front of her. "All done up. I was thinking Felix had hooked up with a supermodel or something."

Unlike most girls who might've blushed at a comment like that, she just smiled and tilted her head. "I'm sure he's had his share of supermodels, Gio. Don't remind me."

It hit him just then. She actually did consider herself Felix's girl. He thought of the girl Felix had just brought to the gym last week and for a second felt a little bad for Bianca.

"Honestly, I don't know if he has or hasn't, I was just saying. Based on your looks, that was my first thought."

"Oh. Well, thank you." *Now* her face tinged with color but just barely. Apparently, she was too caught up with the mention of Felix and a supermodel the first time he'd said it to notice the compliment. He made note of that and would make sure to be extra careful about his Felix comments from here on.

"How the hell did you and Felix hook up anyway? Did you two stay in touch since high school?"

She walked over to the bar area and Gio followed her. "No, it's just a small world that's all. I need water; you want anything to drink?"

"I'll take a water."

She walked behind the giant wooden hand carved bar and opened another door that was also covered in carved wood, but was actually steel—a giant refrigerator. She pulled out two waters, handed him one then opened hers but began talking before taking a drink.

"My grandmother owns a rental shop up here, downtown. I work there and he happened to come in one day, with a girl mind you. They were just shopping for souvenirs and just like you, I told him I remembered him from high school. It took him a moment but he actually remembered—said my name before I even told him what it was." She paused to take a drink.

Gio drank some of his, fascinated by how much she'd changed physically. Yet she still seemed as down to earth as he remembered her.

"We talked for a little bit," she continued. "About school and the old neighborhood and stuff. Then he left. A week later, he comes back and asks if I'd like to grab a coffee with him. We went out for coffee and the rest is well… what it is. This was last summer, so it's been a few months now."

Of course Felix would go back. He'd be nuts not to. Gio wondered if this was who he'd meant when he said he'd met someone that actually made him consider settling down.

"That's crazy. Did you two know each other in high school?"

"No," she smiled. "But I remember having a crush on him even back then. I knew him like I knew you. We had a few of the same classes every year but that was the extent of it." She pointed at his jacket. "Were you going out?"

Gio looked down at himself. He'd forgotten he'd piled on the snow gear. "Just outside. I wanted to check out the rest of the compound."

"You've never been here?" she asked surprised.

"No. This is my first time." Gio glanced around the lavish cabin. "This place is awesome."

Bianca hurried back around the bar toward the sofa. "Oh, well, then I'll give you a tour. It really is amazing."

She put her jacket, gloves and beanie back on. They stepped out onto the porch together. It was freezing but beautiful outside. Living in Los Angeles his whole life and having only seen the snow a handful of times Gio still felt awestruck by it.

"So, you moved up here?" he asked as they carefully walked down the front stairs of the cabin.

"Temporarily, and before you ask, I have no idea how long I'll be here. My grandparents bought a place up here when they retired. Odd, I know. Why would an older couple want to move to such a cold climate? Long story short, until my grandfather met my grandmother, he traveled all over. He actually lived in Alaska for a while. He'd hoped to move back when he retired but my grandmother wasn't having it. So they compromised and moved up here instead. He died early last summer. Me and my mom decided to stay with my grandmother for a few weeks after he died and now months later I'm still here."

"I'm sorry to hear about your grandfather."

Bianca nodded looking up at him. "Heart disease—it ran in his family. His father passed of the same thing. So did his brother."

Gio couldn't help being distracted by her eyes. They were so big, so perfect like something out of magazine. Then it hit him. That's why she'd seemed so familiar. He remembered now. Even back in high school he'd been taken by her eyes. He never even considered asking her out *because* of those eyes. They were so big and innocent looking. He steered clear of the innocent ones. With three younger sisters, he knew what kind of innocence there was behind those often doe-eyed expressions of hers.

Too young and too scared to commit to anything serious back in those days, Gio stuck with more experienced, wilder girls that he knew could deal with his noncommittal tendency. He wasn't about to break any fragile hearts. Bianca's eyes had fragile written all over them.

"Okay," she said as they walked up the stairs of the gym. "Prepare yourself to be amazed."

They walked in. Amazing wasn't grand enough a word to describe the place. It had everything 5th Street had only a hundred times better. Giant black and white stills of some of boxing's greats adorned the wall—Joe Frazier, Sugar Ray, Mohammad Ali, Tyson and, very notably, two of East LA's finest, Cesar Chavez and the Golden Boy himself, De La Hoya. It was a gym fit for a king, no doubt. Felix's picture would soon fit right up there. Gio was suddenly overwhelmed with pride.

"And this is just a gym. Isn't this crazy?"

"Crazy." Gio chuckled. "Yeah, maybe that's the word I'm looking for."

Her phone buzzed and she excused herself saying it was Felix before walking away. Gio barely glanced at her; he was still taking in everything. The guys were going to fucking flip when they saw this.

A door slammed, jolting him out of his thoughts. He turned and Bianca was gone.

CHAPTER 3

Bianca struggled to hold it together but the disappointment was too much. She'd looked forward to today all week—counted the days—the hours. God, she felt pathetic. She prayed her voice wouldn't give. The last thing she wanted was to sound needy. "When will you know?"

"All I know is they just announced we're snowed in for tonight." Felix spoke quickly. "I've been waiting for hours just to get confirmation of that."

"Why did you take so long to get there?"

"Same reason—the weather. Traffic was horrendous. We still got here on time but all flights were being grounded because of the blizzard."

It was just as he said the word blizzard that she noticed his words were slightly slurred. Immediate thoughts of him actually partying instead of sitting at an airport like he was claiming assaulted her. "Have you been drinking?"

"I'm not gonna lie. I've been sitting here for hours with nothing else to do. So yeah, I've had a few."

She exhaled, feeling a little guilty about immediately thinking the worst.

"I'm sorry, babe. I'll make it up to you, I promise, okay?"

The most she would manage was not to frown; a smile was out of the question. She'd been looking forward to seeing him so much, she could almost feel his arms around her. "You think tomorrow for sure?"

"I can't promise," he said. She felt the warm tears fill her eyes again. "But I'll do my best. The storm is pretty bad. The good thing is private jets get first dibs as soon as they open things up again. So I'll be the first one out, okay?"

Bianca nodded, squeezing her eyes, holding her fist to her mouth. She didn't want to speak, afraid her voice would betray her and give away how anxious she was to see him again.

"Hey," he said when she didn't respond. "I love you."

Her eyes jerked opened. Even though they'd been going out for several months and were sleeping together already this was the first time he'd told her this. "What?"

"I do," his laugh sounded a little nervous—a little unsure.

The L word was not something she threw around just like that. As much as she cared for him and as much as she'd begun to miss him when he wasn't around she wasn't sure it was love and she certainly hadn't envisioned the day they did profess their love for one another to be over the phone. She wondered if it was the alcohol talking. "You do? Since when?"

He chuckled again the nervous tone still there. "I don't know. Since now. This has been one of the most frustrating days of my life and I think I just figured out why. Because I'm dying to get to you already and now just hearing your voice...I love you, Bianca."

She tried with all her might not to not get too excited about this but it was too late. She felt ready to jump out of her boots. "I love you, too." The words flew out of her mouth without thought.

She giggled and she heard him laugh on the other

end. "Damn, I can't wait to be with you now. I'll call you the second I know something, okay?"

"Okay," she nodded again as if he could see her. Her mood had completely done an about-face.

The door to the gym opened and Gio walked out. She stood at the bottom of the stairs, her phone still at her ear. Gio mouthed the words, "You okay?"

It was only then that she realized a few tears still streamed down her face. She smiled, wiping them away, and gave him the thumbs up. Gio nodded and went back in the gym.

Felix explained to her he had arranged for dinner to be prepared for them tonight. He'd hoped it'd be a very special first night back together but said the dinner was still being prepared anyway and she should have dinner with Gio and the other trainers. He didn't want her feeling lonely. They said their goodbyes and he promised he'd get to her tomorrow one way or another.

After hanging up she practically skipped up the steps to the gym. What she felt now was such a contrast to what she felt just minutes earlier when he laid the news on her about not making it up tonight. She'd been devastated. She had arranged to have the entire weekend off just to spend it with him. How could three little words make up for it all?

Gio was over by the ring talking to one of the other trainers. He turned when she walked in and smiled at her. She smiled back.

Bianca still couldn't believe what a small world this really was. She'd recognized Gio almost immediately when she first saw him earlier. He hadn't changed much since high school. He did look a little taller and she was sure underneath all those layers of snow gear he'd bulked up even more just like Felix had. But his face was still that same almost pretty face with the chiseled features she remembered from school. The girls went crazy for him even back then. She could only imagine what things were like for him now that he'd grown into his own. And his green eyes were just as amazing as she remembered.

At least three of her friends were in love with him back then. He'd always been nice enough to her in school but except for the times he was hitting her up to borrow paper or a pencil she was invisible to him. Felix at least flirted with her making it obvious that he acknowledged her as a girl he might actually consider. Of course, he flirted with *everyone*.

Gio, on the other hand, only ever gave her very polite, sometimes remorseful smiles when he was borrowing something from her — yet again. At times, it seemed he even avoided eye contact. So, no matter how beautiful it was when the boy smiled, even though it was usually at someone else, she never once allowed herself to even harbor a secret crush for him like she had Felix. Gio was completely out of her league and she never even bothered lusting over him.

"Everything okay?" Gio asked as she reached him. "Is he on his way?"

A twinge of disappointment crept back in but she pushed it away remembering Felix's admission. She shook her head. "No, the airport is snowed in. The earliest he'll make it is tomorrow but he's not sure what time."

"He'll be here." Gio gave her an reassuring smile.

Looking at that face, you'd never believe he was a boxer. Even Felix had a scar over one of his eyebrows and one of his cheekbones was slightly higher than the other from having gotten one too many blows to the cheek. Gio could've been a model as perfect as his face was.

Bianca turned to Ray, the trainer she knew best so far. "Felix arranged for dinner to be made for us tonight so you guys come on into the main dining room around six for dinner."

Ray smiled nodding and tipped the brim of his baseball cap at her. She smiled back and turned to the other trainer Ignacio, who she wasn't as familiar with. "You too, okay?"

After he agreed, she turned back to Gio. "Did you wanna see the rest of the place?"

"Sure." He waved at the other trainers. "I'll see you guys back inside."

They walked out into a third building on the property. This one had a lap pool and cardio equipment. Two treadmills, a few elliptical machines, exercise bike, and televisions all around. "This is probably where you'll be while he's out doing his miles on the trails," Bianca said. "He prefers running the trails to the treadmill so this room gets most of its use from the trainers."

"Nah," Gio shook his head. "I'll be out there with him, too."

"That's right. I forgot. You don't just train, you box, too."

"Not anymore." His expression went hard but he turned away from her and stared at the pool.

It suddenly hit her as she tried to make out his abrupt answer and she winced, feeling like a complete idiot. She remembered now hearing about it on the news and then Felix telling her about it, too. A boxing bout in her old neighborhood gone wrong and one was dead. It was shocking enough but when she'd heard it was Gio who'd been the opponent that killed the other guy it was even more of a shock.

That was almost a month ago and she'd since forgotten about it. "I'm uh… I'm sorry. I heard about what happened. I totally forgot… so you're not boxing anymore?"

"Nope." He walked over to the pool area.

Bianca followed him. "Is that why you're here?"

Bianca had met all of Felix's trainers. Some she knew better than others but Felix hadn't made any mention of any new ones. Not that he was supposed to tell her everything about his training but seeing Gio had been a pleasant surprise and now this explained why he was here.

CHAPTER 4

The last thing Gio wanted to do was talk or even think about Trinidad. He was also beginning to have a hard time not staring at those big innocent eyes. Even under all the glamorous makeup Bianca wore now, they still reminded him of the feelings he'd begun to develop for her way back in high school so he turned away. Taking in the rest of the workout room, he responded without looking at her. "I'm training now so Felix asked me to join him for the next couple of months."

"Oh, so you'll be here for the whole two months?"

"Off and on," Gio said, still taking in the rest of the room. "I'm only two hours away so if I ever need to make a trip down I may leave for a day or two. But yeah, I'll be around for the whole two months."

She showed him the rest of the compound and then they headed back to the main house to thaw out. The fire was already roaring when they got there and it was a good thing because Gio had never been out in such cold weather for that long. The temperature had dropped dramatically from the time they stepped out to the time they stepped back in.

Felix's hired help was fast at work preparing the dinner they'd have a little later. One of the women set up the dinner table and Gio noticed she only put out two place settings. Bianca must've noticed too because she walked over to the table. "We have two others joining us tonight, Amparo."

Amparo glanced up and smiled but shook her head.

"Ray came in already and put something together. He was hungry and didn't want to wait and Ignacio said he'd take his food to his room later—something about wanting to video chat with his wife and kids while he ate."

Bianca turned back to Gio. "I guess it's just you and me for dinner."

Gio shrugged. After introducing him to Amparo, Felix's housekeeper, and peeling off all the snow gear, Bianca showed Gio into the TV room with the fireplace.

She clicked the huge plasma TV on and flipped it over to the weather channel. "Oh, big storm coming our way," she said this with a big satisfied smile, then turned to Gio. "Big storms are good for business. More snow means the ski lifts will be busy and that's always good for us."

"Ah," Gio nodded taking a seat on the brick fireplace. The heat against his back was heavenly. "So a rental shop, uh?"

"Yes," she nodded. "Well, half souvenir shop, half rental shop." She sat on the other side of the fireplace, with an expression that could only be described as orgasmic.

Gio felt like a dick for even thinking it but he couldn't help it. Her eyes had actually rolled back; the smile was so big and content. "God, the fireplace feels good, doesn't it?"

Gio straightened out a bit clearing his throat. "Yeah, it does."

She took a deep breath then those big eyes of hers opened wide. "I didn't even ask you if you wanted something to drink. Hot chocolate, coffee—a beer? The bar is fully stocked."

"Hot chocolate would hit the spot actually." Bianca

stood up and Gio stood with her. "I can get it myself, Bianca. If you'll just show me where it is."

"Don't be silly," she said, but Gio followed her anyway. "I know this isn't exactly my place but in Felix's absence I feel obligated to play host and you're my guest."

Not *exactly* her place? She obviously was taking this relationship with Felix a lot more seriously than he was. Gio hadn't missed the tears earlier when she first got the news that Felix wouldn't be making it tonight. There was no doubt she really cared about Felix. He actually hoped now that she *was* the one Felix had been talking about making him consider settling down. He'd hate to think sweet Bianca was just another one of his many.

They walked through the kitchen where two guys in white jackets were preparing the dinner. Bianca bent over and pulled out a fancy looking machine from one of the cabinets.

"You don't just throw a cup of hot water in the microwave then drop one of them hot chocolate packets in it and stir?" Gio asked, checking out the gadget she was plugging in.

"Oh, no way. We don't even use water for it up here, Gio." She smiled teasingly. "You're not in East LA anymore. You're in Big Bear. Here we use our milk frothers to make it and I keep forgetting but up here it's referred to as hot *cocoa*, not chocolate."

"Milk frother?" Standing this close to her in the kitchen, looking at that playful smile, and God if those eyes didn't still do something to him, Gio had to remind himself this was Felix's girl—well, *one* of them— but still. She was *completely* off limits. Not even flirting would be acceptable.

"Yeah, it's what makes the chocolate milk all foamy and oh, so delicious." She pulled the milk out of the fridge as her expression went all doe-eyed, bringing back memories of her in high school. Her smile disappeared as she glanced back at him. "You're not lactose intolerant, are you?"

Gio couldn't help laughing. "No, I'm cool with milk."

Relief washed over her face and the smile was back. "Oh good. For a moment there it hit me that maybe that's why you used water."

"Nah," he smiled leaning against the counter. "We just don't use these fancy machines down in my part of East LA, is all."

He watched as her perfectly manicured hands put everything together into the machine. It was actually pretty cool to watch the machine *froth* the milk. After only a few minutes, it was done and smelled great. Bianca pulled out a couple of large mugs and poured the cocoa. She pushed the machine back against the back of the counter. "I made enough for everyone," she addressed the cooks in the kitchen, "so help yourselves."

They made their way back to the room with the TV. Even though there were some very comfortable sofas they could've sat on, they both headed straight to the fireplace. That same orgasmic smile washed over Bianca's face again after taking her first sip of her chocolate and Gio *had* to look away, especially because she got foam on her upper lip and he knew what was coming next. "*Mmm*, this is so good."

The erotic sounds weren't helping either. Just the fact that he was having these thoughts and he'd only been around her for a couple of hours was pissing him off. This shouldn't be so difficult. Roni was very attractive in his opinion and not once had these inappropriate thoughts *ever* crossed his mind about his friend's girl. It was wrong and it had to stop, damn it.

He took a sip of his own chocolate and though it didn't make him orgasmic or give him the urge to moan, he had to admit it was damn good. "Sure beats my East LA watered version."

They enjoyed their hot *cocoa* for a few silent moments. Normally boxing would not only be a safe subject but one he happily could go on and on about, but it wasn't one he wanted to get into now. So he was grateful when she asked him about the rest of the gang. "Do you still hang around with Noah, Abel and his brother? I forget his name."

Gio nodded, stirring his "cocoa" with the fancy chocolate stir stick Bianca had provided. "Yeah, we all work at 5th Street. Hector, Abel's brother is still part-time but the rest of us actually help Jack, the owner, run it now."

A sudden squeak from Bianca made him glance up and seeing her turn red, then giggle embarrassedly, had him smiling like an idiot. It was the cutest damn thing. As much of a struggle as it was, he managed to turn back to his *cocoa* chuckling and asked, "What's that about?"

He glanced up when she didn't respond. She was holding her hand against her mouth, eyes closed, trying to muffle her laughing. She put her mug down on the fireplace shaking her head and proceeded to go into a laughing fit. When she gained a little composure she explained, "That just reminded how back in middle school, this group of cool girls wore the 5th Street t-shirts they sell down at the gym." She shook her head continuing to wipe the corner of her eyes. "Me and my friend Anna wanted to be cool too but our moms' were not about to shell out the twenty bucks for a t-shirt." She started laughing again. "So we decided to make our own." Just seeing how hard it was for her to even speak now had him laughing, too. "You should've seen the mess we made of our dads' white t-shirts. We both got in trouble for ruining so many of them and we never did get to wear them." Then she squeaked again and it was all over. They were both laughing uncontrollably now. "Stop!' she begged between laughs. "I hate that stupid squeak!"

Gio caught his breath. He hadn't laughed that hard in a while so the words came out without thought. "I think it's cute. I've always thought you were cute."

That doe-eyed expression was abruptly back as what he'd just blurted out sunk in. Her laughing slowly subsided and she stared at him. Thinking fast he added, "My sister does this hiccup thing when she laughs." He had nothing else. The mood had switched so quickly with his stupid admission he was grasping here.

"You have?"

"Huh?" His thoughts were still scrambling trying to think of something else to say, he wasn't even sure what she was asking. Then she smiled a smile so sweet he had to suck in a fleeting breath.

"Even in high school you thought I was cute?" She tilted her head sideways. "I always felt invisible to you back then."

No way was he telling her she'd been anything but invisible and that just like now there'd been too many times he'd gotten lost in those eyes of hers. Gio sat up straight taking a sip of his chocolate. Son of a bitch if he couldn't think of a proper way to respond to that.

"Well, yeah. I mean, you sat right next to me. How

could I *not* notice you?" He glanced at her. Those eyes were still doing that thing. There was no qualm, no questioning that her *boyfriend's* friend — best friend back in high school — had just told her he'd always thought she was cute. "Just like I said earlier, you're runway model material now. Of course you were at least cute back then."

"Dinner is ready whenever you two are." Amparo stood at the archway opening of the large room.

The second Bianca glanced away, Gio let out a huge silent sigh of relief. His body almost slouched in reaction to the amount of tension being released.

"Thank you, Amparo." Bianca turned to Gio who straightened up quickly. "Shall we?"

Gio nodded and they stood together and made their way to the dining room.

*

Felix had thought of everything. The dinner he'd instructed his cooks to make for their first night back together was excellent. Steamed shrimp, oysters, stuffed mushrooms; crusty bread with some kind of gourmet spread the cook called bruschetta. They even prepared a chocolate fondue with strawberries and pineapple slices to dip. It was so perfect and she'd shared the dinner with Gio.

Not that any girl in their right mind would be complaining about having such a romantic dinner with a gorgeous guy like Gio. He was sweetly attentive and as polite as she remembered him but she couldn't help wishing Felix had been there instead. Still she made the best of it and enjoyed their delicious dinner. When they were done, Gio sat back in his seat looking very stuffed but Bianca reached for another strawberry. "I'm stuffed too but these are so delicious I just have to have one more."

Gio leaned his head back on his chair and closed his eyes. Bianca took advantage of the moment to better examine him. She wondered if he was still single. In high school he'd never had a girlfriend. Not one that she remembered anyway. Sure, she'd seen him with plenty and witnessed those perfect lips of his kissing girls on more than one occasion but she'd never heard of him being exclusive with anyone. For a moment, the very naughty thought of what his lips would feel like on hers, crossed her mind and without thinking, she cleared her throat.

His eyes opened suddenly and caught her gazing at him as she sucked on her strawberry. She looked away dipping what was left of her strawberry in the chocolate one last time as she felt her cheeks warm. "Are you tired?" she asked staring at the chocolate.

"Not really. I just get a little drained after such a big meal."

She glanced up at him finally after staring excessively long at the chocolate. His expression seemed normal enough. Maybe he hadn't thought it strange that she'd been literally eating him up with her eyes but she was still curious. "So what's your story? You still single?"

He nodded, taking a sip of his beer. "Yep."

"Really? A good looking guy like you?" She sat up, leaning her arms against the table as she picked up her own bottle of beer. "Obviously it's by choice, right?"

He lifted a shoulder. "I have too many things going on to get involved in any kind of relationship right now. And just before I left Jack let me know me and the guys are pretty much going to be taking over the gym. So I'll be even busier now."

Bianca's eyes shot open and she noticed that for some reason that made Gio smile. "Really? Like take over, take over? He's *giving* the place to you guys?"

"Pretty much."

"Wow, that's great. But doesn't he have family?"

He shook his head then took another swig of his beer placing the empty bottle on the table. "You want another one?"

"I'll get it." He started to stand, "You need one, too?"

"Yeah, I'll take another," she said standing up. "But let's go over by the bar. I need to stand for a little I'm so full."

They started toward the bar. "Me and the guys *are* Jack's family. And since none of us have dads he's pretty much stepped up and been that father figure we all needed. He's done a great job, too." They reached the bar and this time Gio was the one that walked around to look in the fridge. He pulled two beers out and opened them, handing one to Bianca. "I don't think he's ever told any of the guys because they seem to be under the impression he never married but he told me his wife died when they'd only been married for a couple of months—some rare kidney disease. He knew it was terminal and that she only had a short time but he still married her. She was his high school sweetheart and first love. He never remarried. Instead, he put all his energy into the gym. He said it was the only thing that kept him going."

Bianca brought her hand to her chest. "Oh, my God that's so sad." She actually felt choked up and her eyes began to tear up.

Gio smiled. "Don't cry. That was a long time ago. He's over it now. I promise."

Bianca wiped a tear away feeling silly and smiled. Then she laughed softly. "I get so blubbery when I hear anything so sweet and in this case also sad." Then she laughed a little more. "You don't wanna watch a sad or even touching movie with me. Trust me."

He'd been smiling as he assured her Jack was fine but now his expression got a little serious. "So on top of your good looks, you're also a sweetheart." Bianca stared at his intense green eyes, not sure if that was a question or statement. "I hope Felix knows how lucky he is."

The odd tone to his statement confused her but she took the compliment with a smile. "Thank you and yes, Felix always makes it a point to make me feel special."

He took a drink of his beer but didn't comment further. When they finished their beer, Gio announced he *was* feeling a little tired after all; and that he wanted to be well rested for the next day when he and Felix would most likely start training. Excitement sputtered in Bianca's belly suddenly. Tomorrow she and Felix would be together again and she could hear him say he loved her *in person*.

She called her grandma before getting ready for bed as she promised she would do every night while staying with Felix. Felix had asked her to just move in with him while he was here and she literally hadn't gotten any sleep that night thinking about it. This was so new for her. She'd had boyfriends in the past but never anything this serious and certainly none that were famous.

Felix wasn't the first guy she'd slept with but he may as well be. Her first time was so stupid it didn't even count. She was just about the only girl on her high school softball team who hadn't *done* it yet. When she started dating Gary, a boy she'd known all through school, and he told her he was a virgin too they sort of just rushed to get it out of the way. There was absolutely nothing spectacular about it. It was more of a disappointment than anything.

They did it a few more times after the initial first time and the excitement about *what* they were doing was just about all the excitement she got out of it, because she'd never even climaxed with him. It was always over so fast.

After a pregnancy scare, she decided it wasn't worth it. Even though she'd always been close to her mom and she could tell her anything, one thing she'd promised her was that the first time she did it, it would be with someone she loved and she'd have protection.

Not wanting to disappoint her mom because she wasn't even close to being in love with Gary she decided not to risk it anymore. She told Gary she wanted to hold off on sex for a while and not surprisingly he found reason to break up with her soon after. The only tears she shed were for the fact that she'd given up something so precious to someone who obviously didn't give a rat's ass about her.

Bianca vowed she'd never sleep with anyone again unless she was in love. And while she didn't even know she was in love with Felix until earlier that evening she did know what she felt for him was different than what she'd ever felt for any other guy. When they did make love for the first time it felt right. That's all that mattered to her at the time. And now... now it would be truly different because now she knew he *loved* her. She could hardly wait to tell her mom and nana.

CHAPTER 5

With Bianca being such a distraction today Gio had forgotten to call his mom earlier to let her know he'd gotten there okay. He had a couple of texts he hadn't read: one from her asking if he'd made there in one piece and another from Noah asking him to call him when he had time.

He clicked the television in his room on and tossed the remote on the bed. While stepping out of his shoes he dialed his mom. She was a little pissed that he hadn't called earlier—said she was beginning to worry but she got over it once he assured her he was fine.

The next call he was going to make was to Noah but a commercial on the TV caught his eye. He was fairly certain that being around Felix for two whole months, he might run into a few celebs. He figured he should start brushing up on some pop culture so he wouldn't feel so clueless if he met anyone he should have at least heard of.

The tabloid show on now had just flashed a teaser clip of what was coming up. In the clip were candid photos of Felix walking in the snowy streets of Chicago with an unidentified girl—taken earlier that day. The broadcaster asked if this could be Felix's mystery girl that he'd been rumored to be seeing.

With Felix's upcoming fight getting so much hype Gio was sure the gossip shows were trying to cash in on it by airing even the most insignificant thing they could find on Felix.

Gio closed his door all the way and locked it. Bianca was staying in the master bedroom on the other side of the massive cabin but he still didn't want her walking by and accidentally overhearing the broadcast. He waited out the couple of minutes of commercials while he stripped down and threw on a pair of loose basketball shorts minus a shirt. Maybe it was freezing outside but the cabin was well heated. It was almost hot.

They came back from commercial and Gio sat down on the bed raising the volume just slightly.

"Boxing's current welterweight champ of the world, Felix Sanchez has been linked to many of Hollywood's A-listers including some of biggest athletes in the world. But most recently he's rumored to be in a relationship with an unidentified woman in Big Bear, California. Insiders have suggested maybe that's why he trains at his over twenty acre secluded compound located in Big Bear—to be near her. There have been sightings of Sanchez and this mysterious girl but as of today, there have been no pictures. Just today he was seen strolling through the downtown Chicago area where he was in town to make an appearance on the Stephan Walker show.

"Photos were taken of him and an unidentified woman leaving Michael Jordan's restaurant, One Sixty_blue, then getting in a car Felix himself drove back to the Omni Hotel where all of Walker's guests are put up. Could his Big Bear secret romance be out? You be the judge."

The first few photos of Felix and the girl were harmless, they were smiling and talking seemingly oblivious to the photos being taken but there was no touching.

"We caught up with them at the Omni as they

drove up to the valet and exited their car."

There were more pictures of them getting out of the car; the girl waiting for him to come around the car to meet her and then there it was. He reached over and placed his hand on the small of her back as they walked into the hotel. He might still be able to explain this but the fact remained he was walking into a *hotel* with another girl. Gio shook his head.

And here after spending the evening with Bianca he'd actually begun to believe that maybe Felix was serious about her. Why wouldn't he be? She was everything a guy would want in a girl—beautiful, adorable as shit, but most prominent was how down to earth and incredibly sweet she was. She didn't strike him as someone who would put up with this crap. She shouldn't. But was it really possible she could be that naïve?

Gio never kept up with any of the tabloid crap and here he'd watched *one* episode and already he was getting a blow by blow of Felix's affairs.

"Let's go to Chicago now where Philip is standing by outside the Omni."

"You're kidding me. They actually went on location just to get a glimpse of Felix's new girl?" Gio watched disgusted as *Philip* basically reported he had nothing. They hadn't seen the couple since the photos were shot hours ago. But they'd be looking out and actually had a crew heading to Big Bear as he spoke. "Fucking vultures."

Gio knew Felix had plenty of security and the odds of them getting any shots inside of the compound were slim. But the thought of them hounding Bianca still irritated him. She'd told him over dinner how she'd be staying at the compound during Felix's time here but she was still going to continue going to school and into work at her grandma's shop. No doubt the damn paparazzi would be staked out just outside the compound's entrance. It was just a matter of time before they figured out who she was.

Not only that, then they'd know the girl they'd seen him with in Chicago was not the same girl as Big Bear. Gio wondered how good Bianca would be about handling all the media bullshit.

The show moved on to gossip about another celebrity. Gio picked up his cell feeling even more agitated. Not just at the media but at Felix. How could he be so stupid? He had to know these vultures were watching him all the time. What kind of explanation would he have for her? This would be interesting. But he'd seen Bianca cry twice already since he'd been here. He couldn't be sure about the first time but he was almost certain it had been her initial reaction to finding out Felix wasn't going to make it up tonight. Which meant she cared about him *that* much.

The second time was just a testament to what he'd always suspected about her. Bianca was a sweetheart with a genuinely tender heart—a heart that Felix would most likely stomp. Damn.

Noah answered on the second ring. "G? How's it going up there? Are you cold yet?"

Gio could practically hear the smile in Noah's words. "Yeah, it's colder than shit out there. But Felix has us hooked up. Dude, you should see this place. It's unbelievable."

"I heard about it. He said he'll have us all up at least once while he's still up there. Make a weekend thing out of it."

"That'd be cool," Gio said smiling.

"So how'd it go today? Did you guys get started?"

Noah's questions brought back the irritation of knowing what Felix must be up to that very second. "Nah, he didn't make it out of Chicago. Bad weather or something. He's supposed to make it up here tomorrow. We'll see." He paused for a moment and stood up, then lowered his voice. "Hey, do you remember Bianca Rubio from high school?"

"Bianca?" Noah paused as if he were trying to remember. "Oh, yeah, yeah! The one you were into?" Gio made a dead stop. He'd started pacing but Noah's comment came as such a surprise.

"Who said I was *into* her?"

Noah laughed. "You did, ass. Remember?"

Gio stood there, still not moving, trying to remember ever telling anyone. He'd never even admitted to himself that he was into her. There was just something about her eyes that he found so enthralling. But he'd never told anyone. At least he didn't remember doing so. "No. When did I say this?"

Noah continued to chuckle. *Someone* was in a good mood. Gio frowned and began walking again.

"Maybe it's 'cause we were drunk. But I remember. That time I was all depressed over that stupid bitch that dumped me. I think you were trying to make me feel better. You said you had a thing for Bianca, the chick Felix was always flirting with so she was off limits. Then you made me swear on my bike that I wouldn't tell a fucking soul."

Gio dropped his head back as the memories came flooding back. "That's right. Shit, I forgot all about that." He'd completely blocked out the memory. "Holy, shit. I forgot about Felix and her back then, too. Well, get this. She's here now."

"Here where? In Big Bear?"

"In his fucking cabin. She calls herself his girlfriend and she looks even better than she did back then."

"You're kidding me. Bianca? How the hell did that happen?"

Gio explained everything Bianca had told him then added, as he sat back down on the bed running his hand through his hair, "She's still as sweet as I remember her being and she really does seem to care about him. What sucks is he's probably gonna do to her what he does to all the chicks he goes out with. Use her to his convenience."

"You never know, G. Maybe she's different."

Damn right she was. "The hell I don't know. I just saw his dumbass on TV. They had footage of him and some other chick walking into a hotel together in Chicago just today."

Noah was quiet. He'd been Gio's best friend since high school. Noah knew him too well and Gio knew he sounded a little more irritated than he should. He really shouldn't care about this so much. He never had before when it came to Felix and his trysts. In fact, it'd been fun to hear some of his stories in the past. But this was different.

Before Noah could catch on to what Gio didn't even understand he was feeling, he changed the subject abruptly. "So why did you want me to call you?"

"I need you to leave next weekend open." Noah's cheery voice was back. "Roni's making dinner and wants everyone over."

Finally, Gio had reason to smile. "Why? Is she pregnant?"

"Dude!"

"What?" Gio smiled even bigger.

Noah had told Gio about Roni getting off the pill and that he might be a dad soon. This was no surprise. As much as Noah, who was an orphan, had always put up a front about not caring that he had no family and that his friends were his family, Gio knew having a family of his own was huge for him. Noah had been almost giddy when he told Gio about it. As young as Noah was, Gio had no doubt he was mature enough and could more than handle fatherhood.

"Alright, but don't ruin the surprise." Again the smile Gio imagined on Noah's face practically radiated through the phone. "She is, and since you've already ruined that part of the surprise I may as well tell you the rest. We're getting married. I wanna do it before the baby is here so we'll just have something small but she wants to go to Tahoe."

"Tahoe?"

Noah told him about how since Roni couldn't drink she could at least gamble and how she thought the snow would be extra romantic. They were basically eloping. Noah didn't want anyone having to take time off and spend money to make it up to Tahoe but they'd have a little something when they got back. Noah was obviously excited. Gio couldn't be happier for him. He'd never seen him so happy as when he was around Roni. He congratulated him whole-heartedly and was surprised that even with all the baby and wedding talk Noah went back to Bianca.

"So, you gonna be okay being around Bianca?"

The warm feelings of joy were suddenly overrun with annoyance. "What do you mean? Of course I am." His words were so defensive he almost expected Noah to laugh but he didn't.

Instead, he sounded even more serious. "All I'm

saying is, I know you. You already sound like this pisses you off. And I'm with you. It's bad enough Felix does this to girls in his own league but to dick around with someone like Bianca, who you say is so sweet and probably has no idea what she's in for, sucks. You're a good friend and if she warms up to you at all and vice versa it's gonna make it even harder to know his ass is just toying with her." Noah sighed. "You're out there for a reason, man. To get your mind clear and ready to get back to how things were before. I just hope you're not gonna get all caught up in this shit."

Damn it if Noah didn't read him like a book. He was already getting caught up and he hadn't even been there a day. But he lied. "Nah, I'll be cool. Fuck it. She's gotta have some idea about what she was getting herself into with him. She can't be *that* in the dark about it. Right?"

It was wishful thinking and it only made sense that she did. But something in his gut, something in those unsuspecting eyes of hers told him she was really buying whatever crap Felix was feeding her.

"I don't know. You tell me," Noah said. "Does she seem stupid?"

"No!" Just like that, he was back on his feet. "Just trusting. And she's beautiful. Why wouldn't she believe Felix could really be feeling what he's probably telling her he is? In fact after spending the evening with her I was beginning to think maybe he did, until I saw him on TV."

"Well, let's not jump to conclusions. We all know what the paparazzi can be like. Remember he told us about what they did with that photo of him and that ice skater a few months ago? This could be the same shit. And who knows maybe you can talk some sense into him. Tell him not to be such a heartless ass."

Yeah. That was easier said than done. Just because Gio could talk to Noah like this didn't mean he did with everyone. He'd been as close to Felix as he was to Noah once upon a time. But that was years ago. Gio sighed. He hadn't even realized how much this really bothered him until Noah brought it back up.

"I guess. But I'll be fine. Don't worry, I won't stress over this crap."

Even Gio didn't believe his own words and he was sure neither did Noah but he was ending this now. He wanted to hang up on a happy note. "Hey, congrats again bro. I'm really, *really* happy for you guys. Give Roni a hug for me okay?"

Gio knew Noah wasn't completely convinced about him not stressing out. And as much as he told himself it really wasn't any of his business and his friendship with Felix should come first, *that's* the part that was seriously beginning to bother him.

After only a few hours with Bianca, he already felt sorry for her—and annoyed as hell at Felix. No telling what a few more days and weeks around her would do to him.

CHAPTER 6

The next morning Gio woke to sounds of trucks outside. He peeked out the window and sure enough the plows were going. Gio had seen Felix's private plows on the property last night. Now he knew why he had three. The entire *long* driveway had been snowed in overnight. Gio expected the winter to be white up here. He knew that's what Big Bear was known for but this seemed a bit much.

He showered and dressed in his favorite pair of jeans and a dark thermal. Once fully dressed he walked into the living room where Bianca stood in front of the television holding a mug in her hand. She was still in a bathrobe and her hair looked damp. When she heard his footsteps, she turned giving him a weak smile.

Gio sucked in a breath for two reasons: for starters, she'd washed off all of yesterday's makeup giving her that innocent fresh look like back in school. *This* was the Bianca he remembered and the look brought with it even more memories. Memories of staring at her when she was reading in class, though he'd made sure she never caught him.

But she looked troubled now. From his angle, he couldn't see what she was watching but he could guess. If they were airing the same thing he'd watched last night about Felix, that would do it. "Morning," she said as he got closer. "Did you sleep well?"

"Like a baby."

She smiled again just as weakly as the first time. He

hated to ask but he may as well get it over with. He'd find out soon enough. "Something wrong?"

She nodded and glanced back at the TV. "The storm last night. It's good for the local businesses but only when the tourists down below can get up here. Looks like the main highway up here is completely closed down." The corner of her lip lifted. "Felix is finally on his way but now the airport up here is closed. He'll have to land at the airport in Ontario then wait it out down there. It may be another day before he gets up here." She shrugged. "The only good thing is I took the whole weekend off. I would've never made it out of here in time to get to the shop. Even with three plows they're just now finishing up plowing the driveway. The shop opened a few hours ago. This is the most snow we've had in years. It's a mess out there."

Gio came around to get a better look at the television screen. The news coverage went from pictures of power lines down, car after car stuck in the snow, and then to people struggling to shovel pathways from their front door to their cars. They listened to the rest of the broadcast without saying a word as the newscaster concluded that the main highway would most likely be closed until the following day. Bianca groaned.

"She didn't say anything about the airport." Gio offered. "That might open up sooner."

His phone buzzed in his pocket and Gio pulled it out. It was a text from Felix.

Just landed in Ontario. I'm sorry, man. I'm trying to get up there. I really am.

Gio smiled and started to text back.

"Is that Felix?" Bianca asked.

Gio nodded glancing up at her. "Yeah, he said he just landed in Ontario."

He sent off his response to Felix.

Don't worry about it. You'll get here when you get here. The accommodations in the meantime aren't too shabby so I'm good.

"Is he telling you about today?" Bianca walked past him and into the kitchen where Amparo was preparing breakfast.

Gio looked up at her curiously. "No, what about today?"

"He said once they clear up the driveway I should take you snowboarding." She turned and smiled at him as she poured herself more coffee. "He feels bad that he has us both hanging around waiting for him."

Gio's phone buzzed again and he checked the text again.

So you and Bianca snowboard today. I already talked to her. Enjoy… the snowboarding. NOTHING else ass! Don't worry. I'll hook you up once I'm up there. We'll all go out if this fucking weather ever lets up!

Gio smirked glancing up at Bianca again. "He just told me. Sounds good, but I've never snowboarded." He lifted a hand to give him a second while he responded to Felix again.

Got it. And relax, you'll be up here soon enough.

Gio knew Felix was only kidding about the *nothing else* part of his message. Normally he wouldn't have a problem busting any of his friends' balls. Even on something like this, but this felt different. He didn't want to start any of that kind of talk. Not even in a playful way. So he wasn't even touching on the comment.

He stuck his phone in his pocket and glanced up at Bianca again who was pulling another mug out of the cabinet. "You want some coffee?"

"No thanks. I'm not much for coffee. But I'll take some orange juice if you have any."

Amparo opened the refrigerator and pulled out a glass pitcher. "Freshly made," she said with a smile. "Breakfast is also ready. So whenever you two are ready I can serve it."

Gio met Bianca back at the dining table after she'd changed. Seeing her now no longer glammed up but in jeans, a soft sweater and her sneakers sent Gio right back to senior year World History class. She'd even pulled her hair back in a simple ponytail like she used to wear it back then. Gio gulped, irritated with himself, and forced himself to look away. This time Ray and Ignacio joined them for breakfast so he turned his attention to them, smiling as he took his seat.

"So really? You've never been snowboarding?" Bianca asked, forcing him to look back at her eyes as big and as inquisitive as ever.

Gio smiled. "Nope. The most I've ever done in the snow is tubing." Incredibly, her eyes opened even wider and he was suddenly feeling nervous about snowboarding. Visions of him falling flat on his ass came to him and he was not looking forward to that. Not in front of Bianca. "Maybe snowboarding is not such a good idea."

"Don't be silly. I can teach you." Her eyes were full of all kinds of excitement and as nervous as Gio was, he still couldn't wipe the goofy smile off his face.

Amparo set his waffles down in front of him. Gio grabbed a banana from the fruit basket Amparo had set on the table earlier and sliced it over his waffles. He glanced up to see Bianca watching him. Their eyes met and she smiled. How could something as simple as a smile be so breathtaking?

"Yeah," Ray said, setting his coffee cup down. "It's a little tricky at first but once you get the hang of it you should be good. It's addicting, actually."

"You guys coming too?" Gio asked, glancing from Ray to Ignacio.

They both shook their heads immediately. "Not today," Ray said. "We still have a lot of shoveling to do in the back. That part of the complex piles up the fastest and takes the longest to thaw out. With this storm not letting up we can't let that go. The gym entrance will be buried shut before we know it."

Gio frowned. "Then maybe I should stay and help, too."

"Stop trying to get out of it, Gio," Bianca's smirk teased. "You're going."

Ignacio didn't even try to hide his amused expression as if he agreed with Bianca's assumption of why Gio was offering to help. "We got it, man. We use the plows, too. Piece of cake."

After breakfast, Bianca instructed him on what he'd need to wear. Everything he needed was hanging in his closet for him. He even found a season pass to the ski lift they'd be going to in the pocket of his snow pants. With a sticky note stuck to it.

Get ready for the snow bunnies. =)

Gio smiled remembering the conversation he'd had with Felix when Gio called him to tell him he'd decided to take him on his offer. Felix told him he was looking forward to reconnecting with his best bud.

This was an easy one to figure out. While Felix had always said he'd done some of his best sparring with Gio, Felix didn't really need him to train. He'd won a world championship without him; why would he need him now? And he most certainly didn't need to be pay-

ing him. Felix acted like Gio was doing *him* a favor.
Clearly, it was the other way around. Gio should be
paying Felix for this two-month vacation. Here he was
on day two of his *job* and he'd be spending the day on
the slopes with a full season pass. He knew this was
just the beginning too. Judging from his living arrangements and last night's lavish dinner, not to mention this morning's breakfast, the next two months he'd
be living high on the hog. And all because his buddy
was worried about him.

He thought of the annoyance he'd felt last night
with Felix then as he walked out of his room and Bianca's bright smile greeted him. Noah's words rang
loudly in his conscience. *Let's not jump to conclusions
just yet.*

Noah was right. He shouldn't jump to conclusions.
Felix had a good heart and he wasn't stupid. There's no
way he could be taking someone like Bianca for
granted.

As Bianca approached him, still sporting her beautifully fresh no-makeup look, he breathed in a little easier. She *had* to be the girl Felix had referred to as the
one he could be falling for.

"The driveway is plowed and the driver is waiting
for us outside," she announced cheerfully. "You
ready?"

Gio looked down at himself in his snowboarding
gear and then back up at her. "I guess so."

"You look good," she smiled, looking him over.

Their eyes met and her cheery smile lost some of its
brightness for just an instant then she was back. "Don't
worry. I promise to get you back here in one piece."

"Who's worried?" He laughed nervously which
only made her giggle.

Great, the giggling was already starting and he hadn't even stepped onto the snowboard.

*

Determined to make the best of another day of waiting for Felix, Bianca decided she'd be positive about this and try to enjoy herself. So far, Gio had been pleasant enough company, and he was certainly nice to look at. She giggled inwardly biting her lower lip and pretending the scenery out the window at that particular moment was especially interesting.

"They have beginner trails, right?"

Bianca turned back to see Gio's nervous face, his green eyes momentarily veiled under a slow blink of long lashes. Geez, what she'd give to have lashes as heavy as his. She reached out and squeezed his arm. "Yes, they do. Don't worry I'll take it easy on you." She smiled reassuringly. "Felix was the same way when he first started. Even with all the traveling he'd never really hit the slopes so he was just as nervous but after a few runs he got it."

Gio returned the smile, nodding, but he didn't seem completely convinced. When they reached the lift, Gio appeared even more apprehensive. His green eyes nearly went gray as he stared up at the massive mountain they'd be lifted up to.

The pensiveness Bianca had noticed on their drive there was now replaced with what could only be described as sheer panic. "We're not going up there, are we?"

Bianca brought her hand to her mouth to cover her smile. She wouldn't laugh at him. At least she'd try not to. "Yes, but they have a lot of different trails—beginner's trails. It's not as daunting as it looks. I promise."

Gio glanced back at her but said nothing. The movement of his Adam's apple as he gulped said it all and now she had to laugh. "Will you trust me?"

Her laughter finally got a smirk out of him. "I do but..." He turned back to the mountain. "Damn!"

"C'mon," she said, pulling him by his jacket. "I can show you some of the basics down here first." A giggle escaped her. "Like how to stand on the board without falling."

Gio peered at her but smiled. "I think I can manage standing."

Bianca bit her bottom lip, trying not to laugh. "We'll see." This was going to be just like when she taught Felix all over again. *Felix*—just the thought of him not making it up again was enough to nearly wipe the smile off her face.

They moved off to the side, took a seat on a bench and proceeded to strap their boots into their boards. Bianca finished and stood waiting as Gio struggled to strap his in. "Need help?"

"Nah, I got it."

Bianca smirked watching him continue to struggle when she felt her phone buzz in her jacket pocket. She pulled off her glove, reached in for the phone and checked the screen —a text from Toni. That was odd. She'd spoken to Toni that morning. She'd needed to vent to someone about Felix still not being able to get up. Toni was part of the reason why she was trying so hard to keep her mind off Felix. Bianca had promised she'd do her best to enjoy today without sulking— which she planned on doing before talking to Toni.

Curiously, she clicked on the envelope.

I know you're boarding today. But when you get a

chance give me a call. No biggie. Just something about Felix I thought you should know.

The unease was immediate. Ever since last summer's paparazzi photo, she'd made it a point to stay away from the tabloids. As much as she could anyway. Toni, on the other hand, was a tabloid nut but she had promised to not rile up Bianca unless it was something concrete. Bianca *did not* need to know about every sighting of him with another girl that wasn't even confirmed. Many weren't even recent and lots of them were doctored up.

When she first started dating Felix there were stories all over about him and other girls but many of them were old pictures — old news being revived for the sake of gossip. She refused to drive herself crazy because, as it turned out, every one of the stories she'd confronted him with had proved to have a valid explanation.

Toni hadn't mentioned anything she'd read or heard in months. She glanced up at Gio thankful that he was being stubborn about her helping him and seeing that he was still doing it wrong took advantage of the delay. "I gotta make a quick call, okay?"

Gio nodded not even looking up. Bianca took a few steps away from Gio so he wouldn't hear her and hit speed dial. Toni answered on the first ring.

"Sweetie, I didn't mean to worry you. I even thought of just waiting until later but I was afraid I'd forget."

Bianca took a deep breath. "What? What is it?"

Toni exhaled, obviously annoyed with herself but it was too late. Bianca was already worried. "I just thought you might want to know that the paparazzi have gotten wind of Felix coming up here. They're headed up here as well and they'll be on the lookout for his *secret girlfriend*. I wanted to give you a head's up since I know you stay away from the gossip shows." Bianca let out a slow relieved breath; hating that she still had to worry about this kind of crap. She wanted so badly to just trust him completely. "Any word yet on when he'll be up?"

"Nothing yet." Bianca chewed her pinky nail. "He's supposed to call me a little later. He knows I'm spending the day boarding."

"I know. I'm sorry I interrupted. You know normally I wouldn't but..." she seemed hesitant and that alone put Bianca on edge.

"But what? Is there more?"

There was an unpleasant pause then Toni spoke up again. "No. No, there isn't."

"Are you sure?" Bianca glanced back and saw that Gio had both feet strapped into his board and was attempting to stand. *Shit*. She hurried back in his direction but still held the phone to her ear.

"I'm sure. I just wanted to make sure you didn't get spooked or anything by some eager photographer."

Just as she reached Gio he nearly toppled over and she grabbed his arm with her free hand. "I gotta go," was all she said to Toni before hanging up and sticking the phone in her pocket with her other hand then quickly reaching over to hold Gio up.

His arms came around her in a panic. "Holy shit!"

She couldn't help giggling. "You weren't supposed to strap both boots in yet. Just one." She looked up at him; his face inches away from her. His minty breath so close to her face made her insides flutter but his confused expression had her smiling again in an instant. "I'm sorry I should've told you that first, right?"

"Yeah," he smirked, trying to stand on his own again. "Maybe I wouldn't have taken so embarrassingly long."

She started to laugh but then stopped when she saw him wobble. "Don't!" She grabbed his arm. "You're gonna fall!" Even though she'd just had his big arms around her a moment ago it surprised her just how big and hard they really were now that she was squeezing them.

Her eyes went from his arms to his alarmed expression and she pressed her lips together in an effort to suppress the incredible urge to laugh. The alarm in his eyes turned into humor. "You're loving this, aren't you?"

The only thing that kept her from laughing outright was that the sparkle in his green eyes was so incredible. The urge to sigh deeply won out over the urge to laugh by a mile. She settled for a very satisfying smile and she raised her chin. "Actually, believe it or not, I'm very concerned for your safety." She motioned for him to sit. "Here, unstrap the right one."

He sat and did as he was told. "What's the point of two straps if you only need one on?"

"You'll need them both on when you're actually snowboarding but when you're walking around and getting on and off the lift you only keep one on so your other foot is free to move on and off the board." He glanced up at her as the strap pulled open and Bianca wondered how long it would take to get used to those eyes. "Jesus, Gio. Which one of your parents did you get such amazing eyes from?"

Unbelievably, the sparkle in his eyes got even more brilliant with his smile. "My mom and thank you."

"You're welcome," she smiled back, feeling just a

little bit embarrassed that she was so blunt about it, but it couldn't be helped. "I've never seen anything like them."

His smile waned a bit as those eyes looked deep into hers for a moment. "I could say the same about yours."

She forced her eyes away from his penetrating stare feeling her face warm. "Mine are just plain brown."

"They're anything but plain, Bianca. They're beautiful. But I'm sure this isn't the first time you've heard that." He stood up placing his freed boot on the snow and looked down.

It wasn't the first time but she wasn't about to brag. "Bambi," she blurted out trying to keep the moment from getting awkward.

"Huh?" Gio's eyes met hers again and she smiled at his comical expression.

"It's what Felix calls me sometimes. He says I have Bambi eyes."

A slow smile spread across Gio's face. "Nice. I think he hit it on the nose. Bambi eyes — that's perfect."

As sweet as his smile was Bianca knew it was wrong to be enjoying it so much, so she pulled her eyes away and glanced at his now freed boot. "Okay, so let me show you how to walk in these. Stand like me."

They went over the basics on how to walk around on the board and what to do and what not to do. Then finally they did a little skating. Although she tried her best, she wasn't able to keep from laughing at his clumsiness. After he fell for the third time Bianca meant to keep her laughter to a minimum but she did the stupid squeak thing that got her going good.

She hid her face behind her gloved hands and peeked between her fingers as she continued to laugh.

Gio didn't even attempt to get up. Instead, he brought his knees up and rested his arms on them looking very exhausted already but he couldn't hide the smile. He squinted up at her. "You're having way too much fun at my expense. You know, if I didn't know any better I'd say you planned this. Probably planned the time you taught Felix, too. For your own amusement."

Bianca managed to calm her laughter but still giggled. "I did not!" She pouted but somehow she didn't think he'd buy into it since her lip was still quivering from her stifled laughing. "My boyfriend was supposed to be here today remember?" As the laughter ceased she was able to pout more convincingly until she saw the appalled look on his face and his eyes go wide open.

"Am I supposed to feel sorry for you now after you've laughed at me all morning?"

With that, she was at it again. "I wasn't laughing *at* you." She offered him her hand and he took it. "I was laughing *with* you. We're having fun, right?"

With a grunt and a pull from Bianca, he was on his feet again. "Yeah, my ass is having a blast." Gio dusted his behind off.

Bianca managed to calm her laughing and pulled her phone out. "Not to scare you or anything but let's get each other's number just in case we get separated. Sometimes these boards have a mind of their own. If anything happens we can find each other easier this way."

"Somehow," Gio said, unzipping his jacket, "I don't think I'll hear my phone ringing under all these layers but, if you say so."

"Yes, I say so. You'd be surprised."

They programmed each other's number in their

phones but when Gio stuck his back in his jacket he motioned up to the mountain. "I hate to break it to you, but I don't think you're gonna get me up there today."

"You *have* to!" Bianca's laughing mood was gone now. He couldn't be serious but he shook his head. "Really? A big tough boxer like you is gonna let a few tumbles scare him?"

Gio laughed at that. "Hey, let's not get personal." Taking a deep breath, he took in the mountain again. "Maybe after I've had some lunch. I know we had a big breakfast but I've worked up an appetite."

"Agreed," she said, taking her gloves off and pushing them into her jacket pocket. She reached her hand out to him. "Take my hand. I don't want you falling again and changing your mind."

Bianca meant to just latch her hand in his to help him back to the bench and she thought he'd keep his gloves on. But he took his glove off before reaching for her hand and their fingers automatically laced.

With a gulp she glanced at him as he concentrated on his footing. There was no way he was feeling what she was feeling from the simple touch of his hand. Gio was completely engrossed in making sure he didn't fall. She squeezed his hand as his foot slipped slightly and he squeezed back, finally looking at her with a smile. Her heart rate had already sped up the second their fingers touched. It accelerated even more now. Jesus, could he be more beautiful?

She remembered thinking this even back in high school. Was it possible someone could be just as beautiful on the inside? She would've never thought so, but after spending the evening with him, and the entire morning, that possibility was beginning to feel very real.

CHAPTER 7

Gio could've gone for a simple cheeseburger at the ski lodge but Bianca insisted the food there was overpriced and not worth it. She said there was some place he had to try while he was up here and they may as well try it today.

They now sat at BJ's, a dive off the main strip but Bianca swore they not only had the best cheeseburgers in Big Bear but also the best homemade chili. They also ordered two mugs of beer. Another thing Bianca said was great about this place — their prices. The mugs were under two dollars.

"Now we're talking." Gio smirked, clinking her mug in the air before taking a swig.

"I thought you'd like the cheap beer. You're such an Angelino!" Bianca took a swig.

Gio placed the mug down loving how her always-cheery demeanor was so damn contagious. He hadn't stopped laughing or smiling all morning. Even when he was falling on his ass. "You calling me cheap?"

Her bright eyes teased him. "I call them like I see them. Even Felix with all the money he has couldn't hide his excitement about the cheap beer here." She giggled. "You can take the guy out of the *barrio* but you'll never take the *barrio* out of the guy."

Gio had to laugh. "This is so true. Felix will always be an Angelino. No matter what part of the world he's in."

He thought about how loyal Felix had always been,

not just to him but the gym—Jack—his roots. It almost made Gio feel guilty about how much he was enjoying spending time with the guy's girl. He knew technically he wasn't doing anything wrong but what he was starting to feel every time he looked into those eyes and what he'd felt when he held her hand earlier wasn't exactly admirable.

He took a harder swig of his beer as their food was set on the table. Bianca leaned her nose into the bowl of chili in front of her then did that orgasmic thing with her eyes again. Gio cleared his throat looking away. This wasn't helping his already corrupt thoughts, d-amn it.

"It smells so good," Bianca said as he tried his best to concentrate on their food and not her facial expressions.

"Yeah, looks good, too."

Bianca took a bite of her still steaming cornbread and Gio turned away quickly. Her eyes were already closing at the taste of the apparently delicious bread but there was no escape from hearing the near moaning sounds she made. He fisted his hand pressing his lips together and for an instant wondered if she could possibly be doing this on purpose.

"You're real expressive when you're enjoying s-omething, aren't you?"

The moment the question was out there, he was hit with the visual of her being expressive enjoying *other* things. As if that thought alone wasn't bad enough he remembered something else. He'd be in the same cabin, just yards away from her and Felix's bedroom for two months.

"Something wrong?"

Nudged out of his thoughts Gio glanced at Bianca

who for the first time today wasn't smiling. "No, why?"

"I don't know. You looked upset all of a sudden. Everything okay?"

Her face was so concerned. Did he really look *that* upset? He played it off with a smirk. "Yeah, I was just thinking about…" He couldn't come up with anything so he put a spoonful of chili in his mouth then nodded. It *was* damn good. He hoped the subject would go back to the food. Instead, she surprised him.

"Were you thinking about that guy?"

Gio tilted his head, confused. "What guy?"

"The one that died in the ring?"

For once since it had happened, he was actually relieved that the subject was brought up. Anything was better than admitting what he was really thinking. "Yeah, I guess." It was a stretch. He *had* thought of the guy today. Not just now but he had on their way to snowboard that morning. He looked back down at his chili unwilling to look into her sympathetic eyes any longer. Gio was tired of people feeling bad for him. *He* wasn't the one who lost his life. *He* didn't leave a pregnant wife behind.

Before he could say anything else, Bianca began to speak. "When my grandparents were first married they went on their honeymoon to Acapulco. On their drive back on a lonely road they were assaulted by a gang of thieves. They beat my grandpa with a horseshoe until he was unconscious but before they could rape my grandmother another car pulled up and they all ran off."

Gio stared at her, stunned by her story but she continued, "My grandmother said my grandfather was barely breathing. She was certain he wouldn't make it to a hospital. It took them hours to get him there and by some miracle, he made it. Nana said it just wasn't his time to go. Then just last summer everything was fine. They'd enjoyed a day out on the lake and that evening he fell asleep on his reclining chair and never woke up. His heart stopped in his sleep." Gio didn't think it possible but her eyes grew even darker as she continued to talk. "My dad had something similar happen to him too. When he was a little boy he nearly drowned in a neighbor's pool. The doctors didn't think he'd survive and if he did they said he'd have brain damage because of the amount of time they thought his brain had been without oxygen. Not only did he survive, he made a full recovery. Then like my grandpa, when I was in the fifth grade, very unexpectedly he stepped foot into the street and was hit by a bus. It killed him instantly. Because of his hearing impairment he relied heavily on his sight when doing something as simple as crossing the street but the bus driver said he'd just stepped foot onto the street right in front of the bus without looking up. Something he always did but for some reason that one time he didn't." She shrugged "It was their time."

Gio shook his head, not sure how to respond, then her already dark eyes got even more serious. "I'm sure you've heard this a million times, Giovanni. But you really can't blame yourself. Even if it hadn't happened under the circumstances that it did — an arranged fight that he completely agreed to — when it's your time, it's your time." She reached across the table and touched his hand. "There's only one higher power that decides these things. Believe it or not, you had *nothing* to do with his time being up."

Everyone including his mother, Jack and the guys

had all tried to get him to see the situation for it was—a tragic event that couldn't be helped. But hearing Bianca put it this way made him actually believe it for once. "I'm sorry about what happened to your grandparents and your dad. That really sucks. But I'm glad it wasn't their time so early on."

"And see, that's just the thing," she said squeezing Gio's hand now. "It sucks that this guy was so young, yes. But it *was his time*."

Gio glanced down at her delicate hand. Funny how such a simple gesture could go so far. Her touch was soothing—calming. "He had an untreated aneurism. He should've never been in the ring. The doctor that cleared him is actually under investigation right now." Her hand stroked his now and the pent up emotion he'd held in for so long was back. "His wife is pregnant. She's real young, too. I thought about her when I saw a few couples on the slopes today with their little kids. That's what's bothered me the most about all this. Losing my dad was the worst thing I'd ever gone through, but at least I had my dad for thirteen years. This kid is never even gonna know his dad."

He didn't know why he was telling her all this but it felt good to finally let it out. For so long he'd refused to really tell anyone what he was thinking—feeling. He'd hid away in that garage for weeks; barely speaking to anyone that came and sat with him.

Without warning, Bianca stood up and came around the table, sliding in on his side. She took his hand and leaned her head against his shoulder, giving Gio a heavenly whiff of her hair. "It's okay to feel sad for his child. As long as you're not blaming yourself for it." She lifted her head to face him. Gio refused to move. If he did he'd have to fight the urge to put his arm around her and then…instead he looked in her big concerned eyes. "If we believe my grandma's theory, and I really do, as much as it sucks ass, that kid was never meant to meet his dad. It's just how things were meant to be."

As heavy as what she just said was, Gio couldn't help but chuckle. "Sucks ass? Really?"

Her eyes brightened instantly and she pulled away from him, humor already dancing in her eyes. "My grandma says that all the time."

That made Gio laugh even more and just like that she was laughing with him. "She sounds like my grandma then. Whenever she caught us playing with her things — things we weren't supposed to be touching, like her expensive china, she'd tell us to 'Go play with your *culo!*'" Bianca burst out laughing now and even though Gio had heard his grandmother say that so many times, it sounded hilarious now to him, too. Between laughing he explained. "My mom used to get pissed. She hated the way it sounded. But that didn't stop my grandma." Gio smiled remembering something else. "My mom's always been big on not ruining your appetite between meals with junk but my grandma didn't care what of time a day or how close our next mealtime was. If I or any of my sisters were ever sad about anything she'd load us up with ice cream."

Bianca smiled big. "That's so cool. So you totally get why we women go running to good 'ole Häagan-Dazs with a giant spoon when we're down instead of crying into our beer like you guys supposedly do when you're down."

"Absolutely," Gio agreed, lifting his mug. "Beer's for the good times. But ain't nothing like a big ass bowl of ice cream with all the trimmings to chase the blues away for me."

He told her a little more about his grandma and he was so close to pulling her food over to his side so she wouldn't go back to sitting on the other side. He liked her right where she was. As disappointing as it was when she did move back to sit across from him he knew it was for the best.

Gio had never really been much of a talker, especially with girls. It was rare for him to open up to anyone else but his close friends but Bianca made it so easy. The conversation just flowed so comfortably as if it hadn't been years since they'd last seen each other.

When they were finished with lunch Bianca suddenly looked up at him; her excitement was irrefutable. Instantly, Gio felt the big goofy smile he'd worn all day on his face again. "What?"

"You wanna meet my grandma?"

This was completely unexpected. "When?"

"Today. My mom too, actually." She stood up and he stood with her. "If we take the back way to the resort we'll pass right by the shop. I don't usually go even a day without seeing them and I was planning on going straight back to the cabin after we boarded but since it's on the way, maybe we can stop by?"

The thought of meeting her mom and grandmother made him a little uneasy. Especially knowing her grandmother was the type of woman that said 'sucks ass' *all the time*. Gio had never met any parents of the girls he'd gone out with. Of course, he wasn't the one seeing Bianca. Still, it made him nervous, but after seeing her excitement about such a simple request there was no way he'd refuse. "Sure, we can do that."

Seeing how happy that made her was totally worth

the nerves. On the way there, Bianca got a call from Felix. The girl wore her heart on her sleeve and Gio saw it the moment Felix had given her the news. Felix wasn't making it up to the cabin again.

Gio glanced out the window not wanting to be too intrusive of her conversation but with her sitting right next to him, there was no way of not hearing it all.

"It's all clear up here. I thought you said you'd charter a helicopter if you had to?"

The speaker on her phone was so loud Gio could hear Felix tell her he'd tried everything. Ironically, just as he said it Gio saw not only a plane fly overhead but a helicopter as well. It could be that they were just allowing local touring helicopters but Gio's mind went back to the photos of Felix and that other girl in a hotel and he wondered if Felix was even in California like he claimed to be.

Felix was a player. He'd never denied that and with his celebrity of course he had girls throwing themselves at him everywhere he went. But why lead someone like Bianca on? He had plenty of girls who would gladly agree to a non-exclusive relationship. Why break such a sweet girl's heart? It was totally unnecessary, and completely selfish. It's not like there was a shortage of girls in Big Bear. Even up here in this quaint little town, Felix seemed confident that there'd be plenty of snow bunnies for them.

That made Gio wonder if Felix planned on joining him with the snow bunnies or if he planned on bringing Bianca along.

Gio glanced back at Bianca. There was no hiding the disappointment she now wore so heavily. She sighed deeply. "Okay. Well, keep me posted." A sudden smile illuminated her face. "I love you, too."

Gio jerked his face away and stared out his window, afraid Bianca might see the shock and disgust he was feeling with Felix at that moment. Was he really throwing it out there like that? Telling her he loved her while he was still messing around? He couldn't think of anything more fucked up.

Knowing it would only piss him off but he had to know now, he pulled his own phone out and googled Big Bear Airport. Within seconds, he got what he wanted.

Conditions: Clear

Felix was full of shit. Being a selfish asshole with the girls he dated was one thing but why the hell should Gio get involved in this shit? He didn't mind the time he got to spend with Bianca. In fact, he was enjoying it more than he'd ever admit to anyone. But he just didn't want to be part of or witness to any heartache Felix's heartless ass might put her through.

He didn't even realize Bianca was off the phone and staring out her window now. Her cheery mood was long gone. "So he's not making it up tonight?"

She shook her head but continued to stare out the window. Since she didn't actually answer, Gio pursed his lips wondering if maybe she was choked up. She had been visibly upset the night before when she first got the news he wasn't going to make it up.

"You okay?"

She finally turned and met his eyes. Eyes like hers weren't meant to be sad and at that moment he hated Felix. "You don't think he's just making excuses do you?"

"No," Gio was quick to answer but he'd say anything to make her feel better. "I really don't think he would've had me come up if he hadn't planned on being here."

There was a flicker of hope in her eyes now, as if she hadn't thought of that. "The main highway is still down but this morning he sounded sure that worst case scenario he could charter a helicopter. Now he says that's not looking like it's gonna happen either."

"But it's still a possibility, right?" Gio tried to sound hopeful but the more he thought of the clear conditions at the airport the harder it was to hide the disdain he was feeling for Felix.

The car pulled up in front of a quaint shop. "He didn't sound too optimistic," she said as she reached for the door handle. "More than likely he won't be up until tomorrow."

A very small part of him was glad he'd have another night alone with her. But the bigger part, the important part, the one that was beginning to understand why Noah was worried about him stressing out, had to fight the urge to call Felix and tell his ass off.

Of course, he couldn't. Not just because he was with her at the moment but because even if he walked away to make the call, the way he was feeling he'd probably get loudly worked up and she'd know something was up.

Felix was blowing her off... again. That wasn't something Gio wanted to break to her. What sucked is that she'd eventually find out and Gio hoped to hell he wasn't around to see it. He wouldn't be able to bear seeing her cry.

They got out and walked silently up to the front door of the shop. The contrast of the warmth inside the shop compared to the freezing cold outside felt heavenly. Gio was glad he walked in behind Bianca and didn't have the ability to seeing the crotch-tightening expression she was probably making because it felt *that* good.

A short older woman wearing glasses on a chain that hung around her neck looked up and smiled big. "Bianca!" Another woman, younger than the first, walked out of the door behind the counter engrossed in a figurine she was holding. The first woman tapped her gently on the arm and motioned to Bianca.

The woman smiled and used sign language to communicate with her. Bianca responded with her own effortless hand signs as she approached them. "I'm snowboarding today."

Both women smiled as she hugged and kissed them. Bianca turned to Gio who stood behind her trying not to look as nervous as he felt. This was an absolute first for him and he had no idea how unnerving it could be. "This is Gio, one of Felix's trainers and old friend from high school." She smiled then addressed Gio. "This is my grandmother, Nana, and my mother, Lupe."

After the introductions Bianca's mother signed something to Bianca pointing at her own eyes then at Gio. A shy smile spread across Bianca's face. "She says you have beautiful eyes."

"Thank you," Gio nodded toward her mom. She smiled brightly and though her eyes weren't nearly as big as Bianca's, Gio could see where Bianca got her happy demeanor.

"So, where's Felix?" her grandmother asked.

It was quick. Almost like a flinch and if Gio could stop gazing at her for even a second he might have missed it. But now Bianca hid the initial effect the question had on her. She spoke as casually as ever. "He's stuck down the hill. The highway is closed off and the airport isn't cleared for any landings." She turned back to face Gio with a small smile. "He's keeping me company in the meantime."

Her grandmother peered at him over her glasses. "And how is she doing Gio? She showing you the sights of our little town?"

Gio nodded and was sure his smile came across much bigger than he first intended it to be. "Actually, I thought she was the one keeping me company. But yes, she's showing me around and even though I've been up here a few times before I never realized how beautiful this little town is."

Her grandmother smiled proudly, taking the glasses off and letting them hang from her neck. "It's pretty all year round up here but this is when it's almost magical. Something about the purity of freshly fallen snow does things to the soul and boy, did we get some last night."

Bianca's mom's hands moved quickly signing something at her. Bianca spoke the words almost as if by habit, "The snow even has a healing power."

"Yeah, that too," her grandmother agreed. "It's a very powerful thing." She turned back to Bianca. "How long will Felix be? I'm not kidding about the allure fresh snow has on people. That boy is nuts leaving you to entertain such a good looking friend in this kind of weather."

"Nana!" Both her grandmother and mother burst out laughing at the sight of Bianca's immediately flushed face.

Gio had to smirk but only until he was caught in her grandmother's twinkling but knowing eyes. What was it about grandmothers? He'd been in her sights under five minutes and already she knew what he'd been trying to suppress all day? Maybe he was *that* obvious or maybe she just knew how adorably irresistible her granddaughter was. Whatever it was, what she didn't know was that even if Gio ever stood a chance with Bianca and God help him, as tempting as that would be, moving in on a friend's girl was a line he knew he'd never cross.

He turned to look at Bianca's still horrified expression. And here he thought there was nothing that wouldn't make her crack up. Her grandmother's laugh was down to a chuckle. "Oh, come on. You know I'm only playing."

Gio glanced back in time to catch her grandmother wink at Bianca. He wasn't sure what or if that meant anything and he certainly wasn't asking. As curious as it made him, one thing he'd just realized was that he didn't like seeing Bianca upset or even uncomfortable. She was born to be happy and carefree and at the moment she looked anything but. "So this is it, huh?" He looked around in an attempt to change the subject and to his relief that beautiful smile was back on Bianca's face.

"Yeah, this is it. Our little shop. C'mon I'll show you around."

It was a cute little place. Exactly what he pictured with the exception of the corner of the shop she called the library. They had shelves full of books, a table with a couple of carafes of coffee and cups and a cheery sign that read 'Help yourself!' Then there were comfortable chairs and a sofa strategically placed to face the picturesque window. "We're all insatiable readers." Bianca explained. "My grandma thought it'd be nice to have a reading area for the customers to sit and read by the window. We actually have regulars that do just that.

They come in, grab a cup of coffee and read for a couple of hours. And I've spent many an hour on that sofa myself reading away."

That made her smile as if she'd just told him she had her own carousel. She was something else and he was probably thinking about it too hard. Because he was suddenly imagining himself with her on that reading sofa only what he was imagining doing to her wasn't reading. *Crossing the line.*

Her laughter brought him out of indecent thoughts and he actually shook his head to snap out of it.

"You zone out a lot, you know that?" This obviously amused her.

Playing it off, he smiled back. "I got a lot on my mind I guess."

"Well, you better not do that on the slopes. You'll end up with broken bones.

"Ugh." *The slopes.* "I'd almost forgotten about that."

"You're not getting out of it." And with that giggle of hers, that he now couldn't get enough of, she pulled him by the arm. "Let's go."

CHAPTER 8

For as much apprehension as Gio had about getting up on the slopes, he actually caught on much quicker than Bianca had imagined—even faster than Felix had when he first tried snowboarding. After just a few hours, he was getting fancy and speeding up so much at one point she had to warn him not to get too overconfident.

She watched as he flew by her while she'd stopped to take a breather. Shaking her head her eyes followed him. After spending the entire day with him, she could very easily understand how anyone could develop a major crush on this guy. Not only was he incredible to look at, he was turning out to be one of the sweetest guys she'd ever met. She felt terrible that he seemed so agonized about the tragedy in the ring.

He made his way back to where she still stood. His big satisfied smile gave her silly butterflies reminding her of the days back in high school. Then she remembered how she'd felt earlier when he held her hand. Oh, yeah. She was definitely developing a crush—a harmless one. It wasn't unheard of for girls to develop crushes on their boyfriend or even spouse's friends, especially ones that looked like Giovanni Bravo, right?

She brought her hand to her forehead and nearly blushed recalling her grandmother's comment. That woman said whatever was on her mind without a second thought. Something Bianca had been known to do a lot herself, resulting in some very awkward moments. But she was doing her best to make sure it didn't happen with Gio. Several times today when she kept having to help him stay up and their faces were only inches away she nearly blurted out what she was thinking—that his eyes were just spectacular. But she'd managed to hold it together though there'd been several moments when she'd been lost in them for a little too long and she was sure he'd noticed.

"Ready to race?" he asked as he stopped right next to her.

"Get out of here!" She laughed. "I'm telling you. You need to pace yourself. You don't wanna get hurt."

"I think I got this," he said, straightening out in a proud stance.

She elbowed him playfully. "Actually I think we should call it a day. You're going to be so sore tomorrow."

Gio made an exaggerated face of shock and utter disbelief. She suspected he meant for it to be funny, instead it was as breathtaking as all his other expressions were. "Are you even capable of making *any* unflattering facial expressions?"

His expression dissolved and those eyes now stared at her making her breath catch. "Are you?"

For the first time that day, her laugh was a nervous one and the schoolgirl butterflies were back en masse. She proceeded to scrunch her face up. "See?" Then she stuck her tongue out at him, closing her eyes.

When she opened her eyes, she expected to see him smiling but he was staring at her mouth and he seemed stunned for a moment. Then he smirked, his heavy lashes lowering over the tops of his now smoldering green eyes. With her insides lit, Bianca was totally mesmerized. "I'd say to you what I say to most girls when they show me their tongues but I shouldn't."

Swallowing hard and trying not to let on what his eyes and words were doing to her, she managed to stammer out, "Why not?"

"Because Felix might not like it." His eyes left her mouth and met hers with a smile. "Let me rephrase that. I *know* he wouldn't like it." His eyes locked on hers for an instant making Bianca's heart pound, before having mercy on her and glancing away. "Let's go."

He started off down the small hill leaving her breathless and confused. She squeezed her eyes shut for a moment making a mental note. *Never show him your tongue again.*

With a deep breath, she went after him but only because he turned to see if she was following. Otherwise, she might still be glued to that same spot. She cleared her throat as she caught up to him and tried to sound as casual as possible. "I was serious you know."

He glanced at her, his eyebrows pulled together. "About what?"

"You're gonna be sore tomorrow."

He chuckled now really reminding her of Felix and how cocky he'd been about it his first time out. "Did you forget I work out everyday?"

"I knew you'd say that because it's exactly what Felix said. This is a different work out, Gio. You're gonna feel it tomorrow—everywhere. I promise." He smiled, obviously not worried about it. "I mean it. You might even consider soaking in the hot tub tonight. Felix was so sore the next day and he didn't even go as long or as hard as you did."

A sudden evil smile spread across his face and his eyes just about sparkled with humor. "Is that right? So you're saying I went longer and harder than your boyfriend?"

Bianca felt the flush clear down her neck but she couldn't help laughing and went along with her own smirk. "Yes, you did."

She sped up and away from him no longer able to be that close to him knowing that her apparent crush on him was obviously coming through loud and clear and he was now having fun with it.

"Bianca, wait up."

At first, she didn't wait up. She needed to give her heart time to settle. After a few minutes, she slowed a little reminding herself that even though he'd been a fast learner he was nowhere near her level of skill. He came up alongside her. "You know I'm just teasing, right?"

"Of course." She glanced up at him and his perfect smile.

"I mean I'd say something like that even in front of Felix." He laughed. "Just to piss him off, but I hope I didn't offend you or anything."

"No, not at all." She realized she was blurting out her auto-responses but she wanted to be perfectly clear on this. This was nothing more than innocent flirting. He was just being playful after having spent the entire day with her. Secretly she was surprised, not only by how thrilling it was but how she in no way wanted to discourage it.

The main lodge to the resort was just up ahead, she'd been so distracted by his teasing that the time it took them to get there just flew. "Felix says things like that all the time, too. Nothing shocks me anymore," she lied through her teeth.

"Yeah, but he's your boyfriend."

She shook her head. "But I get it. You two are funny. There's nothing you can say that will weird me out. I promise."

The teasing smile was back and she braced herself.

"You're making a lot of promises today."

That confused her and she searched his eyes then he laughed. "God, those eyes of yours, Bianca." This time *he* shook his head. "Back there, you promised I'd be sore tomorrow." She started to smile remembering but then stopped when she was caught in those molten eyes of his again. "I've made that same promise a few times." He stared at her a bit longer and harder before his lip lifted into a sexy crooked smile. He finally turned away with a soft chuckle leaving Bianca no choice but to laugh along nervously.

By the time they were in the car, she managed to appear cool and collected on the outside but her insides were out of control.

Gio rolled his neck and massaged his shoulder with his hand. "You know soaking in the hot tub is starting to sound real nice now."

"You should. It'd do you good." She smiled innocently, pushing away the visual of Gio near naked in the hot tub.

"Will you join me?"

Was it possible that he knew blinking in that slow motion sort of way had a hypnotic effect on girls? Maybe it was just her weak resolve. She nodded, not looking away and praying her voice wouldn't crack. "Sure. I'll be sore tomorrow, too, you know."

The second her words left her mouth, she saw that evil twinkle in his eye and she fought the flush already creeping up her nape. "You promise?"

Damn him. She wouldn't squirm and he wasn't winning this one. Throwing out the mental note she made earlier she licked her bottom lip and his eyes were immediately on her tongue. "We'll just have to wait and see, now won't we?"

His startled eyes were back on hers and she smiled, hoping she looked as smug as she felt. Got 'em.

*

Unquestionably, what Gio was doing was technically against the man-code between him and his friends. They'd never actually discussed one but was still firmly in place. Coming on at all to one of his friend's girls was clearly breaking all kinds of rules. Rules he never would've dreamt of breaking before Bianca. Not only had he just come on to her, he came on strong. He meant to rattle her. He loved what it did to her. Her reaction to his teasing had completely thrown him.

He couldn't have planned it better if he'd tried. She'd walked right into all his comments but she'd practically challenged him to try to weird her out. He heard it in her voice — saw it in those eyes. She could go from Bambi to bewitching siren in a second and he was hooked. He never would've thought it about sweet little Bianca but she had it in her. She probably didn't even realize she was even doing it and damn it if that didn't make it an even bigger turn on.

Her licking her lip the way she had, had nearly done him in. It took everything in him to laugh with her when she did but Felix better hurry his ass up and get there already. His being there might be the only thing that would keep Gio from considering crossing that forbidden line and if he didn't know any better he was beginning to think maybe Bianca would actually cross it with him.

We'll just have to wait and see, now won't we?

She couldn't be serious. She was just throwing his game right back at him. *Right?* He closed his eyes as he sat there in the hot tub visualizing her licking her lips — how those eyes that at times were almost too full of innocence could look deep into his with an unmistakable reckless abandon.

Hearing the game room door open jolted him. Bianca wore a one-piece black bathing suit with a sarong that covered most of her upper legs but the neckline was low and though her breasts weren't huge they'd do just fine.

Gio sat up a little, mentally slapping himself. What the hell was wrong with him? Not only was this Bianca and she deserved more respect than that, he was certain what was going on in his shorts would not be cool with Felix. He needed to get a hold of himself before he was stuck in the hot tub all night. This was not something he'd in any way be able to hide.

He watched Bianca walk toward him slowly with that ever-present smile of hers. His own smile when he was around her was beginning to feel like a permanent fixture on his face. "How's the water?"

This time he made the orgasmic expression closing his eyes for a second. "Fantastic."

"And the wine?" she asked, placing her own glass in the cup holder on the opposite side of the tub where she now stood and began to climb in.

Normally Gio would've been disappointed and would've even complained about her keeping the sarong on but in this case he was grateful she did. He was already having a hard enough time controlling the rousing in his shorts. It was annoying as shit. He'd seen girls climb in hot tubs wearing much less. On a few occasions, some had joined him wearing nothing at all and he'd never felt this out of control.

One thing was for sure, unless there was another girl there that he could blame it on, he was steering clear of joining Bianca in that tub when Felix was around. He thought it couldn't get worse so he figured he'd indulge in watching her expression when her body sunk in the deliciously hot water. He knew what was coming. That thing she did when something tasted or felt so good. But instead she went all the way in, her head going under the surface.

When she resurfaced, Gio literally held his breath. He didn't think it possible but the effect she'd begun to have on him was intensified a hundred times over now that she was dripping wet. As hard as he tried, he couldn't keep his eyes from wandering down to her breasts. One look at her erect nipples pushing through bathing suit and his eyes darted away. He was so damn hard he was now worried she might actually notice through the water.

Taking advantage of the moment as she tilted her head back and smoothed her hair down, he adjusted himself. He felt like a fucking thirteen-year-old. What the hell was his problem? Any thoughts of doing the flirting thing they'd done earlier flew out the window. He had to think quickly before she got playful on him. If she even thought about bringing out the sexy siren act now he didn't think he'd be able to hold back and this *could not* happen.

"So, was your mom born deaf or did something happen to her?" He was going to ask earlier but he was afraid the subject might be too heavy and he selfishly wanted to enjoy his cheerful day with her. He now welcomed heavy.

To his surprise, she didn't seem bothered at all by

the subject. "My grandmother swears she wasn't born deaf but it's really hard to determine because she was a preemie born way too early. So there were all kinds of complications."

She sunk in resting her head back on the headrest of the hot tub making Gio eternally grateful that a certain distracting area of her body was now safely submerged. He only wished a certain part of his body would do some submerging also.

"My grandmother has always said it was one of the many infections my mom had before she made it out of the hospital that did it. That's how she and my dad met. At one of the many different conferences my grandparents and my mom attended for the deaf. That's why my parents only had one child. My dad insisted he wanted a baby and my mom was afraid I'd be deaf. So when I was born perfectly healthy my mom said 'That's it.' She thanked God for the blessing but wasn't taking anymore chances."

Gio smiled. He would've never guessed someone as perfect and as cheerful as Bianca had been brought up by two parents with hearing disabilities. He was beyond impressed. "So growing up must've been really different for you than for most kids."

She lifted her head slightly to look at him. "That would depend on what you call different. It was all I knew, so to me, it felt normal. And because of my grandparents being so involved and my dad only being partially deaf I never had to attend any special schools for children with deaf parents. I was speaking normally by the time I started kindergarten. Only occasionally would I sign along when I spoke, out of habit." She smiled big suddenly. "And none of the kids made fun of me like my grandmother was afraid they might.

They thought it was very cool that I knew sign language."

They sat in the hot tub for another forty minutes or so but it felt way shorter than that. The mixture of the wine and the soothing water massage of the hot tub was really doing a number on Gio.

"We better get out now." Bianca suddenly declared. "One thing is for sure. You're going to sleep good tonight. So will I."

Thankful to his heavily relaxed body he wasn't immediately at attention when she stood. That is until she turned around and started stepping out as she removed the wet sarong, giving Gio a very nice view of her glorious ass. He squeezed his eyes shut, willing the movement starting up in his shorts to stop. *Think of something else. Anything else!*

"Are you falling asleep?"

He opened his eyes and she was now outside the tub pulling a bathrobe around herself. "No, I'm just gonna finish up this last glass and then I'm out."

"Okay, but don't go falling asleep," she warned. "I'm gonna go change but I'll be back to check on you."

Feeling a little warmed by her concern he smiled. "You promise?"

It was official. He was now in love with her smile. It made him feel… happy.

"I promise," she said softly then walked out.

As soon as he heard her bedroom door close, he was up and out of the tub. He rushed to his room and changed. Suddenly he couldn't wait to be back in the same room with her.

Once dressed he practically rushed out into the game room and even though it'd been just minutes since he last seen her his heart did this weird thing

when he saw she was already there looking so fresh
and in her soft pajamas.

"That was fast," she said.

Gio shrugged. "I just threw on my pajama pants
and a t-shirt."

He had to remind himself where he was and who
he was with because as he walked toward the corner
bar in the game room where she stood pouring herself
another glass of wine he had the incredible urge to
wrap his arms around her and kiss her silly.

He stopped just feet away from her and she turned
to him. "You want another glass? I'm having just one
more and then I'm done."

"Yeah, I'll take one."

This was the first time he'd ever had wine and it
was at her insistence that it would do wonders to relax
his muscles. At first, he'd balked at her offer but now
he had to admit it was good.

"Can I ask you something?"

That gleam he'd seen in her eye earlier when she
licked her lips in the car was back. "Uh, yeah," he said
already trying to conjure up as much restraint as he
could in case she said anything that might push him
over the edge, especially now that he'd had a few
glasses of wine.

"What do you say to girls that show you their
tongue?" The gleam was an all out smirk now.

Their eyes locked. Did she really just go back to
that? For a moment he thought it'd be better if he
didn't tell her — *make something up*. But the longer he
looked in those eyes, the more he wanted her to know.
"That if they're going to show it to me, they better be
prepared to use it."

Her eyes widened a little but he saw something else

in them that scared him, making his heart thump—excitement. If she licked her lips again he wouldn't be responsible for his actions because he was going for it. His breathing accelerated now and he was completely lost in her eyes.

She blinked then her eyes pinched and she looked away as if she was trying to figure something out. "Is that..."

Gio didn't know what she was talking about at first then he heard it too—music. He focused on it as well. It was Spanish music and it was coming from outside. It got even louder now. Bianca walked to the window that faced the front of the cabin and Gio followed her as it became apparent that the music might actually be live.

Her hands went to her mouth when she reached the window. She spun around and darted past him toward the front door. Gio glanced back at her confused then looked out the window. There was an entire ensemble of mariachis out there. Standing with them—Felix. He held a huge bouquet of flowers. Gio watched until he saw Bianca who now wore her snow boots over her pajama pants fly into his arms. Felix hadn't been blowing her off again. He'd wanted to surprise her and in a big way.

Gio wasn't sure what he was expecting but what he felt the moment he saw Felix kiss her, was not it. He swallowed hard, reminding himself maybe this was a good thing. Maybe Felix making such a production to surprise Bianca meant he really did care about her.

The decision was the fastest and easiest one he'd ever made. The short amount of time he'd spend with Bianca was all he needed to know she was special—too special to have her heart torn apart. If Felix didn't have

the sense to see that Gio would make sure he did, even
if he had to beat it into him.

CHAPTER 9

Focusing on the excitement of seeing Felix—feeling his arms around her—Bianca pushed aside any nagging feelings of guilt. Curiosity is all it was. She'd been curious about Gio's comment ever since he first made it on the slopes. The wine had just given her the courage to ask. That's all it was.

"What happened?" she asked, pulling away from him so she could see his eyes. "I thought you said you wouldn't make it up tonight."

"Babe, I was waiting for my driver when I called you." Felix's playful smile warmed her. It's what she loved most about him. She always told him she could totally picture what he looked like as a little boy. Despite his rugged features, he still had such a baby face. "I was this close to just telling you but I knew how disappointed you were about me not making it up yesterday. I wanted to do something special."

Bianca turned to the mariachis who hadn't stopped playing. One moment she was smiling so big she nearly laughed, then just like that the feeling was gone and her stomach dropped.

Andy, Felix's publicist, waved at her from where he stood near the back of the car talking on his phone. She turned back to Felix fighting the scowl that threatened to replace her happy face. "Why is he here?"

"He'll only be here for a couple of days. Just so you know, the media knows I'm up here and they're already on their way. In fact there was already one van parked outside the gates when I drove up." Felix wrapped his arms around her waist and she couldn't help smiling and touched his lips with her finger. He kissed it then continued, "He's here to handle the first few exchanges with the media and tomorrow morning I'm scheduled to make an appearance at some local charity thing."

Bianca couldn't help feeling disappointed and apparently she was no good at hiding it either. Felix kissed her forehead and then quickly began explaining. "It's in the morning. I'll be back before lunch and then we'll have the rest of the day together. I would've said no but Andy thinks it's best if I voluntarily do photo shoots for all these vultures. Says they'll be less persistent about getting that first photo of me up here if I offer it up front."

Bianca shivered. In her haste to get to Felix she'd run out in only her pajamas, barely stopping to put her snow boots on.

"C'mon, let's go get you a jacket," Felix said.

She wrapped her arms around his big arm leaning her head against him and for an instant had a flashback of touching and holding Gio's arms on the slopes when she was first showing him how to stand. Again, she tried shaking the thoughts away until Felix brought them right back. "So, did Gio get the hang of snowboarding?"

"Yes," she smiled. "He got pretty good actually. He wanted to race."

Felix laughed. "Aw, shit! Were you guys out there all day?" Gio stood just inside as they walked in making Felix's smile even bigger. "Hey, brotha!" He pulled away from Bianca to reach out and clap Gio on the shoulder then shook his hand. "Sorry it took me a minute to get here but I hear you had fun on the slopes today."

Gio glanced at Bianca with a smile. "Yeah, she got me up there. And did she tell you what a badass I was?"

Bianca laughed now. She was glad there was no awkwardness. She didn't know what she was thinking. These two had been friends for years.

"Yeah, well, just wait 'til tomorrow. Your ass is gonna be laid up all day. Did you take some aspirin already?"

Gio shook his head. "Not yet."

"Dude, take some. I'm not shitting you. You're gonna be hurting bad tomorrow."

Gio assured him he would. Bianca walked away to grab her heavy jacket, beanie and gloves. She wasn't sure how long the mariachis would be there, but it was freezing out there.

They stood out on the porch having another glass of wine and listening to the musicians play a few more songs. Felix held her close whispering again and again how much he'd missed her. Then Gio joined them as promised after Felix had insisted he have a few drinks with them before going to bed.

At first, it seemed Gio was a little uncomfortable but within a few minutes, he was laughing at Felix's stories about the old days.

When the mariachis wrapped it up Felix walked away and down the cabin steps toward them to pay them. He also needed to talk to the driver who was driving them back to the restaurant where he'd found them.

Bianca glanced back at Gio and to her surprise he smirked playfully. "You happy?"

She smiled nodding and feeling a little embarrassed about how obvious she was. Being in Felix's arms again, hearing him tell her he missed her went beyond making her happy.

Felix walked back up the stairs of the cabin immediately pulling Bianca to him. "So, tomorrow," he said leaning against the railing and wrapping his arms around Bianca's middle so that they were both facing Gio. "I figure there's no way you'll be up to working out and I gotta make an appearance at least once at the festivities they'll be having all month for USASA Nationals going on."

"What is that?" Gio asked.

"Snowboarding and skiing championships." Felix paused to kiss Bianca's temple then took a drink of his wine. Bianca was already tensing up listening to him talk about making appearances. She wondered if he'd noticed and that's why he paused. "Anyhow, tomorrow they're having this thing at one of the bars up here. It's pretty cool. They have bands and shit. I'll have to schmooze a little but Ray and Ignacio will be there. And Andy," Felix made a clicking noise with his tongue. "Don't worry I'll make sure he hooks you up."

Bianca fought the urge to roll her eyes knowing exactly what that meant. As if Gio needed any help getting hooked up. The guy would probably have them lining up as soon as he walked in the place. To her surprise Gio's only response was, "And Bianca?"

"Oh, she'll be there too, right babe?" She glanced at him smiling with a nod. "But she'll probably be with me while I'm schmoozing. So I just meant you'll have Ray and Iggy to hang with while I do my rounds."

Gio nodded taking a drink of his wine. Bianca stared at him wondering what to make of the fact that his only concern about tomorrow's plans was whether or not she'd be there.

They called it a night after that last drink. Andy had long ago made his exit to his own private cabin on the compound but had reminded Felix of their early morning appointment.

The extra glasses of wine Bianca had in honor of Felix's unexpected arrival had done just the opposite of what a few calming glasses usually do—they made her anxious. So were the butterflies in her stomach just thinking about their first night together in weeks.

As soon as the door closed behind them in the massive room Felix called the master bedroom, he pulled her to him sinking his tongue deep in her mouth then moaned. "Damn!" he said, pulling away then looking deep in her eyes without saying anything for a moment. "I had a really long day. I need to shower but uh," he tugged at her pajama top, "you're not gonna need these. The heater is on and I promise I won't let you get cold tonight." He kissed her again, this time a little harder with his tongue exploring her mouth wildly. "Take 'em off and I'll meet you back in my bed in ten." Breathlessly Bianca nodded as he walked away slowly.

She giggled as she fumbled with the buttons on her pajama top then decided to just skip the whole process and pulled the top over her head a little too fast. With her head in a fog and feeling so heavy Bianca nearly tumbled onto the bed making her giggle even more. She managed to get her balance back and stepped out of her bottoms and panties then crawled into the gloriously comfortable bed. She slipped under the silk sheets and lay back onto the many down pillows.

After this morning's disappointment Felix had

more than made up for it and soon he'd be making love to her. She took a deep breath and closed her eyes barely able to believe how wonderful this day had turned out. Heaven... heaven is what this felt like.

*

Bianca's eyes kept going from the back of the driver's head to the rearview mirror as Gio spread her legs. Her heart raced like she'd never felt it race before. She could hardly believe she was sitting in the backseat with him, naked from the waist down.

She refused to pull her eyes away from the driver. Did he know what they were doing? Would he tell Felix? Feeling Gio spread her with his fingers made her breathe a little heavier and a small moan escaped her.

"Shh," Gio hushed her.

She wouldn't look, but her chest heaved up and down and she gasped as his finger began to massage that spot. The one meant for no one else but Felix; yet here Gio was touching, caressing. She bit her bottom lip as his finger sunk in her. She was so wet it was almost embarrassing but at this point she'd beg him not to stop. He worked her in a circular motion while he sunk a second finger in her and she struggled to hold in her moans.

The uncontrollable trembling started and her eyes would open and close as she felt it building. She moaned louder and the driver's eyes met hers in the rearview mirror but she didn't care.

"Come baby," he whispered. That only made her moan louder as her body began to shudder and the incredible sensation flooded her everywhere. "That a girl," Gio whispered. "That's my girl."

She continued to moan squeezing her eyes shut as spasm after glorious spasm continued and she was sure she'd pass out from the pleasure of it. "*You liked that?*"

Something was wrong. This wasn't right. Of course, something is wrong that voice in her head screamed.

"You like that, baby?"

Bianca's eyes flew open and she gasped for a moment unable to breathe. Felix was on his elbow next to her naked. She lay there spread eagle in the middle of the bed. All the blankets were gone. Her heart still beat wildly as she realized what had just happened.

Felix smiled, kissing her softly. "I'm sorry. I was going to let you just sleep but I couldn't help myself. You look so damn good lying there naked and once I started you were enjoying it so much there was no way I was stopping. But damn, if that wasn't a fucking turn on watching you come in your sleep." He moved up over her and she felt his erection graze her leg. "I promise this won't take long at all," he said with a soft laugh.

Her heart was beating even more erratically now. How long had she been out? But what screamed loudest in her head was why the hell had she been dreaming that it was Gio doing this, not Felix?

She wrapped her arms around Felix's neck kissing him long and hard. "I love you."

"I love you, too," he said just as he entered her with a groan.

As usual, he was incredibly gentle—always had been. It was something her mother said she should appreciate. Most young men were brusque and selfish at lovemaking. Not Felix. He said she was different from anyone else he'd ever dated—special—and he would always treat her that way.

Even though she appreciated it, at the moment Bianca needed more. The guilt of her dream washed over her. She didn't deserve gentle. She lifted her hips wanting him in as deep as possible. Guiltily needing to show him just how much she loved him with her body. Each thrust she lifted her hips higher. Each time he went a little harder and deeper and she loved it.

Even though he promised it'd be over quick he made it last until she came again only this time she stifled her moans, squeezing her arms around his neck as he buried himself as deep as he could.

He collapsed atop her breathing hard and for some reason she didn't want to open her eyes. The memory of her climax just minutes ago hadn't faded. Neither had the shock of realizing it was her boyfriend who'd made it happen. Most troubling was the disappointment she felt that it hadn't been Gio. The guilt of it was too much for her to bear. What was wrong with her?

"I love you," she whispered anxiously as she opened her eyes.

Felix lifted his head to look at her and smiled. "I love you, too Bianca."

Her eyes must've looked as dreary as they felt. After what just happened, and not just during the day but the evening, her body felt spent. "Time for bed, sleepy head," he whispered before crawling off her.

He walked away and she supposed he was going to the bathroom to grab a towel but she never found out because within seconds she was out again.

*

No matter how much Gio had been warned, he did not expect to be in this much pain. The walk from the bathroom back to his bed was excruciating. There was no way he was leaving this cabin today or even tonight.

He'd be lucky if he left the bed for anything but to use the bathroom.

Bianca had promised sore. He'd been dealing with sore for years. As a boxer it came with the territory but this was ridiculous. This wasn't sore. This was all out pain. He sat down slowly, wincing, as the pain shot down his upper thighs.

There was a knock on the door and Gio grunted in response. The door opened and Felix peeked his head in then laughed at Gio's pained expression. Gio inched his way back onto the bed with a frown. "Laugh it up, asshole. You should've given me a Vicodin not an aspirin."

Felix walked all the way in now, still chuckling. "I told you it was gonna be bad. Are you gonna eat? Breakfast is ready."

"Hell no. I can barely make it to the bathroom."

"That bad?" Felix stopped and appeared to ponder on something for a second. "Yeah, it *was* that bad now that I remember." He laughed again. "Go sit in the hot tub again. That shit will fix you right up."

Gio couldn't even imagine trying to climb in that thing with as much pain as he was in. "Listen, I'm out of here and Bianca has to work today so she'll be gone all morning but we both should be back by lunchtime. And you're going tonight, by the way, so get your ass in the tub." Felix glanced out the door then closed it softly. Gio looked up at him wondering what he was doing. "So, what do you think?"

"About what?"

"About Bianca. She's something else, isn't she?"

Gio glanced away unable to look Felix in the eye anymore. "Yeah, she's real sweet."

"She's incredible. She's the one who has me considering leaving the whole bachelor life behind."

That should've made Gio feel better. Instead, it irritated him to no end. *Considering?* "What's there not to be sure about? You said it yourself. She's incredible."

"Well, yeah," Felix said, leaning against the dresser. "But my life is too crazy right now to get into anything serious. There's always something going on. I just don't know if I can be there for her like she needs— deserves. You know?"

Gio hadn't planned on having this conversation with him just yet. He was in so much pain, all he wanted to do today was relax. Now every muscle on his body had gone taut. Bianca's words in the car came to him suddenly, *I love you, too.* "Seems to me she's already under the impression you guys *are* serious." He was trying his damnedest to not sound as irritated as he felt. So he didn't know if he could give her what she deserved but he was going to have her think he was in love with her? What the fuck was that about? Unable to hold back he had to ask. "What's up with you and the chick in Chicago?"

To Gio's surprise he didn't get the sly smirk he was expecting. Felix actually looked troubled by this. "You saw that?"

"It's a syndicated show, dude. Anyone in the nation who tuned in last night saw it. Does Bianca know about it?"

"No way." Felix shook his head then lowered his voice. "She doesn't follow the gossip shows. Not since last year and that mocked up photo all over the tabloids. She gets that most of the stories on those shows are for ratings and mostly all are a distant version of the truth." He frowned pulling himself away from the dresser. "But I will have to talk to her about this one."

Gio was just pulling his legs on the bed and leaning against the headboard when Felix's last comment made him stop and stare at him waiting for more. In Felix's case, he was photographed walking into his hotel with another girl. What could the *distant version of truth* be there?

There was a soft knock on the door followed by Bianca's voice. "Felix? You still in there?"

Felix looked at Gio stretching his lips. He was no doubt having the same thoughts Gio was — had she heard anything? "Yeah, come in, babe."

The door opened and fresh faced Bianca smiled. "Morning Gio." Then her eyes went all sympathetic. "Are you in a lot of pain?"

Unwilling to admit just how much pain he was really in, Gio bobbled his head just slightly. It was as much as he could move without creating anymore pain for himself. "A little." He frowned as Felix chuckled.

"You should sit in the tub again. It'll feel even better than last night. I promise." Gio smiled. There she went promising things again. She then turned to Felix. "I just wanted to let you know I'm leaving now."

"I'm leaving too. We can go together." Bringing his attention back to Gio he smiled. "I'm not kidding, dude. Get your ass out of bed and in that tub because you're going tonight. No excuses. There's nothing a little tequila and some nice company won't fix." He winked at Gio as he walked toward the doorway.

"Feel better, Gio." Bianca did a little wave and Gio thought for a moment maybe she was feeling guilty that she hadn't warned him earlier yesterday about how sore he'd be today because there was something off about her usually bright smile.

"Thanks. I'll be fine."

They closed the door behind them and Gio leaned back letting his muscles relax and closed his eyes. He thought of what Felix had said. Would he be telling Bianca about the girl at the hotel with him? Gio didn't even like the thought of Bianca being sad. Not after knowing what a cheery person she was by nature.

His eyes flew open at the knock at the door. "Yeah?"

"Ms. Bianca asked me to bring you something, sir," Amparo explained from the other side of the door.

"C'mon in." Gio sat up a little straighter wondering what it could be.

Amparo opened the door with one hand and held a tray in the other. Breakfast with all the trimmings. There were even slices of banana on the side for his waffles and a couple of aspirins next to his juice. Gio smiled as Amparo placed the tray across his lap. "Oh, wow. This looks real good. Thank you, Amparo."

Amparo smiled. "Is there anything else you'd like?"

He was still taking in everything on the tray when he spotted a folded piece of writing paper with his name on it tucked under his juice glass. Turning to Amparo suddenly anxious for her to leave, he smiled. "No, I've got everything I need. Thanks."

As soon as she closed the door he reached for the note, his heart doing that same weird thing it kept doing off and on all day yesterday. He unfolded the paper and read:

I figured you wouldn't be up to even walking to the kitchen so I had Amparo fix this to your liking. I hope I got it right. I left instructions for your lunch and I'm keeping my fingers crossed that you're feeling better by tonight. I hate these sorts of things but don't tell Felix I said that! See you tonight hopefully. XO B.

Gio reread it two more times, each time fixating on the 'keeping her fingers crossed" and the 'don't tell Felix' parts. She wanted him there tonight. He felt oddly excited about that; which made no sense because Felix would be there, too. Still she was keeping her fingers crossed?

Did she not want him to mention the note to Felix either? For too long his eyes were glued to the XO. He knew it meant nothing but like one of those ridiculous teenage fans reading a response letter from their idol, he touched the X and the O with his fingers. Then feeling like a dumb ass he chuckled before sticking the note in his shirt pocket and dug in.

CHAPTER 10

All morning as Bianca had worked her shift at the shop and answered all her mother's and grandmother's questions, shoving any thoughts of her dream aside. It was just a dream. She'd spent the entire day with Gio. Of course, it would make sense that he'd be around even in her subconscious thoughts. But it was *what* he was doing in there and the disappointment she'd felt when she woke and realized that it wasn't Gio that gnawed at her more than anything.

Why in the world would she be disappointed? She was so excited that Felix was finally here with her. Sure, Gio was gorgeous and sweet but she loved Felix.

She was certain that the hour of online college coursework she'd put in that morning was wasted because the whole time her mind had wandered off to the dream. Bianca shook her head as she turned off her car. It was just a dream. She'd had plenty of bizarre and unexplained dreams before. *Stop overthinking this!*

Toni smiled at her as Bianca walked into her once again empty beauty salon. To Bianca's surprise Toni's hair was still the same color as the last time she saw her but she did have it up in this geisha style, big elaborate hair-combs and all, though she'd passed on the white makeup. Bianca smiled gesturing at the 'do. "Looks good. I seriously doubt now you'll ever find a style that doesn't fit you, Toni."

Toni winked at her as she stood. "Keith, the guy I told you I met at that artsy fartsy film festival in Los

Angeles a few months ago is coming up tonight. He's bringing some Japanese documentary he and his friend worked on together about the history of the Geisha. I figured he'd get a kick out of my hair."

Bianca took a seat at one of the styling chairs laughing softly. "I'm sure he will."

Toni walked up behind her facing her in the mirror. "So, what's it gonna be?"

Bianca had already filled her in on tonight's party when she called to ask her if she was available to style her hair tonight. "Nothing too elaborate. I'm actually hoping to blend into the crowd. I get the feeling it'll be overrun with paparazzi and stuff. I'd just as soon not go but he really wants me there."

Toni looked away but Bianca caught how her expression changed. Ever since the big photo blow up and Bianca making her promise not to fill her in on any gossip with nothing concrete to confirm it, Toni had been real good about not sharing anything she'd read. Bianca knew this expression. She'd seen it before when Toni would tell her about something unpleasant she'd read in the tabloids or saw on TV about Felix.

Toni opened and shut drawers a little too fast and noisily and was avoiding eye contact. "I can do toned down elegance. I know just the thing."

"Toni?"

Toni continued to rummage through the drawer without looking up. "Hmm?"

"You have something you wanna tell me?" Normally Bianca wouldn't even ask if she suspected it had something to do with the many tabloid shows Toni watched but she was acting so strangely now.

Toni glanced at her for a second then went immediately back to searching the drawer. "Uh, no."

"Spill it, Toni." If the discomfort she was feeling wasn't so overwhelming Bianca might actually laugh at how obvious Toni was. Her style and personality went hand in hand. There was nothing ambiguous about her. So she was terrible at trying conceal her feelings.

Toni stopped and looked in the mirror with a frown. "Honey, it's nothing. It's just that with this fight coming up, Felix has been the buzz lately on all the gossip shows. And you know me, anytime they start talking about his elusive Big Bear love interest I *have* to watch and see if by chance they'll mention you or have any photos of you and all."

She went back to rummaging through her drawer until she came up with a red comb and walked up behind Bianca. Bianca was almost afraid to ask but she had to. "Have they?"

Toni finally put on her 'okay, getting to the point' expression and shifted her weight to one side looking at Bianca straight in the eyes through the mirror. "It's always someone else they think is you." Bianca's eyes opened wide at the comment and her stomach dropped. "*But*," Toni added quickly, "I hadn't said anything because there is never anything concrete about the girls in the short clips or photos they show of him. There's never even any solid proof that the pictures are not all old."

Bianca thought of the mariachis Felix had gone out of his way to get for her and how he sounded so genuine when he said he loved her. She wouldn't panic but she also knew Toni wouldn't even be talking about this if there wasn't more to it than just old pictures and rumors with no real foundation. "What else have they said?"

Toni took a deep breath. "You said he was in Chicago last week, right?"

"Yes." Bianca held her breath in worried anticipation.

"They had pictures of him with a girl there. It was nothing bad but one of them did show them walking into a hotel. They were supposedly taken the day he got stuck out there."

Bianca stared at her not sure what to think. "Were they holding hands or anything?" Her own voice was already sounding strained to her own ears and she swallowed hard. Could it be possible that Felix was actually playing her?

"No, they weren't." Toni's voice took on a reassuring tone. "All the pictures were very innocent. It could've been just an associate or something and if wasn't for the fact that they walked into a hotel together and on the very day he was supposed to be flying out here to be with you I wouldn't have even thought of bringing it up." Toni walked around the chair and faced her. "You should just ask him. Like all the other times, I'm sure there is a reasonable explanation."

Bianca nodded, surprised she wasn't already a blubbering mess. But she *felt* Felix's love for her in his kisses now. Saw it as clear as day in his eyes when he looked into hers. If it weren't for that she just might be. If anything, she was angry. Just like she'd promised him she wouldn't jump to any conclusions without asking him first, he'd promised her he'd tell her about anything he thought would get back to her that she might consider questionable. He had to understand things like this could easily, and for very good reason, upset her.

"I'll ask him about it today." Bianca smiled. "Thanks for bringing it up. I'm still not watching any of those shows or reading the tabloids so I would've never known." She smiled even bigger remembering how, just like Toni said, all the other times there'd been perfectly acceptable explanations, there probably would be for this one too.

Once again, Toni did an awesome job of Bianca's hair and makeup. These were the only times she used Toni's services because until Felix came along Bianca rarely even wore makeup. And if she did it didn't warrant having it professionally applied. But knowing she'd be in the limelight she wanted it to look as nice as possible.

The car Felix sent for her was already waiting when she arrived back at her grandmother's house. Her mother and Nana oohed and aahed about her makeup and hair which should've made her feel better. However the knot in her stomach from the news Toni had dropped on her was still firmly in place.

The ride back to Felix's cabin felt longer than normal. She knew there had to be an acceptable explanation. Toni had given her a few more details about the photos. Apparently, they'd gone to dinner alone. And this time there was no other boyfriend or his agent around. It was just the two of them who'd been seen leaving the restaurant together and arriving at his hotel. The more Bianca thought about it the more uncertain she got that this one was explainable.

Felix walked out of the cabin onto the porch as the car came up the drive. He was down the stairs and ready to open her door when the car stopped. As soon as she got out, he pulled her to him and kissed her softly but deeply. "I would've gone with him to pick you up but I just got here myself." He kissed her again then added, "You look beautiful."

Bianca's heart sped up. The thought of this being all one big lie—that he did this with a different girl everywhere he went was too overwhelming. Before he could kiss her again she placed her hand on his chest. "Who were you with the day you got stuck in Chicago?"

His reaction was anything but what she was expecting. She'd let it out that way because she needed immediate reassurance that she had it all wrong again—see it in his loving eyes. Instead, his troubled, almost fearful expression did just the opposite. She pulled away from him.

"I was gonna tell you about that as soon as I got a moment." He reached out for her but she backed away.

"Tell me what?"

"It's kind of a long story but I can explain it."

Explain it? Bianca didn't need any long explanations. There was only one thing she needed to know as her now pounding heart felt near ready to explode. "Did you sleep with her?"

"No!"

"But you took her to your hotel?" He'd made love to her last night and just a few nights prior he had another girl in his hotel with him? She wanted to scream now.

"That's what I wanna talk to you about," he said calmly. "But it's cold out here. Let's go inside."

"I'm not stepping foot in there until you tell me what's going on." Bianca was trying hard not to lose it but she felt so close.

"Baby, relax. I promise you it's not what you're thinking." He exhaled. "Okay. I went out with her a few times in the past. I hadn't seen her in weeks."

"Weeks?" Bianca yelled out, certain now that she

was going to lose it for sure. "You saw her a few weeks ago, too?"

"Yes. *Saw* her." She saw the panic in his eyes one moment then just like that it was gone. "That was it. It wasn't planned. I ran into her is all." He tried again in vain to reach for her hand but Bianca snatched it back taking another step away from him. "I never formally ended things with her. I just sort of stopped calling her once I started seeing you and I wanted to give her the closure I thought she deserved. She lives in Chicago so since I was in town I took her to dinner and I let her know I'm in a relationship now."

"And then you took her back to your hotel."

"To have a drink at the lounge downstairs but I swear to you that's all that happened. And I had every intention of telling you about his. You have to believe me."

He took another step toward her so Bianca took another one back. With every step she'd taken away from him she'd been that much closer to the car and her back now touched it making it impossible to get any further away. He placed his hands on either side of her against the car enclosing her in his arms. "I love you, Bianca. I know this is tough. You hearing about shit like this before I get a chance to explain sucks, but I promise you I won't ever hurt you."

"What's her name?" She demanded making him frown. "I wanna know."

"Shelley. She's an intern at the Chicago Sun-Times. She co-interviewed me earlier last year and we went out a few times. Anytime there's a press conference in Chicago she's there so that's why and how I run into her sometimes but it's over now." His face leaned into Bianca's and he brushed his lips gently against hers. As unsure of this as she still felt, she wanted so badly to believe him. "I love you," he whispered against her mouth. "Please tell me you believe me when I say I won't ever hurt you."

"I want to." Bianca willed the relief to slowly trickle back into her suspicious heart.

He brought his hands up off the car and held her face in them. "You can. I swear to you." He kissed her again but unlike she had in the past, or maybe *just* like she had in the past, only she'd been so deep in denial she didn't *feel* the sincerity. She heard it in his voice loud and clear but something deep in her gut told her otherwise. No one could be this good at lying, could they?

Finally allowing herself to breathe easy she kissed him back, waiting for that sudden liberation from her fears. The exhilaration she'd felt so often in the past when her doubts were wiped away by his words—his touch. Only this time it never came.

She gasped as his big arms picked her up by the waist and off her feet. Soft hopeful laughter escaped her as he cradled her in his arms and he carried her up the stairs toward the front door of the cabin.

Although she felt somewhat content and wanted to believe that he'd done nothing with *Shelley*, Bianca had to wonder if this would ever end. If she'd ever trust him completely. She hated to think this would forever be a part of their relationship and she hated how fast and easy it was for her to believe he could do something like that to her. The knot in the pit of her stomach was now gone but it was replaced with something else. Something that overshadowed what should've been an enormous relief. Instead, it was disconcerting and confusing.

*

As they turned into the back entrance driveway of the club Bianca was relieved to see the entourage of paparazzi that had followed them the whole way there was not allowed in the back way. She let out a slow sigh of relief and Felix squeezed her hand. "You okay?"

She smiled and nodded, glad now that poor Gio, even in all the obvious pain he was in had still come along anyway. He seemed just as unnerved about the paparazzi as she was only for some reason he looked more irritated than nervous about them. But clearly it was new to him too. Felix and Andy, who also accompanied them in the limo tonight, were completely unfazed by the attention.

"It's a private party so the entire club is open only to invited guests. They," Felix gestured back to the paparazzi vans left behind. "are not invited."

Of course, there were reporters present but since they were invited, Felix said they'd be on their best behavior unless they never wanted to be invited back to one of these events.

Bianca had been to this particular club once before with Toni. But she didn't realize it had a VIP section. Then it dawned on her this area had been open to everyone the night she'd been there. They actually created a VIP section just for Felix and his guests by closing off one of the corners of the bar area. They'd only been sitting enjoying their first round of drinks for a few minutes when one of Felix's bodyguards standing by the entrance of the VIP section called him over.

"I'll be right back," he whispered in Bianca's ear before kissing her softly and then stood.

She watched as he walked over to his large bodyguard. As his bodyguard moved out of the way she saw who was standing there waiting for Felix: a tall brunette in a very tight little black dress.

Bianca was immediately on alert. She'd heard about the groupies, even from Felix, though she didn't think his bodyguards would be stupid enough to call him over to meet with any while he was having drinks with his girlfriend.

She noticed Gio was watching Felix closely as well and if she wasn't mistaken he seemed just as irritated by seeing the girl with Felix as she was. She glanced back at Felix when she saw Gio's irritated expression give way to a sudden smirk.

Felix was on his way back to their table with the girl. Bianca sat up a little straighter unsure of how exactly to react to this. "Evelyn, I'd like you to meet my beautiful girlfriend Bianca."

"Nice to meet you, Bianca." Evelyn reached out her hand and they shook. She was tall and gorgeous with dark straight hair. Bianca found solace in that not only had Felix introduced Evelyn to her first but he'd made it clear she was his girlfriend. "Evelyn is a friend of my promoter." Bianca forced a polite smile not sure what that meant.

It also bothered her that Evelyn had obviously met Andy before. Who the hell was she really? And why was she here now? Then her thoughts were muddled when he introduced Evelyn to Gio. "Evelyn, this is my good friend and now one of my trainers, Gio."

Gio stood up, a quick wince escaping him, no doubt a reaction to his still sore limbs. Bianca caught the widening of Evelyn's eyes as she got her first look at Gio up close. The guy was so good looking already and tonight he looked, in a word—delicious. Felix had told them it was semi-formal attire so he'd lent Gio one of his many suits. Felix was ruggedly handsome in his own suit but seeing Gio all done up was something else. The man was perfection on a stick already. Though he'd refused to wear the entire three piece suit he did wear charcoal grey slacks, a long-sleeved white dress shirt and black velvet vest. Since Gio's chest and back were a little bigger than Felix's the vest hugged him showing off the glorious hard pecs she'd been privy to last night in the hot tub.

Things were starting to make sense now and if this was what it looked like, Evelyn was who Felix had mentioned hooking Gio up with last night. Great. She'd been glad when Felix told her Gio would be there tonight. Not that there was anything wrong with Ray and Ignacio who were there now also but she knew what had happened the other times she'd gone out with Felix. Inevitably, there'd be moments when Felix would be pulled away for pictures with fans or autographing.

Felix usually asked Ray and Ignacio to keep her company while he was busy but neither of them were much for talking. Any conversations with them were short and polite and in no way playful or engaging. With Gio here tonight she'd looked forward to at least some entertaining conversation.

She watched as Evelyn spoke with Gio, for some reason hating the incredibly fake way she laughed. The girl was gorgeous and yes, while Bianca could understand why a girl even as beautiful as her could be taken in by Gio, she really didn't have to try so hard. Judging by the smile on his face, he liked what he saw.

"How we doing?" Felix asked as he sat down next to her and slipped his hand in hers.

Bianca glanced at him and then back at Gio and Evelyn. "Is she for hire?"

Felix laughed glancing back at Evelyn. "No, babe. She works for my promoter. She's one of the models that walks around the ring in between rounds holding up the card that tells everyone what round is coming up."

Oh yeah, she could picture this girl walking around in stilettos and a barely there bikini holding up a card high above her head while the ogling spectators whistled and catcalled. *That* made her profession much more respectable than what Bianca was originally thinking.

"She just signed with Budweiser," Felix explained. "That's why she's up here. She's one of the more famous ring card girls in the business and she's super smart about getting her name out there so Budweiser snatched her right up and she's here to sign autographs and take pictures with the audience at the snowboarding events. Of course, she'll be doing it all wearing the Budweiser logo. She wasn't working tonight so I figured since she's single she might enjoy keeping Gio company."

Trying not to have another jealous outburst, it slipped out anyway, "You seem to know a lot about her."

Felix smiled, kissing her on the nose. "I just told you she's one of the more famous ring card girls out there. So yeah, she's worked a few of my fights, too. I'm telling you she's real good about getting her name out there. Of course she made herself known to everyone in my camp as soon as my name started making its way up the ranks. But not like you're insinuating." He glanced back at Gio then smiled at Bianca again. "I'd never ask a girl I once dated to keep a friend of mine company. That would be kind of rude, don't you think? Not to mention insulting."

Bianca sighed softly, already feeling better. "Yes, it would. So what did you tell Evelyn?"

"I didn't. I knew Gio would be coming up for weeks so when my promoter mentioned she'd be up here for the championships, and that I might run into her I asked him to ask her if she'd be interested in hanging out with Gio." He smirked. "My promoter has met Gio before. Even he knows just by looking at the guy no girl would be against spending time with him. Though it'd be only temporary, because let's face it, Gio's never been the committing type. But I doubt any girl is immune to his looks, even her." He stopped and peered at her playfully for a second. "Any girl that is, except you, right?"

Bianca nudged him playfully and laughed a little too loud. Overcompensating much? Visions of her dream made her voice a little shaky, "Of course, silly." As if her ridiculous cackle hadn't been enough. She leaned in and kissed him deeply. "I love you," she added as she pulled away. Could her guilty conscience be any more obvious?

She glanced behind Felix in Gio's direction and to her surprise, he was watching her. Evelyn was obviously very into whatever it is she was telling him but he was paying her no attention. His almost hard stare locked onto her for a moment before turning back to Evelyn.

For one very brief moment, it felt almost as if Gio had read Bianca's thoughts—knew about her dream. But she knew that was impossible. Andy came over and asked Felix if he had a moment for some photos with a few fans. Felix's jaw tightened, clearly annoyed by the interruption. "Go ahead." Bianca squeezed his arm in hopes of assuring him she'd be fine. "I have to go to the ladies' room anyway."

Felix and Andy walked her halfway to the ladies' room before she told them she could go the rest of the way on her own.

Even after she was all done refreshing her makeup she stood in front of the mirror, her reflection staring back at her. This was not at all how she expected this would be. Would she ever get used to this lifestyle? Most girls would probably jump at the chance to be dating a famous boxer. To be given the star treatment everywhere they went—arrive at parties and clubs in limos—and be seated in VIP sections of clubs. Like everything in life, things are always nicer looking in from the outside. But once inside it wasn't all it was cracked up to be.

Felix continued to prove that her first impression of him since getting reacquainted with him was spot on. He *was* still the hometown boy she'd known in high school. Fame hadn't changed him. It had just changed his lifestyle. It wasn't fair for her to continue to distrust him. He had no control over what the media broadcasted about him. She had to stop being so suspicions.

Glad now that she'd bitten her tongue when Felix mentioned his promoter had called to tell him Evelyn would be up here, Bianca still wondered about that. Why would he call him just to tell him that? Did his promoter have reason to think Felix would care? She already disliked Andy for the same reason. Way back before they'd become exclusive, Felix had mentioned his publicist encouraging him to go out and be seen and photographed with as many different girls as possible. Said it was good for his badass image. It'd been his idea to have dinner with the Olympic ice skater Felix had been rumored to be dating. He knew what the tabloids would do with the photos—photos that had nearly broken them up.

Bianca had to start giving Felix the benefit of the doubt. He was obviously giving it to her. He'd just admitted to her that he knew the effect Gio had on women. Knew most women would easily fall for him and yet he hadn't had a problem with her spending the entire day with him. He hadn't even flinched when she told him she'd joined Gio in the hot tub. Of course the hot tub in the game room was party size—big enough for a group of people. Not small and intimate like the one in the bedroom.

Suddenly what was happening too often lately was happening again. All thoughts of Felix were drowned out by thoughts of Gio. She was now visualizing that dream—wondering if Gio would end up with Evelyn tonight and unbelievably feeling a little jealous about it.

Bianca spun around and headed out the door. *This* had to stop. She was being ridiculous and it was embarrassing even to herself. Her stupid feelings were all over the place and she had to get it together. Her face actually flushed at the thought of anyone ever knowing about the absurdity going on in her head.

CHAPTER 11

It'd been over a fucking hour and Felix had still not gone back to sit with Bianca. He'd walked over once, kissed her and asked her something, she'd shaken her head no and then he was quickly whisked away by his damn publicist. Why the hell had he brought her if this is what he was going to do to her?

Gio hated to see her sitting there alone and obviously bored but Evelyn had clung on to him and she wasn't going anywhere. Gio had seen the way Bianca had looked at Evelyn. He got the feeling she was offended by her. So bringing Evelyn over with him to keep Bianca company was out of the question. How stupid was Felix to show Bianca how easy it was for him to whip up female companionship just like that?

The slow song he was dancing to with Evelyn picked up a little and Evelyn swayed her hips against him. He knew how this night could end if he wanted it to but his body was in no way ready for that. Just swaying to the music now made every part of his body ache. He could only imagine how painful it would be to engage in anything more strenuous. And what he'd do to a girl like Evelyn would be all kinds of strenuous. She said she'd be up here for the duration of the events going on and that would be at least a week so he had no doubt he'd nail her eventually. Just not tonight.

His thoughts went back to Bianca and he glanced over and saw she was on her feet now. She walked over to the bar for another drink. He glanced around looking for Felix again and he wasn't anywhere to be seen anymore. God, that pissed him off.

"Something wrong?" Evelyn asked, breaking him from his thoughts and he turned his attention to her big, pretty, hazel eyes. "You seem distracted."

He smiled at her feeling badly that the entire time she'd been talking to him tonight he'd hardly focused on anything she'd said. Earlier because he could hardly think straight watching Bianca with Felix and now for just the opposite reason. He was pissed as shit that she was being neglected. "Nah, I'm just a little tired and sore. Yesterday was my first time snowboarding and I think I overdid it. "

Evelyn laughed, then covered her mouth. "I don't mean to laugh at you but I did the same thing my first time. When I tried to warn my then boyfriend about going overboard he didn't listen either; only he actually broke his ankle that day." She gave him a coy look. "The asshole cheated on me so the memory of him being in so much pain and actually breaking bones always brings a smile to my face."

Gio laughed. "Nice. You have an evil side." He lifted his eyebrow. "I'll have to remember that."

She lowered her eyes to his lips and smiled pushing her body up against him even closer than they already were. "There's a lot to me I'm sure you'd find very interesting." She leaned in and whispered in his ear. "I like being dangerous."

Gio smiled, feeling a little turned on by her declaration. "You do, uh?" he whispered back. "Dangerous like how?"

This could mean anything. He knew girls that were into all kinds of kinky shit. She giggled and nibbled his ear sending a shiver down his spine before answering his question. "I like doing it in public."

Gio tried not to react. He'd be willing to try just about anything at least once but two things he didn't do was anything that involved another guy in the equation and he didn't do audiences. Unless of course the audience consisted of other girls waiting for their turn but he had a feeling that's not what she meant. "You wanna elaborate on that?"

She pulled away from his ear and smiled wickedly. "Like on the sink in the men's restroom."

Before Gio could respond her lips were on his and her tongue thrust into his mouth. He was instantly aroused and the thought of taking her on the sink in the men's restroom consumed him. Maybe his aching body could take a little pain after all. She finally came up for her air licking her wet lips before digging her teeth into her bottom lip.

Glass hitting and shattering on the floor broke his thoughts and not a moment too soon because after realizing it was just a waitress who'd dropped a glass and not a fight breaking out he remembered Bianca. One glance at her table and he was immediately panicked. She was gone. He stopped dancing and looked around from one side of the place to the other as fast as he could. "What's wrong?"

"I just…" At that very moment he caught a glimpse the back of Bianca's head walking toward the back exit — alone.

"I gotta go."

With that, he left Evelyn standing in the middle of the dance floor. He felt bad about it, he really did, but he had to get to Bianca. Something told him she was upset and just the thought of seeing her upset did things to him that had him fisting his hands. He was definitely finishing up that talk he and Felix didn't get to finish that morning. No girl deserved to be treated this way but especially not sweet Bianca.

He bumped a few people in the crowd in his haste to get to her. Any thought of his aching muscles was long gone. Pushing the door open, he lunged out into the freezing air in time to see the car pull up in front of Bianca.

"Bianca!" She turned with a startled expression but she didn't appear to be upset. "Where you going?"

The startled expression softened into one of her sweet smiles. "Back to the cabin. I'm tired."

"Alone? Where's Felix?"

"He was kidnapped," she said with a sideways smile.

"Kidnapped?" As much as Gio was trying to stay open minded about this it already sounded like bullshit.

"The Mayor wanted to have a cigar with him so they stepped outside and I guess after bragging about his boat so much the Mayor, who Felix said has probably had too much to drink tonight, insisted they drive out and see it."

Bianca must've seen the disgusted censure in Gio's eyes because she promptly added. "He asked if I wanted to come. He actually really wanted me to. It's just that being around him and a bunch of guys smoking cigars didn't sound too appealing." She gave him a hearty smile but Gio wasn't buying it. "He just texted me a few minutes ago to say he was doing everything he could to shut the Mayor up already and get back but he said the guy was a talker. So I just told him I'd meet him back at the cabin. He said he'd text you."

Gio frowned pulling out his phone out from his

pocket. He'd turned off the sound before they got there. Bianca started making her way to the car now that the driver had opened the door for her. Gio followed her.

"You don't have to leave because of me." Bianca's eyes did the doe-eyed thing that now drove Gio crazy making him that much more irritated with Felix. How could he do this to her? First, he shows up a day late for reasons still a bit questionable then the first night he gets a chance to spend time with her he ditches her to schmooze with the Mayor?

"I'm done here, too."

He motioned for her to get in the car and she did. He followed behind her flipping through his phone. There were three texts he hadn't read. All from Felix.

The first one was sent over an hour ago:

Do me a favor and check on Bianca for me please. I'm stuck with this drunk windpipe. Let me know if she's pissed.

The second fifteen minutes later:

Dude! Did you check on her?

The third just minutes earlier:

Never mind I just texted her. She's gonna be leaving and I'm meeting her back at the cabin. Stay as long as you want. I'll send a car back for you. Or let me know if you need me to send a car out to pick you up at her room tomorrow. Whatever you decide. Enjoy. =)

As irritated as Gio was feeling, he couldn't smile at that like he normally would've. If it hadn't been for him wanting to get to Bianca he just might've ended up in Evelyn's room but that's not what he was mad about.

Gio wanted to believe in his heart of hearts that Felix had good intentions when it came to Bianca. But more than anything he wanted to believe if Felix didn't, Bianca would see through him. He didn't think her stupid or even naïve enough to fall for his shit. Something told him she had it in her to confront Felix if she ever suspected anything or he upset her in any way. But he'd just left her at a bar by herself. She'd been completely ignored the whole time and here she was headed back to the guy's cabin seemingly okay with the way things went down tonight.

"Are you sure you wanna leave? You looked like you were enjoying yourself in there."

Gio glanced up at her from his phone. "I'm sure," was all he'd give her but she surprised him yet again with her upfront comments.

"Evelyn is very pretty. It looked like she was enjoying your company."

Gio stared at those big eyes for a moment before chuckling. "Yeah, I guess you could say that."

Her lips pressed together. "So go back."

With the adrenaline rush gone now, his body was aching again. He sat back trying to relax his tense muscles and closed his eyes. "I'm still sore."

"You were dancing pretty well out there," she countered rather quickly.

He opened one eye, peeking out at her. She was staring at him so curiously he had to smile but he closed his eye again. "You were watching?"

"What else was I supposed to do? I was bored."

That wiped the smile right off his face. God damn Felix.

"Can I ask you something?" The curiosity in her voice made it impossible for him not to peek again at those animated eyes. He knew they had to be all doe-eyed again and he wouldn't miss that for the world. He opened an eye and she didn't disappoint. He almost laughed at the way she stared at him.

"Go ahead," he said, stifling his laughter.

"Were you going to... you know, with her tonight?"

Gio smirked, wondering if he'd ever get over her sudden out of the blue comments and questions. But he liked them. So much so he wasn't about to let her off the hook. Surely she wasn't a virgin. She was Felix's girlfriend for crying out loud. She could at least say the words. "Going to what, Bianca?" he challenged.

She straightened up fidgeting with her fingers. "You know. Make love."

Now Gio laughed. "I just met her. You don't make love to a girl you just met." Her confused expression made him laugh even more. Then that something that made him say things to her that he normally wouldn't say to sweet girls came over him again and he stopped laughing and looked deep into her big eyes. "Oh, she would've got some tonight. She wanted it—told me so." Bianca's eyes got a little bigger. He'd pay hard cash now for Bianca's reaction to his shocking declarations. It did something to him and he couldn't help himself. "I just wouldn't have called it making love."

"She told you she wanted it?"

She was caught in his eyes now. Gio had seen this happen before with Bianca and it excited him but he was cautious because she never ceased to surprise him. He didn't know what to expect from her anymore. "Not only that she wanted it, but where and how."

Her eyes alternated from his lips to his eyes instantly heating up his insides. They were very close to the cabin where she'd be safe from what he was so tempted to do now. What he was feeling was off the charts wrong but he didn't think he had it in him to hold off if he really thought she'd let him.

"What did she say?" Bianca's question was genuinely curious. Obviously, she'd never asked for what she wanted. That didn't surprise Gio. She didn't seem the type but this had her complete and utter attention; she was practically sitting at the edge of her seat waiting for an answer.

"That she liked being dangerous."

Bianca's mouth opened distracting Gio completely. "Dangerous?"

The driver pulled into the long driveway to Felix's cabin and Gio couldn't be more grateful. If they were any further away he might give in to the temptation and lean in for a taste of that mouth. He swallowed hard. "She wanted to go into the men's restroom and have me take her on the sink."

Her impossibly big eyes grew even wider. "In public?"

"Seems that would be the case."

"And you were going to?"

The car stopped in front of the cabin and the driver got out. Gio waited too long to answer and the door opened, the driver waited to help Bianca out but she turned back to Gio surprising him yet again. Her expression seemed absolutely... *fascinated*? "Were you?"

"I was considering it."

She still didn't budge. "But what if someone walked in?" she whispered.

Suddenly being this close to her felt electrifying. "That's the exciting part," he whispered back licking his lips. "The risk."

Her eyes finally looked away from his and they focused on nothing in particular but she seemed to be contemplating on what he'd just said. Finally, she made her way out of the car. Gio took a giant deep breath, exhaling just as big before following her out. It was only then that he realized how fast his heart pounded in his chest and he was rock hard.

This was crazy. It was just a conversation for Christ's sake! He had to get a hold of himself or she'd be the end of him.

*

Days later Bianca was over the disappointing night out, which Felix had completely made up for by taking her out the following night to a romantic dinner, just the two of them. He followed up the dinner with a very romantic carriage ride where they cuddled up under some warm blankets as they rode around the picturesque little town drinking hot cocoa spiked with Kahlua. They ended the night going back to the cabin where they made love and not once had she thought of Gio.

Then early this morning Bianca awoke to another intense orgasm again only this time Felix was sound asleep. She'd laid there catching her breath trying to remember all the details of her dream as her heart hammered away.

With the visual Gio had placed in her mind about doing it in the men's restroom continually assaulting her thought processes these last few days it was no surprise she'd dream about doing it. Only thing was that it wasn't Felix in her dream. Gio had been the one that lifted her onto the sink, ripped her panties off and then plowed into her like a man with only one mission—to fuck her brains out—and she'd loved it. Just thinking about it now made her warm in unspeakable places.

"You ready?" Bianca flinched at Felix's voice. He smiled coming up from behind her and looking at her in the mirror. "I'm sorry, babe. I didn't mean to startle you." He lifted her hair and sprinkled tiny kisses over her nape. "You look beautiful… as usual."

"Thank you." She turned to face him and kissed him softly on the lips. Desperately needing to chase away the thoughts she'd been having just before he walked in, she changed the subject. "Are you sure about this? I still think this sounds really personal. I hardly know your friend."

Felix and Gio's friend, Noah, from the gym had invited them to dinner tonight at Noah and his girlfriend's place. Noah had been vague but Felix was pretty sure they'd be making some kind of announcement. If that was the case then Bianca thought maybe they'd prefer just their close friends and family members not Felix's new girlfriend who she was certain Noah didn't even remember.

"Yes, I'm sure and don't worry. Noah told me to bring you."

"He did?" That surprised her. From her experience, guys weren't like girls. They didn't go around talking about their relationships. "You told him about us?"

Felix moved over and fixed his hair with his fingers looking in the mirror. "I was going to but he already knew. Gio told him."

That came as an even bigger surprise but she tried not to sound too interested. "Really? What did he tell him?"

Felix glanced at her then back in the mirror and smiled. "Nothing bad I'm sure. But they both remember you from high school so Gio told him about you being up here, too."

They both remembered her? Bianca could see how Gio would, she at least had him for a few classes but she'd never had Noah in any classes and from what she remembered he'd pretty much disappeared senior year. She couldn't think of any other way to continue to pry for more information on what exactly Gio had said to Noah without sounding suspiciously curious so she let it go. She wasn't even sure why it mattered.

The whole ride down to Noah's, Gio and Felix talked about the renovations they'd be making to the gym. Felix was donating some major loot for it. It warmed her how generous he was and how genuinely excited he seemed about giving back to his community.

They arrived at Noah's house in a neighborhood Bianca remembered so fondly. The houses seemed smaller now somehow and the streets narrower but the area still had the same feel. Kids played in the streets. People sat out in their front yards even in the chilly late afternoon.

Noah and the guys were on the porch drinking beer when they pulled up into his driveway. Noah met them at the bottom of the stairs with a big smile. After the hugs, hellos and introductions, Noah offered them all beer from an ice chest he had out on the porch.

They were all just like Bianca remembered them in high school only bigger, especially Abel who had always been the biggest and was now *really* big. Hector, Abel's younger brother, who had always been so much smaller than all of them since he was the youngest was now just as tall as all of them and his teenage frame was like she remembered they all were in high school — bigger than most teens.

Gio immediately jumped up onto the railing of the porch and made himself comfortable. Noah offered Bianca and Felix a seat on the porch bench no one was utilizing. Noah had been leaning against the railing when they arrived and Abel sat on the other side of the porch's railing while Hector sat comfortably on the porch stairs. Bianca sat and took the beer Noah offered, feeling a little awkward as she sipped it. Obviously, they were all going to have a few pre-dinner drinks right there on the porch.

"So what's the big announcement?" Felix asked.

Noah gave him a knowing look. Even Bianca who didn't know them could guess this one. A couple only ever announced one of two things, a pregnancy or an engagement but she kept her thoughts to herself.

"Roni wanted to do this so I can't say anything yet but…" he sort of rolled his eyes then chuckled.

A phone rang in the distance and Noah patted his pants, coming up with nothing. He paused to listen as it rang again. It was coming from inside. "That's me." He pushed himself away from the railing. "I'll be back," he said rushing into the house.

As soon as he was out of sight, Felix scooted up to the edge of the bench they were sitting on and asked Abel. "So what do you think? She's pregnant or they're getting married?"

"If she's pregnant, knowing Noah it's both." Abel frowned turning to Gio. "You should talk to him, dude. They don't have to get married just 'cause she's pregnant."

Gio's reaction to that was defensive. "What difference would it make? They're already living together."

Abel leaned over looking into the front door cautiously then lowered his voice. "Nothing against Roni. You know I love her. But this shit went down real fast, him moving in with her and all. That age difference thing may not be a big deal now but when they get older and it gets more noticeable things could go sour fast."

"That's mom talking," Hector said laughing.

Abel turned to him with a scowl. "But it's true."

"Your mom doesn't like Roni?" Gio asked sounding very disgusted.

Abel brought his finger to his lips in exasperation then peered into the front door again. Bianca watched and listened to all of this fascinated.

"She likes her just fine but eight years is eight fucking big ones," Abel said keeping a watchful eye on the door. "Marriage is huge. Even if she is pregnant maybe they should just live together a few more years. You never know what could happen. He might realize maybe he did jump into this too quick. Maybe the age difference will be too much the older she gets."

Gio shook his head taking a drink of his beer. "Man, he better never hear you say that."

"Why? I'm just looking out for him."

Gio continued to shake his head adamantly. "Dude, I don't care how big you are. He ever hears you say something like that he'll rip your fucking head off."

Bianca felt like she had front row tickets to something girls were rarely given access too. Real live, un-censored guy talk. She was enjoying it just as much as the next nosy person until Felix put in his two cents. "I'm gonna have to agree with Abel on this."

"Thank you!" Abel said, lifting his beer at Felix and turning back to Gio.

"Whoa." Felix lifted his hand then turned to the door lowering his voice. "Not about the age thing. Noah scored with Roni. She's a hot little thing. I don't think she looks older than him now and I don't think she ever will. But the committing for life thing at his age?" *This* is what had Felix shaking his head now and it made Bianca's insides twist. "That's crazy."

Gio's face soured. "He's twenty-one and we all know Noah's always been way older on the inside than any of us. That's why Roni is so perfect for him."

"Why is Roni so perfect for me?" Noah said stepping out the door.

Bianca nearly spit out her beer. She managed to avoid making a total ass of herself swallowing down hard what was in her mouth. Her eyes watered as the gas came back up her nose.

All eyes were on Gio, who now had the burden of explaining what they'd all been talking about and why.

CHAPTER 12

Gio took a slow swig of his beer before smiling at Noah. "Because she keeps your ass in check."

Noah laughed. "Whatever. She's never even had to try." He turned to Bianca. "Speaking of, dinner is gonna be few more minutes but Roni asked me to send you in, Bianca. She's in there finishing up and she wanted to meet you."

Bianca stood up smiling. Felix stood with her. "I wanna say hi to Roni, too." They both followed Noah back in the house. Gio barely waited for them to be out of earshot before looking back at Abel. "Look, I hear where you're coming from but don't even go there with him. It will *not* go over well. I'm telling you." Abel frowned, making Gio shake his head again. "All right, just don't say I didn't warn you."

Gio always knew Abel had his reservations about Noah dating someone so much older than him but he'd kept it to himself for the most part. This is why it surprised him that Abel was being such a hard ass about it now. Gio knew Abel just had Noah's best interest at heart, but Abel couldn't be that blind. Noah wasn't changing his mind about Roni—not now, not ever.

A top-of-the-line SUV pulled up in front of Noah's house, distracting them all momentarily. Gio continued to take sips of his beer as the girl in the SUV stepped out and walked around to the passenger side of the truck. She wore all black—a black sweater dress, black tights and black heels. Even her hair that she wore in a sophisticated sleek bob looked black in the evening light. She leaned into the passenger side door to get something giving them all a clear view of a very nice ass.

Hector, who'd been leaning back on the stairs sat up. "Who's that?"

Both Gio and Abel shook their heads. Unlike Abel, who seemed just as interested as his brother, Gio was curious more than anything. Neither Noah nor Roni had any family that he knew of. As she walked up the walkway and Gio got closer a look, his jaw dropped. "Nellie?"

Abel's head literally jerked back to Gio and was back on Nellie in an instant—Roni's best friend. She'd done a complete one-eighty since the last time they'd seen her. "Hey, guys," she said walking up the stairs.

Gio got up to hug her. "Wow, Nel. You look so different."

Abel and Hector weren't as affectionate they both just smiled nodding their heads to greet her.

"Yeah, I finally put the weight back on that I lost last year." Gio tried not to stare too hard as he took all of her in. She was the epitome of sophistication. Her nails were perfectly manicured, she was draped in expensive jewelry and her makeup was as flawless as the times Bianca said she'd had hers done. "It was a rough year for me but I'm better now."

Gio smiled in agreement. "Well, you certainly look all better." Neither Hector nor Abel said much but Gio caught the way Abel checked her out several times. Gio couldn't help but smirk as he got the door for Nellie. "Roni's inside. They said dinner is almost ready."

Gio watched her walk all the way in, then turned to Abel. "Damn!" He chuckled. "Too bad she's eight fucking big ones older than us, huh?"

Abel rolled his eyes leaning back on the railing. "Even if she wasn't she's not my type."

"Bullshit!" Gio laughed. "I saw the way you were eatin' her up with your eyes."

Abel shrugged with a smirk. "I didn't say she didn't look good. I'm just saying she's not my type. I've talked to her before and on top of being too old for my taste I heard she's got tons of drama going on in her life. No thanks. I'll pass."

Noah opened the door. "Perfect timing." The guys all turned to look behind them at whoever he was talking to and saw Jack walking up the walkway. "I was about to tell these guys dinner is ready. So you're just in time, Jack."

"Good 'cause I'm starved." He held a paper bag with a bottle of some kind of booze in it.

Gio smiled, reaching out to hug him as he stepped onto the porch. "How's it going, old man?"

"I'm still kicking."

"And punching," Hector added laughing. "You should've seen him take a swing me at me the other day."

Jack pretended to swing at him now and Hector dodged out of the way. "I'll swing at you again if your brother tells me you're still gettin' in trouble at school, you wise ass."

Gio turned to Hector. "You still getting in trouble?" Hector shrugged, glancing at Abel who wasn't smiling. "What's your problem?"

"His problem is he needs to stop wasting that brain he's got on bullshit." Abel shook his head, glaring down at Hector. "He can ace his AP stats class but he can't figure out how to stay out of trouble."

Hector rushed by Abel and into the house before Abel who looked ready to take a swing at him got a chance.

Gio laughed as they all walked in together. Roni looked as adorable as ever with her long tight ringlets hanging down around her face and as expected their announcement wasn't much of a surprise. Nellie still stood up and hugged Roni with a squeal. Then she hugged Noah. "I already knew but still. I'm so excited for you guys!"

Noah rolled his eyes but laughed. "I figured that much. She swore me to secrecy but she told you?"

"I had to tell someone!" Roni explained.

Watching them as they talked about babies and marriage and their future there was no doubt in Gio's mind Noah was not making a mistake. Abel's mom was just old school but to Abel she could do or say no wrong. Whatever the woman said was golden as far as he was concerned. As much as Abel could kick some ass for the most part he stayed cool unless provoked. But the one thing that would light his fuse faster than anything was saying something bad about that boy's momma. You couldn't even mess around with *Yo Momma* jokes with him unless you wanted your ass handed to you.

It made sense now. If his mom had told him she thought eight years was too much of an age difference, no wonder he was so damn adamant about it.

Roni and Noah spoke of their plans to turn one of the extra bedrooms in the house into a nursery as soon as they found out the gender of the baby.

Gio's eyes locked with Bianca's a few times as the dinner went on. At first, he thought he'd imagined it. Maybe she'd just looked his way and their eyes had just so happened to stop at the same time. But it happened *several* times after that. As nervous as it made him that someone might notice he *could not* bring himself to stop looking her way.

She may as well have been glowing because regardless of where his eyes focused in an effort to keep them off her she always stayed in his peripheral view. He was aware of her every movement. Anytime she lifted her glass, or wiped her mouth was reason enough to look her way. It came as a bit of a surprise, but it was almost annoying too that he had so little control over something so simple—staying focused on whoever was speaking. What surprised him most was how indiscreet *she* was. Thankfully Felix was too busy yapping and catching up with the guys to notice her wandering eyes.

"So, Abel I hear you're finally getting rid of your truck?" Roni said as she stood lifting her plate from the table.

"Get rid of it? No way. Old Nellie still has a few years left in her. I'm passing her on to this guy if he ever stops getting in trouble." He pointed to Hector not noticing the room suddenly felt like someone had pulled the plug on the cheery buzz that had filled the air just before his comment.

Finally, something drew Gio's attention away from Bianca and he turned to Nellie who was now on her feet also lifting her plate, her lips pressed tightly together.

Gio caught the murderous glare Noah gave Abel.

"I... I didn't mean it like that," Abel stammered understanding now the error of his choice in words. "It's a saying. You know, like old Bessie."

Nellie nodded with a smirk but lifted a very telling

eyebrow. "No worries. I have a few good years left in me, too." She took her plate and glass and walked away to the kitchen. Jack, who sat next to Gio, shook his head chuckling as he dug into his slice of pie.

"What the fuck's the matter with you?" Noah hissed at Abel under his breath.

"It's okay," Roni tried to assure them, continuing to gather more empty plates atop of hers. "I'm sure she knows you didn't mean anything by it. And her middle name is Bessie by the way." Abel's jaw fell open and Roni giggled. "I'm kidding!"

Jack laughed even louder now.

"What's the big deal?" Hector asked. "She ain't old."

"No, she's not." Roni agreed walking off to the kitchen.

Felix laughed a little and Bianca jabbed him with her elbow but he could tell she was having a hard time holding it in herself. As tempted as Gio was to say something, he kept his comments to himself. He could tell Abel was already feeling like a dumbass the way he glanced around as if he was trying to think of a way to bolt out of there. Served him right for what he'd said earlier.

Wisely, Abel didn't make things worse by commenting further about "Old Nellie." He cleared his throat and took a drink of his beer. Then he turned to Noah who was still glaring at him. "I, uh. I thought I'd stick with another truck but when I saw this car my uncle had told me about, I had to have it."

"What kind of car is it?" Felix asked.

"Nineteen seventy-two Gran Torino."

"What?" Noah laughed.

Abel smiled, obviously glad Noah was laughing

now instead of glaring.

"Figures you'd get a muscle car." Gio chuckled, still struggling from keeping his eyes roaming into dangerous territory especially since all eyes were on him for the moment.

Roni and Nellie strolled back into the room and sat down. Roni reached for a dessert plate while Nellie reached for her glass of wine and took a sip. Gio couldn't help smirk at Abel's noticeable discomfort.

"So when do you get it?" Noah asked.

"In uh... ," Abel cleared his throat again.

Gio's eyes were on Bianca again as she tried to hide her smile under her napkin. Apparently she was having as much fun with Abel's discomfort as Gio was. He smiled at her then turned quickly away his eyes now stopping on Roni who'd caught the exchange. She smiled and turned back to her dessert.

"... a few days."

Unlike Gio, who couldn't go more than a few minutes without looking in Bianca's direction, Abel did an excellent job of looking everywhere but in Nellie's.

After grilling Abel for a few more minutes on the specs of the car Bianca wiped her napkin over her evil little grin and addressed Nellie. "You said you just bought a new car too, right? What kind did *you* get?"

Gio laughed inwardly. Way to have fun by pointing out that these two had something in common albeit it was minimal. And doing it in front of everyone, especially given the fact that Abel was already uncomfortable was genius.

Nellie seemed surprised. Bianca hadn't said much up until now and to speak up suddenly and address the other person who'd hardly said anything clearly threw her. Everyone's attention was on Nellie now.

Everyone that is except Abel who had a sudden interest in reading his beer label. Gio almost threw his balled up napkin at him so Abel could see that Gio knew what he was doing. He wasn't fooling anyone. But he had to remind himself they were all adults now and refrained.

"It's a Denali." Nellie smiled.

"Her divorce-is-final gift to herself," Roni added with a big smile and a wink at Nellie.

Now they had Abel's attention.

"That took a while didn't it?" Gio said as he took a swig of his beer.

"Yeah, it got a little messy. Court days kept getting rescheduled and what not." Nellie shook her head. "But finally it's over and I couldn't be happier."

"Time to move on." Roni smiled. "And girl, as good as you look, you're gonna enjoy your freedom. You better."

"Oh, I plan to. I'm already going on that weekend party cruise with the girls from work."

"I know," Roni pouted. "If I wasn't pregnant I would've gone with you."

Noah's expression immediately soured. "No, you wouldn't have."

Roni laughed and leaned into him. "I meant with you, silly. I've never been on one. It could've been sort of a honeymoon."

"This was so last minute. Someone canceled and I took their place. But," Nellie smiled lifting her eyebrow, "we can plan another time. You can still go if you're pregnant. There'd still be lots to do or we could wait until after the baby is here."

"You know in all my years," Jack spoke up, "I've never been on one of them damn cruises either."

Nellie turned to Jack her eyes even brighter. "We should plan a group thing." She turned back to Roni. "If we all go after the baby is born, you can take the baby and we can all take turns watching the baby so you two can have fun, too."

Roni sat up with a very excited smile. "Oh my God, yes! That would be so fun!"

"I'll coordinate it." Nellie shrugged. "It's what I do for a living after all. Getting this together should be a breeze." She turned back to the table at no one in particular. "When the time gets closer I'll get with everyone to find out who's in and we can decide what week is good for everyone."

Gio had glanced at Abel and was already smirking at his way too disinterested expression when he caught the exchanged smiles between Felix and Bianca. It wiped the smirk clean off. Someone would have to stay home and run 5th Street while everyone was on vacation. Gio suddenly got a good notion of who it would be—him and Abel.

They finished dinner and said their goodbyes to everyone, congratulating Noah and Roni once again before they left. They dropped by Gio's house so he could pick up a few things and say hello to his mom and sisters before heading back up to Big Bear. Felix didn't want to waste even a day of training, since this week he had a couple of gigs in Hollywood that would cut into his training time.

Gio picked up a couple of jeans and a few more changes of underwear then grabbed what he really wanted—his iPod and earbuds. He told Felix he wanted it for his runs but really he was counting on it to keep his mind and eyes off Bianca on their drive back. The drive down had been fairly painless for the most part. But he'd had to endure watching Felix run his hands up and down her thighs and even witness a few kisses. Not to mention hear Felix whisper things to her that made her giggle softy. He'd listen to his iPod all the way back and pretend to sleep if he had to but he wasn't going through two more hours of that crap.

Almost as soon as they were back in the car, the whispering and giggling started. Gio put his earbuds in, blasted it, and sat back in his seat with his eyes closed. The whole way he must've opened his eyes no more than three times. The last time he opened them was at the very moment Bianca kissed Felix and it had him slamming his fist into his seat. He squeezed his eyes shut immediately not caring what they thought of his slamming fist. Maybe he was jamming to his music, maybe he was having a bad dream, but he wasn't explaining shit.

Gio's phone buzzed in his pocket a couple of times on the way up but he dare not risk opening his eyes to check it. It hadn't seemed like a big deal to him before but he wondered now how he'd make it through the next few weeks. What he felt for Bianca was beyond a doubt the most confusing thing he'd ever had to deal with.

They were finally at the cabin.

"Bed time," Felix said, pointing at his watch. "We're up bright and early tomorrow."

Gio agreed saying goodnight and headed to his room. Once there he checked his phone. He had a missed call from Noah but no voicemail and he had a text. The text was from Noah as well.

I didn't notice shit but please tell me what Roni and Nellie thought they picked up on tonight is not true. There's nothing going on between you and... you know who. Right?

Gio sat onto his bed lying down and texted him back. He should've known girls were more apt to pick up on shit like this and he didn't even know what *this* was. So he responded the way he knew he should. If anything ever did happen, Noah would be the only one he'd consider telling but there was nothing to tell yet and he could only hope he'd have the willpower to keep it that way.

You're right, they're wrong. Nothing's going on.

Because he knew his best friend wouldn't leave it at that Gio lay there thinking about the whole damn situation as he waited for Noah's response. *Was* there even a situation? And did he want there to be one?

Just thinking about Bianca made Gio smile. His first impression of her, and he still thought so, was that she was sweet and innocent just like he always had even back in high school. There was something so intoxicating about the way those big innocent eyes of hers hung on his every word. She was like a sponge. You could almost see her brain working through her eyes, soaking it all in but what was even more fascinating was watching her react to the things he knew he had no business saying to her. Things Felix would just as soon drop Gio on his ass for if he knew he'd said them to her and rightfully so.

So why couldn't he stop himself? It's like something came over him when he'd see her get caught in his eyes. It would happen so fast and without warning — like a switch she'd turn on with just one look and as wrong as he knew it was, he was helpless to fight it.

His phone buzzed again and he read the text:

You sure? These two went on and on about it.

It was tempting to just call Noah and spill his guts but it was too soon. Truth was, as intense as some of the moments they'd had, it could mean nothing. He kept saying it to himself. Bianca had this innocence about her. It was highly probable that she was completely clueless about what she was doing to his horny ass.

Yes, I'm sure.

Gio was purposely being vague. He could add things like 'I wouldn't do something like that,' but that statement was no longer one he could say or even text with steadfast conviction.

He closed his eyes trying to push away what was beginning to feel like obsessive thoughts of her. The most pressing questions of all and what had Gio tied up in knots were: Did she know she was doing this to him? Could it be possible that sweet little Bianca knew she was driving her boyfriend's friend fucking nuts? But even more burning, why? Gio had heard her tell Felix she loved him. Saw the tears and hurt in her eyes when he hadn't made it up on time. She'd run out and greeted him with such excitement the day he finally did get there.

It made no sense. Gio had met plenty of girls who'd been willing to have a go with him even though they had boyfriends. But they weren't anything like Bianca. They were wild ass skanks whose boyfriends probably knew exactly what they were dealing with.

After the night they'd all gone out Gio had begun to think maybe it was better if he left—told Felix he couldn't stay—made something up. The ride home that night and his conversation with Bianca had been as close to the fire as he could get without touching it.

Now he had proof that he hadn't imagined what had happened at Noah's dinner—he wasn't the only who'd seen it. Would he be more tempted now to play with fire? He couldn't even be sure what her reaction would be if he did the unthinkable like give into the urge to taste her mouth just once.

Just a few weeks ago Gio might've punched someone in the face who so much as insinuated that he could be the type of friend that would even be thinking something like this. Felix may be flawed and probably unworthy of Bianca but he was his friend and they went way back.

Another text from Noah:

That's what I thought. Sorry I even questioned you, man. Girls are quick to jump to conclusions. I'll keep that in mind from here on. Goodnight.

Gio brought his fist to his forehead with a groan. Great. No guilt there. He'd be sleeping *real* soundly tonight.

CHAPTER 13

For the next three days Bianca had managed to keep herself preoccupied with school and work in the mornings and early afternoons while Felix worked out. Then in the evenings, she'd be back at the cabin with him.

Toni had called and texted her in the past few days excited that she'd seen her on TV and in the tabloids. Well, photos and some footage of her getting into her car or walking onto the small satellite university campus where she attended the only class she wasn't taking online. They'd been pretty sneaky so far and surprisingly respectful of her space because most of the photos Toni had mentioned Bianca hadn't even been aware when they'd been taken. Only once had she noticed a photographer across the parking lot aiming his camera at her. She'd never understand how celebrities could stand it. It had totally crept her out.

Bianca had to laugh at how giddy all this made her friend. The woman was glued to the television and her computer now that she had friend who was actually part of her favorite pastime — reading the gossip columns.

She was on the phone with her now, as Bianca drove back to the cabin. Usually Felix either picked her up himself or he sent a car if he wasn't done training but he'd be leaving early the next morning for Los Angeles to do some promoting and wouldn't be back until the following night. Felix could have a driver drive her around in one of his fancy Towne cars while he was gone but Bianca felt more comfortable in her little Civic. She still felt a little weird about knowing there was a driver waiting on her when she went shopping or stopped by to visit with Toni.

"Why aren't you going with him?" Toni whined.

Bianca crinkled her nose. "Because he'll be busy the whole time and I'll be cooped up in a hotel room."

"I'm sure he'd find a way to keep you entertained," Toni countered.

"By myself? No thanks. Besides I have school and work."

"He's doing the Late Night show. You could meet Conan O'Brian!"

Toni's exasperation made Bianca laugh. "I'm sure I'll get a chance to meet him some other time." Bianca had already met a few celebrities because of Felix and she never felt quite as star struck as she knew Toni would've been but at the risk of having her friend pass out she wouldn't mention her lack of interest in meeting the late night mogul.

"So, are you staying at his cabin tomorrow night anyway or are you going home?"

The question was one Bianca had contemplated for days. Felix had actually suggested she and Gio go do something tomorrow. Go snowboarding again or catch a movie. She knew it was only because he felt bad about leaving Gio up there on his own. The past few nights he'd hung out with them after dinner watching television or playing pool. Felix had even asked him if he wanted to join them in the hot tub last night which Gio immediately declined. Ray and Ignacio weren't much for socializing. They were always calling it a night and heading to their rooms right after dinner. Some of the nights, like the first night Gio had got there. they didn't even join them for dinner but took their food back to their rooms instead.

The dreams hadn't stopped. If anything they'd become even more intense now. One of the most intense being the night they got back from dinner at Noah's. They were so intense she was beginning to get nervous. She'd been known to talk in her sleep in the past. Although her grandmother had teased her once that it was more aggravating than anything because it was impossible to make out any real phrases. She said mostly it was just a word here or there that wasn't even all that intelligible. Too often the only word she remembered crying out in her dreams was *Gio*.

Bianca felt her face fire up as she pulled her car into the dairy parking lot. She wasn't buying anything but she needed to talk to someone about this already and she didn't want to have this conversation while she was supposed to be concentrating on driving in the snow.

"Toni?"

"Yeah?"

Biting her lip, she tried to think of where best to start. "Have you ever been in a relationship where you were happy but still found yourself attracted to someone else?"

"Oh, honey this sounds juicy. Hold on. Let me turn my sign over to closed and lock this door."

Bianca heard her giggle and she smiled trying to shake the anxiety she'd been feeling for days. She turned the key, shutting off the ignition to her car.

"Okay, so who is it and how come you hadn't told me?"

"First, you answer my question," Bianca drummed her fingers on her thigh. "Have you?"

"Of course I have. It's perfectly normal. Even married women can be attracted to other men. Nothin' wrong with that unless you act on it." Bianca thought about that last sentence for a moment without responding. "Oh, Bianca. You're too cute. So you have a crush on someone else and you're worried about it? I think it's especially normal for you since Felix is gone so much."

"But it's not just someone else. It's his friend. His friend like from way back. They're real close."

"Ooh!" Bianca could tell by Toni's excitement she didn't get the magnitude of this and how could she? "What friend?" Then in a much less excited tone, she scolded again, "And I can't believe you hadn't told me!"

Bianca took a deep breath and started from the beginning—way back in high school beginning. She filled her in on the important details feeling like she was slowly building a case against herself and why she was guilty of something only she hadn't done anything.

Toni listened intently, responding with "uh-huhs" in all the appropriate pauses. When she got to the part of the first dream, the night Felix arrived, Toni was quiet for a moment then she burst into laughter. As nervous as she still was about all this Bianca couldn't help laughing with her. "It's not funny, Toni!" she said but continued laughing. "Can you imagine if I would have said Gio's name as I came?"

Toni cackled even louder now and as funny as Bianca knew this *wasn't* she continued to laugh, too, barely able to catch her breath. Bianca was grateful she hadn't squeaked or this conversation would've gone nowhere. As the laughter calmed, she wondered if she should even go on. The dreams were even worse but somehow she knew Toni would find them more humorous than inappropriate. This was not the outcome Bianca had hoped for when she pulled over. "Toni!" she tried to sound firm as Toni continued to giggle. "I need clarity. Get it together, woman!"

"Okay, okay." Toni cleared her voice. "So the guy is beautiful, crazy sexy and he's obviously attracted to you too but you did say he's respectful, right? And he was mindful of making sure that you were not offended by his playfulness. If that's all it is then I wouldn't worry. You're very attractive Bianca, of course, the two of you are gonna flirt."

"There's more."

"Oh?"

Now that Bianca had her full attention again, she told her about the night they'd gone out and the ride home with Gio—what Evelyn had said to him. "Oh, what a slut! And pshaw! The men's restroom? That is so nineties!"

"That's not the point, Toni." Bianca wasn't feeling humorous anymore; the incredible unease was back and she was beginning to feel choked up. She needed someone to understand and tell her she wasn't crazy for feeling so incredibly guilty and selfish. "The point is there is this... I don't know how to describe it. It's like there's something bigger than the both of us when we're alone. I'm left completely breathless sometimes—I'm utterly mesmerized by him and I'm pretty sure I've seen it—*felt* it in him. We both know it's wrong but it's beyond any comprehension. If we can't even understand it, how can we control it? And I know it sounds like a bunch of bullshit. A huge cop-out." Her voice broke and she stopped unable to go on.

"Bianca," Toni's voice was full of remorse.

"Sweetie, don't cry. I didn't know this was bothering you *that* much."

Bianca sucked it up and took another deep breath feeling like a blubbering idiot. "It's just that I keep having these dreams, Toni. In the last one I got out of bed with Felix, tip-toed over to Gio's room, took off my clothes and climbed in his bed. And the thing is it's always so real yet it's so easy for me to do it. I know it's only a dream but even in dreams I usually think the way I would in real life. And in the dreams I want him *so* desperately." She breathed in, thankful that she was completely in control of her emotions now and continued. "I can barely look at him for fear that he'll know. He'll see it in my eyes. And the worst part is, I talk in my sleep."

"Oh, shit. You do?"

"Well, I used to. I haven't slept in the same room with my grandma in years but years ago she told me I did. What if I do one of these nights and I say his name? Say the things I do to Gio in my dreams—that I can't stop thinking about him—that he's on my mind constantly now even when Felix is making love to me. It's *so* wrong!"

Bianca heard Toni breathe in deep and then hum. It was something she did when she was brainstorming or trying to figure something out. Bianca could almost picture her walking around her little salon. So, she waited patiently hopeful that Toni would have some words of wisdom for her.

"I'm gonna be honest with you, okay? Don't be mad but I need you to really think about this before you answer, okay?"

"Okay." Bianca had an idea what her question might be.

"Are you really in love with Felix?" That wasn't it.

"Yes! Of course I am." Bianca snapped.

"No. I asked you to really think about it, girl." Toni snapped back. "Now think, because I'm just being honest here, so again, don't get mad. When you told me about how you told him you loved him, you said it just like that. You said, 'He said he loved me and I told him I loved him too.' Then you got all squealy and I had no choice but to do what any good friend is expected to do and squeal with you. But I did think it was weird you never actually said you loved him or that you were *in* love. You said you *told* him you loved him. It's different."

"Well, I *am* in love with him." Bianca tried not to take offense or sound defensive but it did bother her that Toni would think she could be so immature she'd be more excited about the idea of being loved and saying it for the first time than actually being in love.

"Really?" Bianca could tell by Toni's tone she *really* wasn't buying it. "And when did you know you were in love? Do you remember the moment you knew? That's usually a pretty big moment you remember forever."

Bianca didn't. All she remembered was being stunned when she heard Felix say it to her for the first time. But she was hurt. How could Toni be thinking this all this time and not mention it?

"I do," she lied, hoping she sounded convincing and not as angry as she suddenly felt.

"Bianca, don't be mad —"

"I'm not." She shoved the key into the ignition pulling her seatbelt on.

She *was* mad. God, was she ever. Just not at Toni. She was mad at herself. How stupid was she really?

Was it possible she'd convinced herself she was in love with Felix just because she got all caught up in the way it felt to be in love — liked hearing him say it back? And what, if anything, did her not actually being in love with him have to do with her feeling what she did when she was around Gio? She did at least have feelings for Felix. She cared about him and her feelings of jealousy when hearing about him with those other women were genuine. There was no way she was faking those.

Then she remembered what she'd felt when she saw Gio kissing Evelyn. She'd just texted Felix back agreeing to meet him back at the cabin but glancing up to see Gio and Evelyn kissing had been enough to make her spring out of her seat and bolt for the door. Bianca squeezed the steering wheel feeling her face flush, utterly mortified. She was ridiculous. What was wrong with her?

"I'm not mad," she repeated as she pulled out of the parking space. "I'm just confused and all of this is just making me so insane."

"And that's perfectly normal." Toni had her reassuring voice on and Bianca appreciated it because what she needed right now more than ever was reassurance. "From what you tell me Gio sounds like a sweetheart — a sweetheart that also happens to be eye candy. I'd question your sanity if you *weren't* attracted to him. Shit, I think I want him and I haven't even seen the guy."

Bianca laughed feeling completely grateful for having a friend like Toni. Toni would never judge her and she was always there when she needed her. She'd always told Bianca she could call her at any hour for any reason and unless she was stone cold dead asleep that she didn't hear it, she'd always answer. That had almost happened these last few nights when she'd awakened from her Gio dreams.

"I just wish I didn't feel so incredibly guilty about waking up right next to Felix in his bed having a full blown orgasm brought on by his friend." Just the thought made her wince.

Toni exhaled heavily. "Okay, I'm only gonna say this because I hate that you're beating yourself up about innocent dreams but I'm warning you're probably gonna be pissed." She paused, probably waiting for a response but Bianca didn't give her any. She could never be pissed at Toni. "I've been looking into this Shelley girl he met up with in Chicago and I haven't said anything to you because I have nothing solid but it's not looking good. Now, I could be totally wrong about this so don't start getting all upset or anything. That's all I'm gonna say about that because I could be on to something or like all the other times it could turn out to be nothing. All I want you think about is this. What you're doing—dreaming about his friend—is harmless. It's *just* a dream. He, on the other hand, well, let's just say his complete and total innocence is questionable at best."

Bianca thought about that for a second as she drove into the cabin's driveway. She could see Felix, Gio and Ray sitting on the porch holding coffee mugs. Probably tea for Felix and hot cocoa for Gio and Ray just like they'd been drinking the last two evenings she'd driven up. What was it about these guys and liking to drink on the porch?

"I'm here now," Bianca said as she pulled the car up across from the cabin facing the porch where the guys sat.

Felix smiled at her and Gio glanced up at her for a second before turning back to Felix who'd said something that made him laugh. "Okay. I'll let you go then," Toni said. "But let me just leave you with one last thing. In all the times you've been going out with Felix, when you were so excited about him coming up for a couple of months and when you told me he'd said he loved you—I've never once heard the emotion I heard from you today when you spoke of Gio."

Bianca stared out her windshield at Gio and Felix. Just a couple of weeks ago she was certain there was nothing or no one that would make her happier than Felix. Now, not only was she not sure if she was even in love with him, she may've fallen and in a way she didn't even understand for someone else—someone she could never have—his best friend.

She'd never forgive herself for breaking up their friendship. Only she was already feeling it from this far away—the pull. She needed to be near Gio now. She wasn't ready to walk away—didn't think she could if she tried. But she had to before she did something she could never take back. What in the world was she going to do?

CHAPTER 14

Last night had been rough. Each day that passed having to see Bianca with Felix was that much worse than the last. It made Gio wonder how much longer he could take being here. But then they'd have another one of their moments and the more urgent question became how in the hell would he ever bring himself to leave? He couldn't decide which was worse—having to see her with Felix—or never seeing her again. At least only as often as he ever saw Felix which if he wasn't training him was only every six months or so.

Felix had left early that morning. Gio hadn't even been up when he left and if he had been he would've pretended not to be. Felix would be gone for almost two days. The last thing Gio wanted was to witness their long goodbye.

After taking a shower, he called his mom to check in. She'd asked him to call at least once a day so he figured he'd get it out of the way now. Then he called Jack. The night of Noah's dinner Jack had discreetly asked him to call him when he could. Gio had the next day and Jack told him he was going to hold off on adding the rest of the guys to the title of the gym because of a lawsuit he had pending. He didn't want any of them getting dragged into it as part owners. He even offered to take Gio off the title because if the lawsuit got ugly, which his lawyers didn't anticipate it would, they could come after Gio as well. Gio had told him he wasn't worried and to do whatever made him feel better. Since getting Gio's name off the title would involve a lot paperwork and getting them signed and notarized Jack said he'd hold off on that for now.

In this morning's call Jack told him things were moving along. The lawsuit was going to be dismissed but it'd still be some time before he could get the guys on the title. He seemed worried that somehow they'd find out he'd only added Gio's name and be hurt. Gio told him what he was sure was the truth. None of them would think anything of it and would understand but guaranteed him they wouldn't find out from him. His lips were sealed until Jack told him otherwise.

Bianca was having breakfast alone when he walked into the dining room. "Morning sleepyhead," she said smiling brightly when she glanced up and saw him. "Feel good to sleep in?"

"I didn't actually," he said taking the seat across from her and already feeling his heart rate speed up just from being this close to her. "I had some phone calls I needed to make."

Gio knew Ignacio and Ray had both gone home yesterday to be with their families until Felix got back. Felix had flown them out first class and had offered to fly Gio to Los Angeles also but Gio passed saying he wanted to get some more snowboarding in on his days off. That's when he and Bianca had had another one of their moments. It had obviously surprised her he wasn't leaving like the other trainers. They'd all gone snowboarding a few times since the time he first went alone with Bianca but he hadn't gone back with her alone since.

Amparo poured him a glass of juice and let him know she'd be back with his breakfast.

"So who's snowboarding with you today?" She

glanced at him then back down at her plate. "Evelyn?"

Gio had just picked up his juice but stopped before taking a sip. He'd been in the room with her for less than five minutes and already he was getting the urge to say things he shouldn't. Last night Bianca had mentioned she had class this morning and an online seminar she *had* to watch today. It was disappointing to say the least that she wouldn't be going with him but at the time he'd thought it for the best. "Nope. I'm going alone."

Her eyes met his, a little surprised. "Really? Why?"

Gio shrugged. "No one else to go with. I haven't even called Evelyn." He knew it didn't matter but he wanted that clear. He hadn't called Evelyn or responded to her texts and had no intentions to, though he'd told Felix otherwise to avoid any questions. "So I'll be flying solo. Unless…" he smirked. That did it. She was caught in his eyes again. And though he felt a little evil and like a bad influence the thought of spending an entire day with her beat out any hankering to do the honorable thing here and not dangle the bait. "Unless you play hooky and join me."

The doe eyes made their appearance and Gio breathed in deeply. "I shouldn't…" She bit her bottom lip then smiled.

That wasn't a no and that alone made Gio's heart step it up a notch. "But?"

"I guess I can skip class but I really have to watch that stupid seminar." She smiled as brightly as she had when he first walked in the room. "I can do that tonight though."

The excitement Gio felt was different from any he'd ever felt because it was laced with something else. Something perilous seeped in along with the exhilaration. Something that took a little from the thrill of knowing he'd have her all to himself today. Strangely, the silent warning is what made the time he spent waiting while she got ready after breakfast that much more agonizing.

By the time they were in the car Gio felt like a kid ready to board a rollercoaster. It was as if his body and soul were already anticipating what was to come. The whole way to the ski resort they spoke just as comfortably as they always had with the difference now being that, unlike in those first few days, they kept stopping sometimes mid-sentence to just stare in each other's eyes.

The only thing that kept Gio from kissing her was he had no way of knowing how close Felix was to all his staff. The driver would be witness to it with one glance in the rearview mirror. If Gio did give into the insatiable urge he had now it wouldn't be just a soft kiss that could be construed as a friendly kiss. If he did this, he was going for it all the way.

They reached the resort and the driver got out. Gio knew he had less than a minute before the driver opened the back door for them. He couldn't stand it any longer; he had to at least taste what he'd been obsessing over for days now.

He leaned into her as she undid her seatbelt and her head jerked up at the feel of his body pressed against hers. Her eyes were immediately on his lips and he leaned in licking her bottom lip softly, making her gasp. For one horrific moment, he thought she might protest and that he may have just ruined everything. Then to his surprise, she brought her hand around his neck and pulled her to him kissing him wildly, making him groan in her mouth. The door opened and they flew apart. Gio was certain this was what it felt like just before you had a heart attack, because his heart had never beat so violently. He gulped hard, trying to get it together as he got out of the car and at the same time savored the taste of her still in his mouth.

They didn't say too much as they made their way to the lift. Bianca mentioned the crowd not being bad and maybe trying a new, more difficult trail this time. Gio could barely think straight. He could still feel her soft lips on his, taste her tongue in his mouth. Once they were on the lift, he turned to face her. "Bianca?"

She looked in his eyes but said nothing. Gio had considered possibly apologizing or at the very least explaining why he'd done what he'd done, but he saw her eyes on his lips again and the moment she licked her own his entire train of thought was shot. He leaned in and kissed her again only this time it wasn't nearly as wild as in the car. She let her head fall back as he kissed her deeper, his tongue seeking out every inch of her delicious mouth.

Knowing that getting carried away could be dangerous up on the lift he refrained from doing all the other things he wanted to do. Like suck her lips and taste her neck but just kissing her was already working him into a frenzy. Her hand was on his thigh and she kept sliding it up and down, squeezing at times. That alone was driving him insane, making him kiss her even deeper.

They kissed the entire way up, the only times he'd pulled away at all was to look deep in her eyes. He wanted to make absolutely sure she wasn't regretting this. Gio had no idea how this was going to work or how far this would go. Was this the only time she'd allow this? He didn't even want to consider that. There'd be no way he'd be able to fight this anymore. Not knowing what he knew now. That she was just as hungry for him as he was for her. Not once since he'd started kissing her had she so much as slowed it down. Her tongue kept up with his, matching every swirl, even sucking on his tongue like he did hers.

When they reached the top, Gio was thankful for the thick ski pants. But if anyone was looking closely they'd see the evidence of their ravished marathon kiss the whole way up.

As soon as they got off Gio took her hand. Just like that first day when he held it for just a moment, he felt the current-like blaze that shot through him from simply touching her. It was insanity. This after just kissing her nonstop all the way up the mountain.

Bianca shivered. "You cold?" It dawned on him just then these were the first words either of them had spoken since he said her name at the bottom of the lift.

She shook her head. "No." She smiled and he was relieved that she wasn't having second thoughts yet about what was happening.

That was just it though. What *was* happening? Did he dare ask and ruin it or should he just go with it and enjoy it as long as it lasted?

She turned to him her beautiful eyes bigger than ever. "You're not gonna tell Felix, are you?"

"Of course not." Okay, maybe they *were* going to talk about it.

"I've never wanted to kiss someone so badly in my life," she explained, stopping in front of him. This was just one of the things that had Gio falling for her fast. The way she just said what was on her mind regardless of the circumstances. "No matter what happens, I just want you to know kissing you will probably be one of, if not *the* most gratifying experiences of my life."

As nice as that sounded Gio obsessed over every one of her words searching deep into her eyes. "No matter what happens? What do you think is gonna happen?"

She shook her head unable to break the hold he had on her. He could feel it just like all the other times she was locked in his gaze and he loved it. It meant something but he didn't know what. "We can't..." she started to say then she whispered, "Felix."

Bianca didn't even have to say it. Gio knew all too well. He'd thought of it before and he was still thinking it now. He couldn't—shouldn't do this to Felix. Only now, there was something even more profound he was feeling. There was no way he'd be able to keep this from happening again. In fact, he could hardly stand it now. He leaned in and did what he *had* to do and kissed her again. To his relief just like the first two times, she didn't protest, kissing him back eagerly.

"Gio," she finally spoke breathlessly in between kisses.

He wanted to shush her—tell her they shouldn't talk about it. Just go with it. Whatever *it* was. Then just like she had so often done in the past couple of weeks, she surprised him with her next question. "You really wanna snowboard today?"

Gulping back excitement along with the anxiety of what she might possibly have in mind he stared at her. "What would you rather do?"

She laughed softly her face turning a slight shade of crimson. "No, please don't think... I'm just saying. I have no idea what's happening here...*Why* this is happening." The last part she said almost to herself as she glanced around. "We should talk. But this is making me so nervous. Maybe we should go somewhere else. Somewhere where the paparazzi won't get any pictures of us that might get back to Felix."

Gio glanced around, stepping away from her immediately. He hadn't even thought of that. Thankfully, they were too high up now for any paparazzi to be following them. Then he thought of their ski lift kiss and remembered they'd been pretty low when they first started but he hadn't spotted any of the vultures earlier. Not that his mind was thinking very clearly when they exited the car. After the first week they now had plenty of photos of Bianca. So the paparazzi's interest in her and Felix had died down significantly.

Bianca moved a stray strand of hair away from her face. Gio watched her mesmerized. "I mean if all we do is snowboard we could stay here—"

"Let's get out of here," Gio said bending over to strap his free foot onto his snowboard. He hoped she was saying what he thought she was saying; that she wanted to go somewhere more intimate where they could continue what they started. He'd leave the rationalizing and thinking this through for later. Right now, he could think of nothing better he'd rather be doing.

They made their way down the slope at an even pace, glancing at each other every now and again with knowing smiles. Gio pushed away any negative thoughts. This already felt like a betrayal on his part. How much further would he take this? How far would Bianca allow him too? Would he even try? Should he?

This was already far more than he had ever hoped for—even let himself consider. And leaving the slopes to possibly do more was *her* idea. That thought alone had his insides detonating. Gio breathed in deeply as they reached the bottom of the slope. He glanced around as they stopped looking out for any possibly paparazzi. There didn't appear to be any but as much as he was dying to kiss her again, he couldn't chance it.

The moment they were in the car and the driver closed the door Gio turned to her. "We could —" she started to say but Gio's lips were already on hers, devouring the taste of her mouth then it hit him and he stopped, pulling away to look in her eyes.

"We could what?"

She smiled, her face once again tingeing with color. "I was gonna say we could go to the movies. It's nice and dark in there."

Not exactly what Gio had been envisioning but he'd take it. "Sounds good to me," he said, sitting back with a frown at the sound of the front door opening and the driver getting in.

Bianca had already instructed the driver to take them back to the cabin so they could change, explaining to him briefly that they'd decided to call it a day early after she'd pulled something she was afraid would get worse if they continued.

Gio had been torn between being impressed by how quickly she'd come up with an excuse or being disturbed by it. He never would've pegged her for a being a good liar but he supposed after today they both would have to be or this could blow up in their faces in a very bad way.

He played with her fingers on their drive back as they sat in comfortable silence. An automatic insta-smile was plastered on his face the moment their eyes would meet and she matched it each time. It was everything Gio could do to keep from kissing her right there. Take her face in his hands and just claim her, even in front of the driver. Claim her — because even if it was only for today she was his and he was going to make the most of it. But he knew they'd have to be careful.

The car pulled up to the front door of the cabin and Gio once again took advantage of the seconds it took the driver to walk to the back of the car to kiss Bianca like it was their last kiss ever.

Warily he pulled away when he heard the door handle pulled. They exited the car and made their way to the front door of the cabin. Bianca turned to him suddenly her worried doe-eyes at full attention.

"What?" he asked, anxious to get inside where he might sneak in a few more kisses.

"The entire compound is full of security cameras." She glanced back at the car. "I have no idea if he has cameras in the cars."

The thought was not one that panicked Gio immediately. Felix had talked to him about the security measures he'd taken when they'd spoken of the paparazzi last week but he didn't mention cameras in the car. He did, however, mention the amount of cameras on the property and he was glad Bianca had reminded him of it because he was already having visions of taking her in his arms the moment they got inside.

He frowned, knowing that any thoughts of cozying up with her anywhere on the compound were now all shot to hell. There was no way without it instantly getting back to Felix. Gio did worry that their kiss in the car might have been captured by one of the cameras on the property. Felix had told him he could check the video even when he wasn't there. "We talked about the security system last week and he never mentioned cameras in the car." This was going to be tough and he wondered again, why on earth he was taking such a gamble. Was doing this worth the risk of getting caught and possibly losing a friendship he'd had since he was a kid—losing the respect from his friends and Jack when the news got back to them?

Their hands caressed as they reached the door and instinctively he took her hand instantly, feeling the fire scorch through him from just her touch. He dropped her hand remembering the cameras and their eyes met again.

Gio had wondered about something for days. There was something he saw in those eyes during moments like these when Bianca seemed caught in his and he'd finally figured it out. It was as if he was seeing himself in her eyes. Because she was feeling that same unexplainable fixation that he was feeling. It was plain as day now.

The wait to get her somewhere where he could hold her was going to be excruciating and just like that, he had his answer. Maybe if it was anyone else. Someone he didn't have this strange yet fascinating connection with it wouldn't be worth taking such a risk.

He smiled as he observed the very moment she was finally able to pull away from his gaze. Yep, the answer was as palpable as the blood thrumming in his ears now in anticipation to the rest of this day. Bianca was hands down abso-fucking-lutely worth the risk.

CHAPTER 15

The angora scarf Bianca wrapped around her neck should have brought on a little guilt. She'd purchased it just a few weeks ago with thoughts of Felix caressing the soft fabric. Now all she could think of was that she'd soon be snuggling up next to Gio in it.

She'd been tempted to call Toni while she was in the bedroom changing. A very small voice in her head wanted Toni to talk her out of this. Tell her she was making a huge mistake. But the much louder, more compelling voice all but snuffed out the little one. It screamed what she really wanted to do and that was to be with Gio all day. Have him hold her and kiss her like he had on the lift when she'd nearly melted into one huge puddle. As dangerous as she knew this could be, Bianca could hardly wait for it to happen again.

On the ride to the movies, Bianca struggled to concentrate on what she was saying as she looked into Gio's eyes. "There's this really nice hiking trail we can check out after the movies. It's well kept for wintertime hikers and on the easy side." She lifted her fingers to air quote. "Kid friendly," she smiled, feeling her insides warm as Gio's eyes traveled down to her lips again. "It um…," she licked her lips noticing his eyes widen and hoped he didn't think she'd done that on purpose, "leads into a meadow where families with young kids can take them for snowball fights and build snowmen."

Bianca paused to inhale deeply. She had to. The

way he was looking at her did something to her that left her in need of catching her breath. "It's really beautiful but the best thing is it's kind of a local secret. So it's never crowded and the times I've gone out there during the week I usually have the whole place to myself."

"Why do you go by yourself?"

Her eyes were immediately on his lips at the sight of them moving. "I um... just love the trail. You'll have to see it to understand. Even when it's not wintertime. I went up there a lot when I was deciding whether I was going to stay up here or move back down to Los Angeles. It's a great place to think."

She licked her lips again. "Stop doing that," he whispered, closing his eyes.

They reached the theater and the driver got out. Just like all the other times Gio's lips were instantly on hers. She loved the way he kissed her with such need. A need she could barely fathom. This guy could have any girl he wanted. Evelyn had obviously been ready and willing to do it in the men's bathroom with him after knowing him for only an hour and he'd passed it up—passed *her* up. He'd never even called her. If all he needed was one thing, Evelyn was a phone call away. Yet here he was *needing* Bianca as if she were his last fighting breath. She'd never felt anything like it but it completely captivated her.

The door opened and Bianca could feel the enormous effort it took Gio to pull himself away from her. Getting it together or at least trying to after every limb in her body had gone flaccid, she struggled to compose herself as she climbed out of the car. The driver had to use a little extra strength as she held his hand to get out.

They bought popcorn and soda though Bianca got the distinct feeling they weren't going to be doing much eating or even watching of the movie. The theater was as empty as she expected it to be. It was the first showing of the day on a weekday. They were literally the only ones in the theater. No sooner had they sat than Gio's big arm was around her and she let her head fall back onto it as he dove in. She was rewarded with one of the longest, deepest kisses he'd given her yet.

It wasn't until many minutes later when they came up for air that she noticed there were now a handful of other people in the theater. Since they were in the very back row, and she could only assume Gio had led them there purposely, she didn't have to wonder if anyone sat behind them.

They spent the rest of the two hours doing much of the same, stopping only briefly a few times to take sips of their soda or when they had to shush each other because their moans would escape them a bit too loudly. Mostly Bianca, but at times even Gio got carried away. That usually led her into a giggling fit where she'd have to bury her face in his chest to muffle the sound. She was grateful that the theater was so empty, although she was certain they'd annoyed a few people. Not that Gio seemed to care or even notice.

After the movies, they walked across the street and grabbed a couple of slices of pizza. "This is probably the best pizza up here," Bianca said, biting into her slice.

Gio once again attempted to make an unpleasant expression and as usual failed miserably. He still looked every bit the amazingly hot guy that he was. Bianca laughed.

"What?" he asked raising his brows.

"You may as well give up trying to look anything but delectable."

He smiled the smile that now made her insides flutter. "Delectable, huh?"

"Yeah," she said, biting into her slice of pizza.

She finished chewing as he stared at her, wiped her mouth and then, without even realizing it, licked her lips. Before she could respond any further, his hand reached out and squeezed her arm. "You're gonna have to stop doing that. Don't you realize I can't keep my eyes off you and each time you do that..." He scooted his chair closer to her side of the table, leaned in and pecked her a couple of times before really going in for it with a long ravenous kiss as if they hadn't just made out for over two hours straight and ended it with a groan.

With her legs gone to mush again, she blinked as he pulled away slowly but stayed close enough to look profoundly in her eyes. "Every time," he said, then glanced down as if to make sure she wasn't doing it again. "Every time you do that, that's what's gonna happen."

Bianca gulped, knowing he couldn't possibly mean when Felix was around, too. She wouldn't ask because she wasn't ready to discuss that subject yet but she did wonder exactly what would be discussed when the time came. When this flirtation started, she thought that's all it would be. Even when she'd allowed herself to fantasize about the possibility of something like this happening—maybe just one kiss—nothing more. She never imagined feeling this kind of intensity from him or herself. The very thought of being in the same room with him and Felix now made her cringe and she should've been mindful of Gio's words when he'd said he couldn't take his eyes off her because he'd been watching so closely he noticed.

His eyes were immediately troubled. "What's wrong?" She shook her head and attempted to look away but he watched her so closely it was impossible to hide any emotion from him. "What is it?"

"I just thought of Felix for a moment... of being in the same room with the both of you after today."

Gio's features went instantly hard. "Let's not worry about that now."

Bianca nodded, agreeing quickly. She too didn't want to ruin the rest of the day. There was still so much time left and then they had tomorrow morning. Her heart began to race but for a different reason now. It suddenly hit her that once Felix was back this would be over and the thought nearly made her gasp but she held it in knowing how closely Gio still watched her.

Gio cleared his voice. "I was gonna say before you interrupted me by laughing at my expression." The hardened countenance he wore just a moment ago was now replaced with a sexy smirk. "It's just that once you've had my mom's pizza you'll know why nothing else even compares. There's nothing like real Italian homemade pizza."

"Hmm," Bianca smiled hoping her comment would not sound cynical. "Maybe someday I'll get to try it."

His smirk went flat as their eyes met and he did that thing that rendered her virtually helpless to so much as glance away from his beautiful green eyes. Then he smiled again. "Yeah, maybe you will."

They finished eating and Bianca gave the driver instructions on how to get to that special meadow she'd told Gio about. She'd taken Felix out there once and even though they'd had a nice little walk he hadn't seemed too excited about it. This was one of those things that either you loved as much as Bianca did or she wasn't sharing it with you. So they hadn't gone back since.

Toni was the one that turned her on to it and she'd loved it from the moment she took her first hike there. Of course, that was late last summer when the leaves were just starting to turn colors so the spectacular views were breathtaking. But she'd been going back at least once every two weeks. So far it had been just as amazing no matter what the season.

They reached the beginning of the trail and Bianca told the driver where it would be best to park. Like the theater, there were very few people there. A few couples and a man walking his dog. The sun shone so brightly against the white snow for a moment as the clouds opened up they actually had to squint.

"Wow." Gio was looking at the area with that same admiration she remembered feeling when she first saw it.

"And this is nothing." Bianca smiled, relieved that she hadn't talked up the place too much and he actually seemed genuinely impressed. "Just wait until you see the meadow."

Bianca would never tire of the way he gazed at her. "Then lead the way, beautiful."

Such a simple compliment and Bianca felt her face flush. She'd just sucked face with the guy, heard his moans, felt his hunger for her and *this* made her blush? It was so silly she had to look away and he laughed. "Wow. Really?"

She covered her face with her gloved hands trying to keep from going into a laughing fit because she felt so stupid and the worst thing that could happen did — the squeak. It was loud and one look at Gio's laughing face and she was in near tears laughing.

He pulled her to him laughing and moved her hands away from her face. "Don't cover your face. I love seeing you laugh."

Bianca buried her face in his warm jacket as he brought his arms around her waist holding her tighter. The enthralling smell of him, his aftershave, his skin as she lifted her face to his. It was enough to calm her laughter, get her heart pounding again for a different reason now.

She glanced back at the car glad the driver was back in it and the car was facing the opposite direction but one look back and he'd see them because they were in plain view. When she glanced back at Gio his lips were on hers again. One soft kiss was all he gave her and she sighed. "Don't tell me no one's ever called you beautiful before."

It was hard to keep a straight face but staring in his eyes made it easier. It practically immobilized her. This was getting embarrassing. No person should have this much power over another. But she couldn't hold it against him. There was no way he was doing this on purpose. Was there? "Yes, I've been called beautiful once or twice in my life," she said down playing the amount of times Felix alone had called her that among all the others who'd used that word to describe her over time.

"Once or twice? Get out of here." Another couple came around the corner of the trail making Gio and Bianca move out of the way.

Gio took her hand and they began to walk down the trail. The one thing she hadn't mentioned to him were the caves along the trail to the meadow. She'd been afraid he might construe her suggesting they come here as something more mischievous. The thought of being alone in one of the caves with him had crossed her mind and just thinking about it now warmed her insides. What they were doing was already bad enough. Taking things even slightly further was going past her one time indulgence to do what her heart wanted instead of what her head told her. Which is what she was calling this — a one time indulgence.

Even in her thoughts, it sounded like what she knew it really was, pure bullshit. This was wrong no matter how you looked at it. Yet, not once, other than the little voice that had barely made a peep when she went back to the cabin, had she considered fighting it. And now that it was happening she couldn't even begin to imagine how she'd ever go back to the way things were before today.

"What's that?" Gio pointed with a smirk.

"A cave," she said, trying to sound as casual as possible. "There are a lot of them around *the trails.*" The trails. In other words not just this one. The one she'd brought him to on a day when she'd known they'd have the entire trail mostly to themselves.

He gave her a knowing look. Damn it. She knew it. But the truth was she was beginning to wonder now if subconsciously she *had* been thinking that way. "Can we go in them?" He looked up on the mountain above the cave. "Or are there bears and mountain lions around here?"

"There's all kinds of wildlife out here but didn't you ever watch cartoons growing up?" She giggled, willing herself not to get into any more of her stupid laughing fits that would have her squeaking like a mouse on crack. "Bears hibernate in the winter; so it's rare to see one out here in the snow."

"Where do you think they hibernate, Bianca?"

That wiped the smile off her face and she stared at him as his words sunk in. The thought of a bear being in one of those caves hadn't even crossed her mind. This time he laughed taking her face in his hands, kissing her lips and cheeks and finally her forehead. "God, Bianca." was all he said before hugging her close to him with a grunt.

She hugged him back taking in the smell of him again. He smelled so good and it felt so perfect being in his big arms she could barely stand it.

Finally loosening his hold on her, he kissed her, a little longer this time, then took her hand in his again. "Let's go check it out."

Bianca had been in them before, mostly nervous about any possible snakes, but now she wondered why a bear being in one of these caves had not crossed her mind. The whole damn town was called Big Bear for Pete's sake!

She followed him cautiously as he made his way down the trail toward the cave. It was big enough for them to walk in without having to duck their heads. "This trail is probably too busy for any bear to want to make it their place." There was a lot of writing on the inside walls and names etched into the rocks. "Oh, yeah. Way too many people visiting this place for any bear to feel comfortable here."

He turned to her with that sexy little smirk of his that made her insides liquid. "A lot of young couples probably turn this place into their own little love cove." He pulled her to him and in the next second had her pinned against the cave wall. "Is that why you brought me here?"

Before she could respond, he kissed her roughly pressing his body against her. Bianca wasn't sure if she should panic or go with it. He pulled his lips off her and moved her already loosened scarf out of the way. "Take this off." Staring into his eyes, she did so methodically. Completely aroused and caught in his eyes again, she let the scarf drop but he caught it and stepped away from her stuffing it in his jacket pocket. "Is this why we're here, Bianca?"

She shook her head but no sound came out. He took a step closer to her again, bringing his face next to her ear, causing her body to tremble in response. "What do you want?" he whispered. Again, her head began to shake but she froze when she felt his tongue on her neck.

"I'm not usually like this. I want you to know that."

"I do." He continued to kiss and lick her neck making her legs weaken with every stroke of his tongue.

"I don't condone cheating. That's not the type of person I am."

He stopped his kissing and pulled back to look at her. "Yet, here you are with me. Why is that?"

"I don't know," she whispered.

"Would you feel better if we stopped?"

"No!" She felt her face heat with her abrupt answer.

Staring at her very seriously and thankfully not smirking at her rejecting the idea of them stopping so vehemently, his eyes came down to her lips. "Why'd you bring me here? Tell me what you want, Bianca."

With her body still trembling, she shook her head, for once her mouth holding hostage the words that she really wanted to say for fear he'd think her absurd. "I don't know," she whispered, staring now at his lips. "I don't know anymore. I don't understand what I'm feeling — or know what I want."

"I know what I want." He leaned in whispering the words against her neck making the trembling more pronounced. And she felt him chuckle. "Is that your body telling what *you* want?"

She tried pushing him away, suddenly feeling angry — or hurt. It made no sense, she *did* want him — this. And doing what he was suggesting was probably the most she could ever expect from him but she didn't like that he was okay with just that. "No, Gio. That's not why I brought you here."

He pulled away to look at her and damn it if she wasn't caught in those eyes of his in an instant. "I know that, sweetheart." He hugged her hard. "But Jesus. What I want... I could only dream of..."

He didn't finish his sentence burying his face into her neck, then lifted his head and took her mouth in his again kissing her so hard it was alarming but at the same time so thrilling she moaned. He bit her lip the arousal she felt by the slight pain was surprising, leaving her to only imagine would he could only dream of — what other parts of her body he wanted to bite. Then like they usually did in reaction to him the words now flew out. "I've been dreaming of you." His head lifted immediately — his near frantic eyes eagerly searching hers for more and suddenly for the first time in all the times she'd spoken so freely with him, Bianca was speechless.

CHAPTER 16

Gio waited but Bianca said nothing more. She just stared at him in that same way she'd been doing since they left the cabin that morning. Those eyes owned him now—completely. It was almost painful to look into them now and know she belonged to someone else. That she was his for just a few stolen moments and tomorrow she'd be back in Felix's arms... his bed.

He hugged her, squeezing his eyes shut, not wanting to be looking into those eyes when he asked her, "What've you been dreaming, Bianca?"

Did he really want to know? He realized only moments ago when he found himself getting carried away that as much as he wanted to take her and do all the things he'd been fantasizing about on a daily basis now he couldn't—shouldn't. Not just because she was Felix's girl but because what was happening was exactly what he'd been afraid of.

Kissing her today had been a leap of faith. One he'd hoped would get her out of his system. Instead, it'd backfired on him. His need for her now had magnified in a way he hadn't expected. Making love to her would only make that a million times worse. If she told him now that that's what she wanted he couldn't even begin to imagine rejecting the idea—but he had to.

"Bad things," she finally whispered. "This isn't like me. I swear to you. That's why it's so hard for me to understand why this is happening."

Earlier he would've looked at her. Watched her as

she gave him any further details of her dreams but now he couldn't. It was hard enough just listen to her.

"What kind of bad things?" He gulped, now afraid of what her answer might be.

"The kind of bad things that have me waking up with my heart pounding and breathless but very content."

Gio froze and he could feel Bianca do the same. One thing he loved about her so much was how easily she put things out there. Only now he was wishing she'd have been just a tiny bit vaguer. He was having visions of the kinds of things he could do to her to leave her heart pounding and breathless. Although today he'd had a heavy dose of her breathlessness and felt her heart pound straight into his several times like now.

She still didn't move but she began to speak again. "In my dreams—"

"Don't." He had to stop her before she went on. "I don't think I can take it." He backed up taking in the delicate features of her sweet face—he was in love with every one of them now. He forced a smile. It took everything in him to let it go—not stay there and listen to her tell him what he'd done to her in her dreams. "Let's go check out that meadow." He pulled out her scarf from where it was half pushed into his jacket pocket and placed it gently around her neck, then kissed her one last time before taking her hand and walking her out of the cave.

For the rest of the day she was his. They walked the trails hand in hand and played around in the snow when they got to the meadow. They each made a snowman and, since she obviously was more experienced at this then him, hers was much better than his half-assed crooked excuse of a snowman. Of course she laughed at it openly.

They then decided they would take their own snowmen down with snowball bombs. Being the gentleman that he was, Gio let her go first. Her first bomb was a direct hit that took his snowman's head right off. Her jaw dropped and in the next second was laughing uncontrollably. "I didn't mean to do that," she squealed as she took off when she saw him give chase.

"What do you mean you didn't mean to? You aimed right at his head!"

She laughed even more as he caught up to her, quickly pushing her down on the soft hill of powder she was going to try to climb. She flipped around still laughing and out of breath. "I'm sorry!"

Gio couldn't stand it. He loved everything about her. Her laugh—her smile—the way she made him so impossibly happy by doing nothing more than laughing. Nothing else seemed to matter as long as he was around her. Laying there in the snow next to her looking in her eyes was pure heaven. His eyes on hers calmed her laughter but she still smiled big. She lifted her hand and touched his hair.

"You're so beautiful," he whispered, staring at her. "I mean that." He lifted himself to rest his weight on his elbow. "Don't take this the wrong way but I've had my share of beautiful women." The flicker in her eye told him maybe his dumb ass should be careful with his wording. "I mean I'm not just talking about looks, Bianca. There is something so special, so beautiful about you. I hope you know that."

He bit his tongue before telling her that he didn't think Felix worthy of her. Hell, Gio probably wasn't either but at least he wouldn't take her for granted. He knew a good thing when he saw it and Bianca was as good as it got.

Bianca sat up making him sit up with her. "I don't think there is anything special about me. And I'm not saying that to fish anymore compliments out of you. What you've said is enough. Thank you." She glanced out into the open meadow. It was as amazing as she had described it. Even as Gio glanced around at the huge snow covered pine trees that surrounded it so perfectly he suspected it wouldn't be quite as amazing if she wasn't there with him. "It's just hard to feel special when I've spent one of the most wonderful days of my life kissing my boyfriend's best friend." She turned to caress his face. "I should be missing him, you know? I did before you came along. I haven't thought about him even once today. What I'm feeling for you, Gio..." She shook her head. "It's scaring me."

"Noah's my best friend," Gio said, as if that bit of information made the situation any better.

He should be happy about what she'd just admitted but how could he be? If she were with anybody else, Gio would already be doing—saying anything and whatever it took to convince her to leave the guy. The way he was feeling right now begging would be the obvious and easiest next step. He'd never begged a girl or anyone for anything in his life but if he thought it could make things different he'd gladly be on his knees already.

The problem was it wouldn't change things. Her boyfriend was Gio's longtime friend and, just like all his other friends, loyalty might as well be Felix's middle name. He just couldn't do that to him. The only thing Gio could hope for now is when he finally got a moment alone with Felix that he could get the truth out of him about his loyalty to Bianca—the only place where ironically it appeared to be lacking.

"Felix is still your friend from way back and he speaks very fondly of you."

Gio frowned. He didn't need to hear this right now. He stood up, frowning even more when he realized his ass was soaked. Jeans and snow—not the smartest combination. He held his hand out for Bianca and she took it standing as he pulled her up.

"Ugh! My butt's all wet," she said turning and giving him a glimpse of that perfectly round behind.

"Yeah, mine too," he said, trying not to be too obvious about enjoying the view.

Bianca giggled. "We better get out of here before we literally start freezing our butts off."

Halfway back to the car Gio pulled her aside and into his arms. He needed to alleviate the ache he was already feeling from just the thought that their time alone was almost over. This was going to be torture.

He kissed her so desperately he hoped it didn't freak her out but he couldn't help himself. "I wish…" he started to say between kisses but stopped to kiss her again.

"Me too," she whispered against his lips, sounding just as desperate. She took his hand and placed it inside her jacket against her chest. Her heart pounded as wildly as his did. "That's not just excitement, Gio. It's fear that this feeling is only gonna get worse." He stared in her eyes suddenly seeing the fear—the very fear he was beginning to feel himself. "What's happening?" she whispered. "I've never felt this way."

"Me either," he said quickly.

"We can leave again tomorrow, he won't be back until tomorrow night."

He leaned his forehead against hers. "Yeah, let's do

that." That did ease the ache a little but Felix would be back tomorrow night and spending the day with Bianca had epically failed in getting her out of his system. In fact, his feelings for her now were at a level he didn't even know existed in him. What the fuck was he going to do?

*

On the ride home, Bianca's stomach turned when she saw she had several missed calls and texts from Felix. Lying to him was out of the question. All it would take was one call to the driver to get an update on her if he was worried. She felt weird about even reading his texts in front of Gio so she waited until she got back to the cabin in the bedroom to read them. But she did tell Gio that if he talked to Felix before she did not to lie. She was telling him almost exactly what they did today leaving out, of course, all the parts about making out with his friend all day.

Most of the missed texts were basically the same, asking her how things were except for the last one about a half-hour ago.

Babe I'm getting worried. Please call me as soon as you can.

She listened to the voicemail that he left just a few minutes after the text.

"Look, if this is about that story they've been airing. I promise I can explain that, too. We talked about this already, remember? I'm supposed to get a chance to explain before you shut me out." He paused for a moment taking what sounded like a very frustrated deep breath then exhaled. "I'm sorry this keeps happening but I wish you wouldn't turn on me so quickly. Call me… please?"

Unlike all the other times something like this happened, Bianca felt oddly relieved. In her rush to read his texts she'd skipped the texts from Toni. Toni was probably already all over whatever story Felix was referring to. Knowing that Toni was under strict warning that she wasn't supposed to pass on any gossip about Felix unless there was something concrete, Bianca felt like a huge hypocrite afraid to read her texts.

The first was a safe one saying only that Toni knew Bianca was in class and to give her a call when she could. The second was what she was dreading:

I'm not sure if you've seen what I've seen all day today on TV but I hope your not responding has nothing to do with you being too upset. Call me please I'm worried now.

How was it possible that after spending such an incredible day with Gio she could possibly care about this? Her insides were instantly on fire as she hit speed dial and called Toni back. She needed warning before she turned on her television.

Bianca was angry—more than angry but it felt different this time. If she was going to be deprived of being with someone as amazing as Gio her only consolation was that she at least had Felix. Someone equally amazing just a few days ago, right? At least she'd thought so until Gio had come along seeping slowly into her every waking—and sleeping—thought.

Before Gio, Bianca had been excited about her future with Felix. Sure, he wasn't without his flaws but for the most part the only one she'd found in him was the possibility that he wasn't being completely honest with her and so far all her suspicions had been all for nothing. He kept proving time after time that he was in fact in love with her and the rumors were all without merit.

What she'd done today with Gio was inexcusable. But even though she'd kissed his friend — *all day*, something told her whatever Felix had done was much worse. Not only that if he'd really done anything he'd probably been doing it for quite some time. It made her feel like the biggest fool on the planet because she should've seen something like this coming sooner. The signs had all been there. She just refused to see them — clung on to the hope that he was really telling her the truth and now she could very possibly be left with nothing.

More than anything, she knew why she'd lit up so fast. And it was almost humiliating to admit it. Her stomach had been in knots from the moment she and Gio snuck their last kiss in the car tonight. The countdown had *just* started until their next chance to be together like they had today and Bianca didn't think she could make it. It had just started! She'd never felt anything like this. She was already tempted to skip this whole business of finding out what Felix did and run out there to be with Gio now. So the idea of ending things with Felix and leaving here never to see either of them, but most dreadfully never seeing Gio again, was what really had her falling apart.

Toni answered. "I'm sorry Bianca. I didn't mean to alarm you but when I didn't hear back from you —"

"I haven't seen or heard anything, Toni. But can you please warn me. How bad is it?"

Bianca held her breath in anticipation. "It's not too bad. The only reason I brought it up is because you usually respond fairly quickly and I hadn't heard from you *all* day so I had visions of you curled up in bed crying or something."

She'd begun to exhale slowly but that last comment made her breath hitch. "Curled up crying? I thought you said it wasn't bad."

"No, no, it's not! But if you see only parts of it I could see why you might think it is. It's basically the same stuff I uncovered digging on the Internet about him and that Shelley girl. Now that they have photos of you and him they're making this big thing over who is he really with. They have some really cute ones of the two of you on that horse and carriage ride you two went on, by the way."

It was the strangest mixture of relief, excitement and guilt all rolled into one. For one she was incredibly relieved that it wasn't as bad as she was expecting. However, the guilt all but consumed her. She wasn't relieved that her boyfriend hadn't cheated on her. She was excited that she wasn't going to have to leave him and in doing so leave Gio as well. Felix was the one thing keeping them apart but at the same time, he was the only thing keeping her there with the possibility and hope of a few more stolen moments. This whole thing was crazy and not to mention incredibly selfish. But even now she could hardly wait to meet Gio in the hot tub.

Bianca had purposely called Amparo ahead to tell her she and Gio had picked up fast food on the way home and were already eating in the car so she could go ahead and close up the kitchen early and call it a night.

Even though they wouldn't be engaging in anything incriminating for the security cameras to catch, just knowing that she'd soon be in the same room alone with him again did things to her—had parts of her body already reeling with anticipation. It was unreal.

Toni finished telling her about the photos and the stories the media were trying to twist into something. None of them had it straight, except they were all insinuating that it appeared Felix had two girls—one in Chicago and one in Big Bear. But none of the stories had any real facts other than some old photos of Felix with Shelley and the more recent ones of the day he'd been stranded in Chicago.

Bianca thanked Toni for the update then took a deep breath before calling Felix. He answered on the first ring. "Bianca?"

"Hey."

"You had me worried, baby. How come you hadn't returned my calls or texts?"

"I had my phone put away most of the day." She closed her eyes before continuing hoping the rest would sound as innocent as possible. "I went to the show today with Gio and then we went to that meadow I like to go to. I forgot to turn my phone back on after the we left the show."

Felix was quiet for what seemed too long and Bianca could only imagine what he was thinking. It was so unlike her not to check for his calls or texts and even more unlike her to not respond to them as soon as she got them. "Are you sure this is not about the stories they've been airing all day?"

She almost didn't but then decided at the last second she would. "Maybe." And so the lying began.

"Babe. You have to stop doing this. These stories are gonna continue. You have to let me explain before you go believing the worst. I don't know how else to assure you that it's all a bunch of bullshit." There was noise in the background and she heard him tell someone he'd only be another minute. "I got a live radio interview to do right now. You can tune in to listen if you want. But we need to talk when I get back tomorrow. I hate that this shit keeps happening. More than anything I hate for you to be upset."

Bianca squeezed her eyes shut, the guilt nearly blinding her. "I'm okay, really."

"Are you sure?"

"Yes."

"Okay, but we still have to talk." He gave her the information on where she could tune in to listen to the interview and she pretended to write it down saying she would listen. Then just before he hung up he caught her completely off guard. "So what did you see today?"

"Huh?"

"At the show — with Gio?"

She shook her head, drawing a blank and panicked. "Oh, uh." Bringing her hand to her forehead, she spun around in the room, desperately trying to remember what movie they'd purchased tickets for. Without exaggerating, she could honestly say she hadn't watched even a minute of it. And at the moment couldn't even think of *any* movie. She snapped her fingers annoyed that her mind had completely zoned out. She finally blurted out the last action flick she'd watched.

"Really? Isn't that old?"

Shit! She had no idea. It was just the first thing that came to mind. "Not the first one." Was there even a second one? Not sure what else to do, she hit end and stared at her phone waiting for it to ring but it didn't.

After a few minutes, she figured he'd been hauled off to do his interview and she relaxed. The anxiety of the nearly botched call hadn't even worn off yet when the anticipation of being with Gio again began swirling inside her and she hurried to change into her bathing suit.

CHAPTER 17

Out of habit, Gio had clicked the TV on in his room as he walked in. Halfway through rushing to change into his swim trunks, the words of the reporter on the television hit him like a bolt and he grabbed the remote clicking record like he had back home anytime something about this aired.

"Felicita Morales, the widow of Trinidad Morales gave birth today to a baby girl, Trini Morales, named after the father she'll never get to meet. Trinidad, who lost his life just over a month ago in the ring after a blow to the head during a fight that burst an aneurism in his brain, was only twenty-two when the tragedy occurred."

Gio went numb. He stared at the screen as they went into detail retelling the story of the fight, Trinidad's death and the ongoing investigation of the physician who released him to fight. He picked up the remote turning up the volume as the cameras zeroed in on Trinidad's father who was being interviewed at the hospital. He spoke solemnly about the birth of his granddaughter. "It's bittersweet day for our family," the reporter translated from Spanish. "Even though we are very happy that God blessed us today with a part of my son." The man's eyebrows pinched and he brought his hand to his mouth unable to hold back the emotion.

Gio felt the anguish in his own heart as the man tried to continue speaking and suddenly he felt himself struggling to hold back tears as well.

"My son was so happy when he found out he was going to be a father." The man went on even as the tears ran down his face.

Gio immediately thought of Noah and how horrible it would be lose him. To leave Roni behind with a baby that would never know him would be even more devastating.

The reporter went on to say that mother and daughter were doing well and that they would most likely be released from the hospital tomorrow then moved on to the next story.

The knock at his open door came just as Gio rewound the story and he gulped hard not wanting Bianca to see the emotion he was feeling.

"Hey," he said, unable to even look at her so he hit play and watched the TV instead.

"You okay?" She stood next to him and watched silently as the entire story replayed. As soon as it was over Gio rewound it again. Just like the other stories he watched over and over again back home, he thought maybe he'd grow immune to the fact that Trinidad's entire family and now his fatherless daughter were still mourning the loss of the family member *he* had killed.

He hit play again as he stared at the screen gulping hard because the emotion was not going away.

"Gio, stop." Bianca's voice was cautious. "Why are you gonna watch it again?"

"Can you give me a minute?" he asked, still staring at the screen.

"Remember what we talked about? It's not your fault. It's sad but—"

"Bianca, please!" His words were louder than he'd intended and he felt her flinch so he finally turned to her, lowering his voice. "I just need a minute."

She nodded and without another word walked out of the room closing the door behind her. Gio watched the whole thing a few more times then finally threw the remote on the bed. The temptation to turn the lights off, sit in a corner and lock everyone out again like he had just after this first happened was overwhelming.

The knocking on the door again, made Gio frown. He didn't want Bianca to see him like this. He could feel himself getting pulled back into that same darkness he'd been in for weeks after Trinidad's death and he didn't want her to know how fucking weak he could be.

Instead of telling her to come on in, he walked to the door ready to tell her he was calling it a night — say he wasn't feeling well and he would just take a pill or something and go to bed. He opened the door and Bianca stood there holding a tray. On the tray — two bowls of ice cream with all the trimmings.

"I thought you might be in the mood." She gave him the most adorable hopeful look as she waited for his response.

Gio smiled, wishing now that she wasn't holding a tray between them because he was overcome with an incredible urge to hug her — hold her like he had all day and never let her go. She was his magic pill. The one thing that brought light into his darkness. Because of her, he'd barely even thought of Trinidad the whole time he'd been here until tonight.

"Yeah, ice cream actually sounds perfect right now. Thank you." He leaned in a little closer. That same familiar warmth he felt when he was around her was already pushing away what he'd been feeling just before he opened the door. "I'd kiss you if I could," he whispered and her eyes did that thing that drove him insane. "I swear to God, Bianca. If you lick your lips I *will* kiss you. I don't care where we are."

She giggled. "Don't tempt me." Gio dropped his head back with a groan and she laughed. "You wanna eat it here or in the kitchen?"

Having Bianca in his bedroom all to himself was way too dangerous. Reminding himself that he'd already come to the conclusion that he'd be willing to risk it all for her, he decided he didn't trust himself. "I think the kitchen would be safer."

She smiled, turning around and he walked after her. The tray was set on the counter and they each took a bowl and a spoon. Gio dug in immediately. Then watched and waited as she took her first spoonful making that face she did whenever anything was delicious. "Why do you do that?" he asked, exasperated.

Instantly her eyes went into Bambi mode. "Do what?"

Gio laughed shaking his head. "Never mind."

"No. Do what?" She insisted.

He leaned his hip against the counter taking another spoonful of ice cream before responding in a hushed voice. "Make that expression whenever something feels or tastes really good." He glanced around wondering just where the damn cameras were and placed the spoon strategically over his mouth on the off chance Felix could read lips. "Like you're enjoying a hell of an orgasm." He laughed at her shocked expression. "It's scandalous."

"I do not."

"Oh, yes you do. That expression of yours haunts my dreams." He paused when that reminded him of something. "Speaking of." He used the spoon to shield his lips again. "Now that we're safely somewhere where I have no choice but to behave, you wanna tell me about those dreams you've been having?"

Gio decided earlier that maybe he did want to know exactly what she was dreaming of. It's what he planned on asking tonight before the newscast of Trinidad's baby interrupted his thoughts. He didn't think he'd get any sleep from wondering if he didn't ask.

Bianca blushed just slightly and he wondered if that meant the dreams weren't too explicit. But as usual she surprised him yet again. "They've all been different but you remember what Evelyn said she wanted you to do to her?" He nodded slowly, their eyes now locked like they'd been doing so much of lately. "I couldn't stop thinking about it and I finally dreamed you did that to me."

Gio swallowed hard, turning his body to face the counter to hide the evidence of his rapidly growing affection for Bianca from any cameras. "And you woke up content?"

"Very." The sexy siren was back and he nearly gasped at the wicked smile. "I do every time."

"I see." He nodded, trying to appear as unfazed about this conversation as she was. How the hell did she do it? Sweet, innocent, little Bianca — but from what he was hearing and seeing and from what he'd witnessed all day maybe she wasn't as innocent as he made her out to be. Could this girl get any hotter? "What else have I done to you in your dreams?"

She licked her lips causing Gio to straighten up with a jerk. "Don't do that," he blurted out.

"Oh." She touched her lips with her fingers. "Right, I'm sorry."

Bambi replaced the siren in an instant and Gio had to laugh. "It's okay. Just don't do it again. What else?"

"Are you sure you don't wanna talk about..." She gestured toward his bedroom. "You know, what you were watching?"

Gio lifted his eyebrows amazed that just being in the same room with her watching her so closely, listening to her talk about the fantasies about him could put him on such a cloud that even the reminder of Trinidad had no effect on it. "Seriously?" He took a few steps closer to her. "You're asking me if I'd rather talk about Trinidad than hear about the wet dreams you've been having of me?"

They were locked in one of their moments again. The corners of her lips began to slowly curve upward. Sexy siren was back and nothing excited Gio more.

Music once again interrupted their moment. Only this time it didn't come in the form of a mariachi band outside. It was coming from her robe pocket, reminding Gio she wore nothing but her bathing suit underneath. He could've been sitting in the hot tub with her right now having wine instead of standing in the kitchen eating ice cream like the wuss that he was.

Bianca pulled the phone out of her pocket and now Gio could make out a song he'd heard somewhere before. She held up the phone showing a picture of her grandmother on the screen, as the lyrics to the song became clearer.

I hope you still feel small when you stand beside the ocean.

"That's Nana's song to me." She smiled, then pouted. "I need to get this and I'll probably be a while. I haven't talked to her or my mom in over a day. That's unheard of." She opened her eyes wide playfully. "I'll have to catch them up. Plus I still have that seminar I absolutely need to watch."

"That's okay," he said hiding the disappointment. "We have tomorrow."

Bianca answered but asked her grandmother to give her a second then held the phone to her chest and whispered, "I already miss you."

God, what he'd give to be able to kiss her that very moment. "I miss you, too," he whispered back and those incredible eyes of her brightened. She waved her pretty fingers at him before walking away and mouthing the word, *goodnight*.

Gio took a very big deep breath before setting his bowl of half-eaten ice cream in the sink. Tomorrow couldn't come fast enough.

*

They lay in a meadow. It looked very different than the one Bianca had taken him to because there was no snow, only grass and flowers in every color. Gio was certain it was still the same one. He lay there next to her, his weight on his elbow while his other hand stroked her hair as he stared into her eyes. "I wanna kiss you," he whispered.

Bianca smiled, making the day suddenly brighter, the intoxicating scent of the flowers that much stronger. "I want you to."

Gio leaned in with anxious anticipation of tasting her mouth and kissed her — for a very long time. He didn't need to breathe. He didn't need anything anymore. This was all he needed — forever. To be lost in Bianca's world, in her mouth, her kisses. He'd never felt happier in his life. Finally, he pulled his lips away from her and instantly he was lost in her eyes. She smiled again. A smile so blissful — so content. "I love you, Bianca."

"I love you, too," she whispered back.

The strong smell of coffee suddenly trounced the smell of the flowers.

Gio opened his eyes for a moment annoyed that he'd been awakened from such a perfect dream. In the next second, he was smiling. The smell of coffee in his nose and the noise coming from the kitchen meant only one thing. It was morning and in a few hours, he'd be holding and kissing Bianca again.

Springing from the bed, he'd never felt this eager to jump in the shower in his life. He took what was probably the fastest shower in the history of the world and even did a little dancing as he dried off and got dressed. It couldn't have been more than fifteen minutes between the time he got out of bed to the time he took one last look in the mirror before heading to the kitchen.

It was worse than the screeching sound of nails scraping across a chalkboard. Because it wasn't a sound. It's what Gio's insides felt like when he came around the corner. Bianca's eyes met his before Felix's. Her eyes said it all. She hadn't been expecting this either. Gio's eyes were immediately on Felix's hands. One was holding hers, the other caressed her belly as he leaned in to kiss her.

"Gio," Bianca said before Felix's lips touched hers.

Felix turned, realizing they weren't alone in the dining room and smirked. "Hey, dude. I'm back."

"Yeah, I can see that."

The disappointment Gio felt knowing he wouldn't get to spend the day with Bianca after all, didn't even come close to what he was feeling that very moment as he watched Felix pull Bianca in front of him wrapping his arms around her waist. He kissed Bianca's temple and she stared at Gio, her usual beautifully intense eyes now as lifeless as he felt. "You ready to train? I lost enough time already. So when they canceled this morning's gig I shot straight up here."

Gio concentrated on Felix's face unable to look at Bianca anymore. "Sounds good." He spun around grateful about not having to stand there anymore and see Felix wrapped around Bianca for even another second.

"Nah, dude. Have breakfast with us first."

"No." It was abrupt and a bit too loud but Gio didn't care, he kept walking to his room refusing to look back. His heart pounded erratically now. He turned his torso halfway back, lifting his hand but made sure he didn't actually look at them. "That's cool. If I'm gonna train I'll just grab some orange juice. Maybe a protein shake. I forgot I gotta make a phone call, too. You two have breakfast. I'll meet you in the gym."

Without waiting for a response from Felix, Gio rushed into his room and closed the door behind him. With his heart at his throat, he paced the room back and forth breathing harshly. "I can't do this shit," he muttered under his breath. "I can't."

Feeling like a madman, he stalked into the bathroom and stared at his red-rimmed eyes in the mirror. "Either you man the fuck up and do this or get the hell out now and never see her again."

Before seeing her with Felix again today he'd thought the latter would be worse but after what he'd just experienced he didn't think anything could feel worse than that.

It was time to call Noah. Gio needed to be talked down before he slammed his fist through the mirror.

Noah would be pissed. Gio knew he would. Last time he'd checked the number one unspoken rule between them all was you didn't sleep with any of your friends exes. This wasn't even Felix's ex. This was his girl. But Gio hadn't slept with her—yet. He knew now with every fiber of his being that if he ever got the chance to he would in a heartbeat.

But what he'd thought yesterday when he rationalized that he shouldn't still stood. If he ever did, that could really be trouble because if he felt like a madman now, and all he'd done was kiss her, he couldn't even imagine what his reaction to seeing her with Felix after he'd made her his would be. Because, damn it, if he ever did sleep with her she'd be his. As perverse as that sounded—there'd be no rationalizing with his heart at that point.

It occurred to him he should maybe go outside to make the call. He didn't want Felix accidentally overhearing him. But the risk of running into them again and in a compromising position was one he was *not* willing to take. So he locked the bedroom door then went into the bathroom and locked that one, too.

He ran his fingers through his hair after hitting speed dial, still trying to calm himself. It rang several times before Noah picked it up sounding a little breathless. "I'm in the middle of something. Can this shit wait?"

"No." Gio and his friends rarely called each other. He knew Noah had to be wondering about his early morning call.

He heard Noah curse and the phone muffle while he said something then he heard Roni and Gio knew what he'd interrupted. "This better be important," Noah barked and if Gio wasn't still reeling from seeing

Bianca with Felix he might've laughed.

"It is."

Gio heard doors open and close and he knew Noah was walking through his house. "So what is it?"

Leaning back against the wall Gio slid down until he was sitting on the cold floor. He rested his elbow on his knee and leaned his forehead against his fist. "You know that text you sent me that night after we had dinner at your house?"

"Yeah?"

"It's true. What Roni and Nellie were talking a-bout—it wasn't then, but it is now."

Noah was quiet for a moment then, "Are you kidding me, G?"

"Noah, I tried to fight it. I swear to you but he left yesterday and it'd just been building for some time now and—"

"You slept with her?"

"No!"

"Then what? Wait. I need coffee for this shit."

Gio waited for what seemed like forever, then finally Noah spoke again. "All right, what happened?"

Gio gave him a quick run down of how things just started building, how incredibly sweet she was, her amazing eyes and what they did to him. He mentioned her licking her lips, and then yesterday. Without giving him too much detail Gio told him about how they'd made out the whole day, but made sure to add, "But it's not just a physical thing. I would've never gone for it if that's all it was. You know me, man. I wouldn't do something like that to Felix. She's just different, Noah. I've never felt anything like this for any girl. The only connection I've ever had with a chick where I can actually talk so openly like this is maybe Roni but that's different. With Bianca—"

"Whoa, whoa, whoa. Back the fuck up. Roni?"

"No. Not like that."

"You just said it! A connection with Roni? Are you shitting me?"

"About watching our parents die from cancer. It was the only thing I could think of that even came close. Roni's the only one who's ever really gotten it when I told her about my dad dying." Gio shook his head. "Okay, bad example. Maybe I shouldn't have used Roni. That's totally different."

"Yeah, thank you. Can we not bring her into this conversation about you being tempted by your *friend's girl*?"

Gio rolled his eyes. "Not tempted. It's more than that. I wouldn't be calling you if it was just a temptation. I have feelings for her now and I didn't even realize how bad I had it until I saw them together this morning." He banged his head against the wall just thinking about it. "I don't know what I'm gonna do. I feel like I need to get the hell out of here. But I can't. I can't just walk away now but seeing them together..." He banged his head again. "It's gonna drive me crazy. I almost lost it today."

"Well, don't do that."

Gio shook his head. "This is impossible. Even if they did break up, it still wouldn't be cool."

"Look," Gio heard Noah take a deep breath. "I'm gonna tell you what the girls' theory was that night after you guys left. There are a few things you should consider before getting too caught up with her. First of all, what does she have to say about all this crap they're saying about him and that other chick in Chicago?"

Gio pinched the bridge of his nose. "Nothing. She's never talked about it and I've never brought it up. I don't even know if she knows."

"She's gotta know," Noah said quickly. "It's funny that this chick who seems to be talking so openly and freely with you wouldn't mention something this big to you. They've been talking about it all over. The girls had a theory."

Gio didn't say anything but he didn't like Noah's tone when talking about "this chick" so he waited.

"First thing, I will say they thought the attraction between you two went both ways. According to them, she seemed to have just as hard a time keeping her eyes off you as you did her."

Gio waited for the big "But" he could feel coming.

"But they also wondered if she could possibly be doing this to get back at Felix for what he might be doing to her. Maybe she's using you—"

"No." Gio sprang to his feet. "She wouldn't do that."

"What else could it be, G? You really think she thinks this is gonna have a happy ending? Think about it." He paused to take what sounded like a drink of his coffee.

Gio took the moment to pace in the spacious bathroom. Noah was starting to irritate him. Bianca was just as surprised by yesterday's turn of events as he was. She'd planned this about as much as he had.

"If what the girls were saying is true," Noah continued, "she's the only one in this equation getting exactly what she wants—the famous rich boyfriend and his hot friend on the side."

"Nope," Gio said, stopping in front of the mirror as his insides began to ignite all over again. "This wasn't planned."

"It's just something to consider."

"Not considering it. Because it's not true." His irritation with Noah had just reached another level. "So Roni thinks I'm hot, huh?"

"All right!" Noah snapped. "Don't be an idiot. I'm not *trying* to piss you off. But you gotta admit it's a possibility."

"That's not Bianca, okay? If you knew her like I do now, you'd know why that's not even a *possibility*. I've been with girls like that and Bianca isn't one of them. So let's just throw this little fucking theory of yours out the window, okay?"

Gio heard Noah let out a low whistle. "I guess you have fallen hard."

He ran his hand through his hair completely frustrated. "Yeah, and you of all people know what that feels like, so help me out here. What do I do?"

Noah exhaled. "Damn it. I had a bad feeling the moment you first told me she was even up there. Whatever happens this isn't gonna end well. You know that right?" Gio nodded as if Noah could see him. "Have you talked to Felix?"

"About this?" Gio stared at his own stunned expression in the mirror.

"No. Remember we talked about maybe you telling him not to be such a heartless ass. He may not even be that into her. Maybe he is seeing that other chick in Chicago. Find out. It might not be such a big deal if you wait for him to dump Bianca and then go after her."

That had been Gio's only thread of hope since the beginning. But after getting to know Bianca even better, the idea that Felix wouldn't really be into her seemed even more impossible now.

After talking to Noah for a little longer and not getting much more help, the only conclusion he'd come to was he needed to talk to Felix and find out exactly where things stood. How concrete was the relationship between him and Bianca? And what chance, if any, did Gio have of walking away from this with his heart still intact?

CHAPTER 18

It kept happening. As much as Bianca tried to act normally, she couldn't help but tense up every time Felix snuggled up to her. It was just a matter of time before he noticed there was something very wrong. He'd already noticed it earlier when he kissed her neck on their way into the bedroom and she all but moved away. When he asked what was wrong she played it off but she saw it in his confused expression, though he let it go.

After a day away she'd normally be all for a quickie before she had to leave to go work but today she'd told him she was in a hurry even though she didn't actually have to be at her grandmother's shop for another hour.

What had she been thinking? That it would all go back to normal? That being with him again after yesterday would feel the same? Nothing felt the same now. This was all wrong but Bianca didn't know how to fix it without calling the whole thing off and walking out of not only Felix's life but Gio's as well. That was a sacrifice she just wasn't willing to make — didn't think she could.

Bianca was just finishing putting on her shoes when Felix walked out of the bathroom wearing only his training shorts. Before she could finish he was by her side on the bed caressing her face. "You have no idea how much I missed you," he said before kissing her lips softly. She immediately tensed up and he stopped and pulled away looking at her very seriously. "Okay, we need to talk. I know why you're acting like this. My gig wasn't canceled, Bianca. I canceled it so I could get back here as soon as possible."

Bianca stared at him, her heart speeding up a little. He couldn't possibly know.

"There's something I need to tell you. I was gonna wait until tonight but I gotta get if off my chest now." His nervous eyes went from hers to the ceiling and all around the room until they came back to her, unnerving her even further. "I did go out with Shelley even after I started seeing you." Bianca pulled back and he tried to take her hand but she pulled it away. "It was way back in the beginning," he said urgently. "Back before I knew how serious things were gonna get between me and you."

Bianca thought back to his words 'way back in the beginning.' Back when *he* made *her* promise she'd wait for him.

"Before you knew? You mean when you told me you were going to be dating me exclusively and so I should promise to do the same?" She stood up from the bed and he stood with her.

It amazed her how if they would've been having his discussion just days ago, she might've cared more. As angry as she was that he'd lied to her all this time — assured her she had nothing to worry about and that all those stories were just to sell magazines and boost TV ratings — the hypocrisy she felt was just too blatant. Though the anger helped blanket her guilty conscience.

"Listen to me, please." He reached out for her and she pulled back, glad she had good reason to reject his touch now. "This was in the very beginning, Bianca. I saw her just a few times. It was so insignificant I wouldn't even be telling you about it now but the damn tabloids are blowing all this up. I didn't want you to find out that way."

"So that's the only reason you're telling me now? Because you knew I'd find out?"

"Yes and no. I'll admit it I was a selfish prick, okay? I had a different girl in every city. But that was then. That was before you. You changed everything. I'm begging you—"

"Don't!" Bianca wouldn't be able to stand there and listen to him beg for her forgiveness knowing she was just as guilty if not worse.

"I will, Bianca." He started to get down on his knee.

"Stop that." She reached out for his hand. "You don't have to."

Taking advantage of her outstretched hand, he took it and pulled her to him and spoke so close she thought he might kiss her. "Please forgive me. I'll do anything to make it up to you. I'll prove I've changed—changed because of you. You mean everything to me now. I even told Andy to cancel half the shit he had planned for me in the coming weeks so I could spend less time away from you."

Bianca couldn't take it anymore. She was drowning in guilt now. Guilt because here Felix was saying everything she would've been thrilled to hear just a few weeks ago, because his surprise arrival this morning should've been as exciting as the night he showed up with the mariachis. Instead all she felt now was disappointment. Disappointment that now she'd have less time with Gio.

She pulled away. "I need to think."

"Think all you want. But please don't leave."

Leaving was the last thing she wanted to do. She could hardly stand knowing that Gio was just a few rooms away and she couldn't run to him like she wanted to. But to be away from him for good with no chance of even seeing him, that thought alone nearly suffocated her.

How had this happened so fast? She still cared about Felix but what she felt for Gio was a whole other monster. She'd never felt anything like it and right now all she wanted to do was get out of there. Run away and try to regain some composure. Her mind was spinning and she could barely think straight anymore. "I gotta go to work."

"But you're coming back, right?" He squeezed her hand, his pleading eyes burning into her.

She nodded and he began to hug her but she pushed him away. "Don't," she whispered and he lifted his arms away immediately.

"Okay. Just come back… please."

She grabbed her purse from the nightstand and started to the door. "Bianca."

Bianca slowed as she reached the doorway then stopped and turned around. "What?"

"I love you."

After spending a day like yesterday with Gio and feeling something so much more powerful than she'd ever felt for Felix, Bianca couldn't return the sentiment. She vanquished the idea that what she felt for Gio was love only because it was clear that she'd already been too hasty in her declaration of love to Felix. Something she was now certain was untrue. Deep down she'd always known what she felt for Felix wasn't that profound feeling she'd read and heard so much about.

She obviously didn't know much about love. What she did know, without a doubt, was this thing she felt now for Gio was something so incredibly strong that even as wrong as it was, she knew with all certainty that the moment she got the chance she'd be back in his arms.

A strained smile was all that she managed. That and a nod as she turned and walked away.

There was no way she could face Nana and her mother right now. They'd know immediately something was wrong and as close as she was to them she couldn't tell them about this. Both of them had always been very liberal when it came to Bianca's personal life. They trusted her and the choices she made.

The only times they ever had serious issues with was anything that compromised her safety. This situation now had dangerous written all over it, but Bianca felt helpless to pull herself out of it. She couldn't stay away now.

With just under forty-five minutes to spare before she had to be at the shop, the obvious direction to head was to Toni's place, to tell her about the mess she was in now. But she had a feeling even Toni would attempt to talk her out of going back and that's the last thing she wanted to hear. No amount of reasoning was keeping her from going back.

The fact that this was so unlike her was what scared her the most. Growing up Bianca had always been the voice of reason in her crowd — the good girl. She never took risks or did anything that would disappoint her mother even before her father died but more so after.

When her father was killed her mother made a huge sacrifice to keep them in the same house by taking on an extra housekeeper job during the week and another one on the weekends. This after her grandparents had offered to let them move in with them in their more than ample Big Bear home. Bianca knew it was tough on her mom but her mother said she wouldn't traumatize Bianca further by uprooting her from the only home she'd ever known and from all her friends.

To show her mother her gratitude Bianca never even dreamed of doing anything bad. She never ditched, snuck out or even drank before she was of legal age. What Bianca was doing now felt so wrong—so bad. Something she knew her mother wouldn't approve of but even that couldn't stop her now.

With nowhere else to go, Bianca parked in front of a coffee shop, and got out. That morning when Felix walked in so unexpectedly just as she was pouring her coffee she'd been so crushed about her day's plans with Gio being ruined she'd all but lost her appetite and barely got in a few sips. She needed the caffeine now. It would help her think.

Taking a seat in one of the booths after getting her coffee she took a long swig and closed her eyes. Then it came to her. Here she thought she'd have to wait until she had a moment alone with Gio to find out what, if anything, more was going to happen between them. She'd forgotten all about the fact that they'd exchanged numbers that first day on the slopes.

Feeling the butterflies in her stomach going wild, she pulled her phone out of her purse and searched her contact list for Gio. Always the fast thinker she edited it to read the first name that came to mind—Lala—the name of the coffee shop. She always locked her phone anyway but had been known to forget on occasion and she wasn't chancing Felix accidentally coming across any texts between her and Gio.

After changing the name on the contact she stared at her screen not sure what to text him. Three words came to mind over and over. The same words she'd said to him last night. So she typed them in.

I miss you.

Her heart fluttered as she hit send. And then she waited, her stomach churning. She'd seen the look on his face that morning. Saw how after the initial shock of walking in on her and Felix just as he was about to kiss her, his eyes traveled immediately to Felix's hands caressing her. She wondered now if perhaps he was upset with her but how could he be? He knew what he was getting himself into when he first kissed her. Knew just like she did how impossible this situation was.

Despite the impossibility of it all and knowing the huge risk she was taking just sending the text, here she sat eagerly awaiting his response. This was crazy. She felt like she was back in middle school waiting for the boy she was crushing on to pass the note back in class. But this was *so* much more than a crush.

The phone beeped and a tiny squeal escaped her. She covered her mouth glancing quickly around the small coffee shop feeling silly. No one seemed to have noticed her ridiculous little outburst. Fumbling with her phone nervously she hit the envelope from "Lala."

I miss you too.

Her heart nearly doubled over as she brought her hand over her mouth again. How was it possible she could get so excited about something like this? Toni was right. As excited as Bianca had been in the past about anything with Felix she'd never felt anything quite like this. She was still thinking of how to respond without sounding too needy when a second text came through.

SO much.

If Bianca was excited before she was bursting now. She didn't care how needy she sounded she was telling him exactly what she was thinking. Her fingers couldn't type the words fast enough.

I can't wait to be alone with you again. I can't! This is insane. It's all I'm going to think about from now until then.

She held her phone after sending her message, staring at it obsessively, willing it to beep. After an excruciating few minutes, he responded and she read it anxiously.

You and me both. We'll think of something. We have to. Insane? Don't get me started. You have no idea! But I gotta go for now. We're about to go for a run. I'll text you later. MISS YOU! G.

Her only response to that was a very excited set of x's and o's. She stood up, her lips outstretched to capacity. Now she could start her day and just like she'd felt that morning when she woke, the butterflies swarmed around her belly in anticipation of when she'd see him again. She wasn't exaggerating when she said it to him. This was pure insanity. Insanity that now seemed to fuel her heart and run through her veins but the craziest thing about it was that she welcomed it.

*

Gio's magic pill had come through again. Just reading those three little words had been enough to calm him from the torment he'd been feeling ever since he'd seen Bianca with Felix earlier. Then reading her follow up text confirming that she was feeling just as anxious as he was about being forced to be apart was enough to convince him that staying here was the right thing to do. Even a moment alone with her would make it all worth while. Though he still worried about how he

would handle seeing them have their moments together. He didn't even want to think about that right
now. For now, he'd concentrate on the positive news
that she was feeling just as tortured by all of this as he
was. That had to be good thing somehow.

Since Gio started training with Felix, between the
other trainers and Bianca always being around, he
hadn't had a moment alone with him. Because Felix
showed up unexpectedly early Gio finally had time
alone with him. The other trainers wouldn't be back
until later that afternoon.

From the moment Felix had met him at the gym,
Gio had picked up a strange vibe from him. He wondered if by any chance Felix had noticed anything between him and Bianca. But he couldn't have. Gio had
been in the same room with them for just seconds before he'd bolted out of there. The real test would be
later tonight and every evening from here on that Gio
would have to spend time around them.

After his taste of what that might be like Gio wasn't
beyond feigning sudden illness to leave the room
abruptly if he had to. Judging by his reaction this
morning it wouldn't be hard to fake feeling sick to his
stomach.

They wrapped up their run and were enjoying a
water break in the gym. Felix sat on the edge of the
boxing ring and Gio sat across from him on a bench.
After downing his water, Gio decided to just go for it.
"I saw you on TV the other night. So what's up with
you and that chick they keep talking about? Any truth
to that?"

Unlike most of the times when Gio or any of the
guys inquired about gossip they'd heard on TV about
Felix he didn't smirk and give his generic response of

"You know me."

Slam dunking his crushed water bottle into a box next to the ring Felix frowned shaking his head. "Not anymore. But now that the word is out about Bianca the media is having a fucking field day with old photos trying to generate a story when there isn't one. I hate having to explain this shit to her over and over."

Gio thought about the photos of him and the girl the day he got stranded in Chicago. "So all that is old stuff? What about the stuff in Chicago the day you got stuck out there?"

"That's the only recent one. And that was just dinner and a few drinks. Sort of a farewell thing." Felix stood up and shook his arms in the air loosening them up. "I explained to Bianca about that. It's all this other shit they're bringing up that sucks. What girl wants to hear about her boyfriend's exes right? I sure as hell don't wanna hear about hers."

Or about who she's currently messing around with on the side. Lost in thought Gio pondered what Noah had said. She was the only one in the equation getting everything she wanted. He was the guy on the side. This wouldn't be his first time but in the past he actually liked it that way—no need to even talk about committing—he was just the guy on the side having his fun and then waving goodbye. No hard feelings. Only now, he didn't want to be that guy. He didn't even want to be the main guy. He wanted to be the *only* guy.

"Hey, Bravo!"

Gio looked up a little startled by Felix's sudden raised voice. "Huh?"

Felix laughed. "Did you even hear what I said?"

Gio peered at him feeling stupid and smiled. "Sorry, my mind was…" he shook his head. "I don't know.

I didn't hear you."

"Yeah, no shit. I asked what you thought of Bianca's meadow?"

Gio had no idea how they'd gone from talking about Bianca's exes to the meadow but the thought of the meadow, especially the one this morning in his sleep made him smile. "It was cool. I liked it." Understatement of the decade.

"Really?"

Gio stood up when he saw Felix walk over to the cabinet and pull out the hand wrap. His mind was still enjoying the memory of his dream as he walked toward Felix ready to help him wrap his hands. Felix turned around to face him making a face. "I thought it was kind of boring. I guess I'm not the hiking type." A smirk replaced the face he was making and he chuckled. "Although rolling around in the grass, having my way with my girl was fun."

Gio was sure even Felix heard it—the visual of his dream shattering violently like a glass frame into a million pieces. He couldn't even respond to that. Not even with a chuckle like he normally would've. "Give me that," he said holding out his hand and Felix handed him the wrap.

If Felix noticed the hasty change of subject when Gio started talking about sparring techniques, he didn't say anything. This would've been the best chance to find out what Felix's thoughts were on his and Bianca's relationship—how serious he was about her. But Gio decided he'd rather not know. This was worse than he thought. Gio's heart had already begun to claim Bianca as his. He wouldn't even be able to stomach hearing Felix speak in terms of *his* girl. It was happening already and he hadn't even slept with her.

CHAPTER 19

The three days following Felix's early return Bianca managed to keep him at arm's length. She spent the days working and at school. Then in the evenings, Felix was understanding of the fact that she was still hurt about his betrayal to even cuddle much less do anything else. The guilt would start to become too much to bear. Then she and Gio would have one of their silent moments where she was caught in his eyes again or he'd send her a text that would have her walking on air and she'd be back to square one feeling ready to do or say whatever it took just to be near him.

Felix was doing everything he could to try and remedy things. Now that Bianca didn't really care and since he supposedly confessed to the real truth behind the stories, she'd begun to watch more of the tabloid shows. It helped ease her guilt. At the same time whenever she came across any of the stories while he was in the room with her, it helped support why she wouldn't be engaging in any intimate activity with him any time soon. She just couldn't—not anymore. She had to take full advantage of the tabloid stories now.

Tonight they were all going to Winterfest, a rail jam event in town. The festival was part of the ongoing events surrounding the Snowboarding championships. It was a nice break from the last two awkward nights and she was looking forward to the possibility of getting a moment alone with Gio. So far, since Felix had gotten back they'd had a few but in the cabin it was impossible to do much more than exchange knowing and longing gazes.

They reached the downtown area of Big Bear where the event was taking place. They hadn't been there very long when Felix was recognized and the fans requesting pictures with him started up. Felix's bodyguards allowed a few and then they started again through the crowd. Though they tried to remain inconspicuous it was impossible to do so with two burly bodyguards in front of them and two behind them. The one time she wished his busybody publicist Andy were here to distract Felix and pull him away like he usually did at public events, he wasn't here.

Gio had been quiet ever since they'd gotten out of the car and for the first time in days she'd allowed Felix to hold her hand. It was out of habit. They were walking through a crowd and it was more of a protective measure on his part so as not to get separated in the crowd.

Now that they'd stopped and a breeze blew, making Bianca cringe, he wrapped his arms around her from behind in an effort to warm her. Bianca knew holding his hand was probably what Felix was waiting for to work his way back to the way things were before and she now regretted it. She'd hoped to hold onto the no touching rule for a while longer. If she did anything with Felix the guilt would eat her alive because these last few days Gio's texts had become more and more heartfelt. He was feeling exactly what she was and if she had to see him with someone else, it'd be worse than anything she ever felt when hearing about Felix with other girls.

As if on cue, Felix reached over and tapped Gio on the shoulder. He'd turned his back on them the moment Felix had wrapped his arms around Bianca. "Check out who's here."

Bianca turned at the same time as Gio in the direction where Felix was pointing. Over by the beer booth, Evelyn stood posing with two guys holding beer cups. She wore a white ski suit that appeared to be painted on, with the word Budweiser written down the front of it. The matching white high-heeled boots that went up to her thighs, were in no way made for the snow. Her long dark hair looked perfect even in this God forsaken weather. Even with all the men standing around waiting for their chance to be photographed with her, Bianca knew the moment she saw Gio he'd have her full attention.

"You should go ask her what time she's off," Felix said. "Maybe she could join us after for drinks somewhere or come back to the cabin for some and hang out."

Bianca had to bite her tongue to keep the word *NO!* from flying out. She stared at Evelyn for a moment then turned back to Gio who smirked then shrugged. "Maybe later. She looks busy right now."

Normally her ears, like the rest of her extremities in this weather were freezing cold but right now, they were on fire. If Evelyn rode back with them or worse, Gio left with her in her own car, Bianca didn't know how she would deal with it.

Feeling her throat already swelling she suddenly knew what Gio must be feeling watching her with Felix and she pulled out of Felix's embrace. She knew it was abrupt and she'd surprised him but she didn't care. "I need to find a ladies' room."

The startled look on Felix's face eased up a bit. "Oh." He looked around.

"I know where they are," she added quickly. "Just wait here. I'll be right back."

"Is the men's' room near there, too?" Gio asked and their eyes instantly locked.

"Yeah, I might as well go too." Felix said, squashing any hope of sneaking a moment alone with Gio. "I had a couple of beers before we left and it's just a matter of time before the urge to go kicks in."

They all walked slowly through the crowd of bundled up spectators. Bianca knew of closer restrooms in the vicinity where they'd been standing but it meant walking past Evelyn's Budweiser stand so she led them to the ones in the opposite direction. The image of Gio and Evelyn making out on the dance floor flashed through her mind. Bianca dropped Felix's hand. She'd make every effort tonight and from here on to not give Gio any reason to even consider bringing Evelyn back to the cabin. That would be the only thing that would have Bianca running far from that cabin for good.

Felix was stopped by some fans asking to take a photo with him and Bianca gestured to him that the restrooms were just a few feet away and kept walking. The mere thought of Gio bringing a girl back to the cabin had her in near tears. Feeling like a complete hypocrite, she wiped at the corners of her eyes as she entered the restroom before she could shed even one stupid tear.

Because the restrooms were further from the main crowd they were less crowded like she knew they'd be. She was in and out quickly.

Feeling a bit more composed, she glanced around for Felix and was completely startled when someone suddenly pulled her hand. She turned to see Gio and followed him quickly behind the small building that housed the restrooms. Once behind it Gio backed her up into the wall and kissed her frantically.

Breathlessly and oh-so-happy, Bianca kissed him back just as madly, savoring the familiar taste of his mouth. Her heart pounded now as both the excitement and the reality of the enormous risk this was set in. Even as desperately as he kissed her, the boy obviously knew what he was doing because his kisses were anything but sloppy. They were just as perfect as she remembered; his tongue maneuvered magically in perfect rhythm with hers.

She pulled away just long enough to say what she had to. "Don't bring Evelyn back to the cabin."

"I won't," he said simply and continued to kiss her.

"I haven't been sleeping with him," she said against his lips. "I'm not going to anymore."

Gio stopped and stared at her breathing hard. "You're not?"

"No. I promise. But promise me you won't see Evelyn anymore."

The response to that was a longer, even more vehement kiss. Then he stopped and looked at her. "I've no interest in Evelyn — none."

Taking a step away from her, he glanced around. "We gotta go. Felix was just caught up for a few minutes with one of the skaters. Go this way." He pointed to the quickest route back to where Felix was, then pointed in the opposite direction. "I'll go that way." He started to walk away then rushed back and took her face in his hands kissing her deeply one last time before letting go and sped around the small building.

Bianca walked around her side cautiously, her mind still swimming in a blissful daze as her heart continued to attack her rib cage with each wallop. Her phone buzzed in her pocket and she was certain it was Felix looking for her but it was a text—from *Lala*. With her body still reveling the euphoria of having finally quenched her aching need to be near Gio again—feel his touch—kiss his lips, she stared at the screen elated. Just seeing the envelope with the code-name for him now like she had so much in the past few days made her want to do a little dance but she refrained and clicked on the envelope instead.

God I missed your lips.

She smiled, inhaling deeply as she touched her fingers to her lips, still warm from his kisses. "Wow. Now there's a smile I haven't seen in a while. Where's that coming from?"

The phone nearly slipped out of her hands at the sound of Felix's voice. He stared down at her phone, his eyes full of curiosity—or suspicion.

"I, uh." Unable to put even one coherent sentence together, Bianca slipped her phone in her pocket. She cleared her throat. "Toni... she..." Bianca glanced up at Felix but unable to look him in the eye too long she glanced away quickly. "She was just being silly."

Beginning to walk and pulling a strand of hair behind her ear, she snuck a peek in Felix's direction. His brows had pulled together. "Yeah? What's she up to?"

"She's seeing some new guy." Gio was up ahead waiting for them and smiled when his eyes met hers, making her already wild insides go even wilder. As anxious as the feel of this conversation was making her, she couldn't help smiling back. "Some indie film maker from Los Angeles."

Felix nodded, looking up at Gio who stood waiting for them a few feet ahead. "I meant to tell you earlier this week but things have been kind of weird. I'm having the guys up from 5th Street for the weekend. We'll probably all go out. Maybe you can invite Toni since it'll be a group thing."

Bianca turned to him. The pulled together brows and any sign of suspicion were now gone. "I'll ask her." She smiled softly, and nodded. "That would probably be fun."

Of course, that meant letting Toni in on her situation which she now absolutely had to tell her anyway. There was only so much longer they could keep this up without something going horribly wrong and Bianca would have to make a decision soon. Toni would no doubt be helpful in that decision making. Although the idea of walking away from Gio was one that became harder to even consider with each passing day.

There were no further moments the rest of the evening and for the next few days Bianca spent her days dodging Felix's advances and melting over Gio's texts.

Determined to not only keep her promise to Gio about not sleeping with Felix but to keep the touching to a minimum, Bianca upped the hurt act every time a new story about Felix and his other women was aired. It helped that the media was relentless and she was more than thankful that her feelings for Gio were so overwhelming they'd completely purged any feelings she'd previously had for Felix. Otherwise she would've been going crazy with all the stories. Her grandmother had asked her several times already without mentioning the gossip about Felix if she was okay. Bianca reassured her that she was.

Her impetuous feelings for Gio were a bit alarming. Especially given the fact that she still had no idea how this would ever work. She wondered at times if it was their circumstances that created such an urgency to be

with each other. The need was profound—the willing-
ness to take risks becoming greater.

With Felix and Gio's friends coming up early for the
weekend Bianca took the weekend off, including Friday, but left the cabin Friday morning before any of
them got there to get her hair done and have a much
needed talk with Toni. Toni had already agreed to
come with them later that evening when they went
night boarding. With Roni being pregnant Bianca planned on hanging out with her at the resort while the
guys snow boarded so getting her hair done wouldn't
be a waste. Toni had been excited about meeting them
and since Felix's previous visits had been limited up
until now, this was only the second time she'd be
around him. She was still a little star struck.

Knowing Toni's salon got busy Friday mornings Bianca ran a few errands first. Toni was still busy when
she got there but told Bianca the wait wouldn't be long.
Bianca sat down in Toni's tiny little waiting room and
began sifting through all of Toni's tabloids. She stopped when her phone pinged with a text. It was from
Felix. The whole week she'd calculated leaving when
he was already in the gym so there'd be no danger of
him attempting more than the goodbye peck—the only
affection she'd given him since his admission of having
gone out with Shelley. And she made sure that happened only in the privacy of the bedroom. The master
bed in his room was so freakishly big it was easy
enough to steer clear of his side and so far he'd re-
spected the boundaries. When she'd left that morning
she barely stuck her head in the gym to let him know
where she'd be.

*Will you be home before noon? The guys will be here in a
couple of hours and we were thinking of going out for lunch.*

She'd just finished reading his text when she got another one from Gio.

This weekend should be interesting. We might even get some time alone. How long till you get back today? I miss you already.

They'd probably just finished their morning workout and Gio was back in his room. Felix said today's workout would be a short one. As usual, her insides were already mush. And like she always did, she reread the text smiling brightly before responding.

I miss you, too! I shouldn't be too long. Just getting my hair done then I'll head back. I hope you're right about this weekend. This is torture!

She hit send and waited flipping through the magazine again until she heard the ping again. She smiled hitting the envelope again.

I know it is and something's gotta give. SOON. Things can't stay this way much longer. I've been giving it some thought. But I'm not sure if this is what you want. We'll have to talk as soon as we get a chance.

Bianca reread and stopped at the most intriguing part. *If this is what you want?* She hadn't put much thought into what she wanted. All she'd allowed herself to do was to be grateful for what little he could give her under the circumstances. Up until that moment, she didn't think anything more could come of their relationship except a forbidden one even after she and Felix broke things off, which she knew was inevitable and barreling down on her.

Is was only a matter a time before Felix would question the point of having a girlfriend he wasn't allowed to touch. Especially since there were a million girls out there who'd be more than willing to oblige.

"I'll be with you next, Bianca," Toni informed her as

she walked her previous customer to the register.

Bianca clicked back to the main screen of her phone to check the time. It wasn't even ten yet. She had plenty of time. "That's fine," she said, getting back to her text screen and responding to Gio. Afraid to ask and agreeing with his final comment, she'd wait until they could speak in person to find out what he meant by what she wanted. So she kept her response simple but sweet.

I can hardly wait. Xoxo

She stood slipping her phone in the front pocket of her jeans. As she made her way to the salon chair, still thinking about Gio's text, her phone pinged again and she pulled it out. How something so simple could excite her was beyond any reason. She smiled big then quickly frowned when she saw the text was from Felix. Her stomach dropped when she saw she'd sent that last text to him, not to Gio. His response was nothing more than a question mark.

"Oh my God." She brought her hand over her mouth.

"What?" Toni asked as she walked back toward her.

The salon was empty now that her last customer had walked out. Bianca couldn't be happier about that because she had so much to tell her. Things she didn't want others hearing. But right now she had to figure out how to explain this.

She was still standing there her hand over her mouth trying to calm herself. This could've been so much worse. Some of the responses she'd written to Gio's texts this past week would've completely buried her. Especially since she'd been so cold and indifferent toward Felix. Even sending x's and o's to him now might be questionable. And it obviously was, judging by his response. "Shit," she muttered as any suitable response eluded her.

With her mind still racing she gasped when her phone rang. It was Felix. Not only did she have to lie, she wouldn't be able to hide behind a text to do it. *Damn it!*

Toni must've seen the panic in her eyes because Bianca saw the worry in hers when she asked, "What's wrong?"

Bianca lifted a finger to her lips then answered her phone bringing her hand to her forehead. "Felix, Toni was about to wash my hair. Can I call you back?"

He was quiet for a moment then spoke slowly and a bit cautiously. "Bianca, was that last text you sent meant for me?"

She laughed nervously. "No, actually. I meant to send that one to my mom. She's making my favorite *empanadas* this week."

More silence then. "Oh, okay. I thought that was weird. I'm glad it was for your mom and not anyone else." Bianca couldn't be sure but his laugh sounded as forced as the one she responded with. "So, you'll be back in time for lunch?"

"Yeah." Her hand was now firmly over her closed eyes. He suspected something. She could hear it in his voice—his strained laugh. This was bad. How could she be so careless? "I should be out of here in under an hour."

"Okay, I'll see you then."

She was about to say okay and get off the excruciatingly uncomfortable call when he interrupted her. "And hey."

"Yeah?"

"I can hardly wait." His chuckle was more genuine

this time.

As much as she tried, her own laughing response to that wasn't even remotely genuine. "Me either. I'm already hungry."

She knew that's not the response he was going for but she didn't care. She was finally off the call and walked over to the salon chair, plopping her emotionally drained body into it while Toni stood there and stared at her.

"What in the world?"

"God, Toni. Where do I start?"

CHAPTER 20

Jack, Abel and Hector arrived first. Gio and Felix walked out to meet them. Felix had offered to send a car for them but Abel insisted on driving his newly purchased Gran Torino. Gio and Felix laughed when Abel revved the heavy engine as they pulled in.

"Hey," Gio said tapping the hood as he walked around the car. "You should paint it red and white. Then we could call you and Hector Starsky and Hutch."

Abel laughed getting out of the car grabbing Gio's outstretched hand for a quick handshake and a pat on the back. "This shit is badass," Abel said turning back to the car. "I hardly had to do anything to it."

"And it's *fast*," Hector added from across the car.

It hit Gio suddenly. Both Abel and Jack were sticklers about Hector missing school for *any* reason. "You actually let this guy miss school today to come up here?"

Before Abel responded, Hector announced almost proudly. "I got suspended yesterday."

Gio brought his fist to his mouth with a smirk but was surprised neither Abel nor Jack seemed too pissed about this. Usually Abel had a fit if Hector, who lately had been getting into a lot of trouble, even got written up for anything. He turned back to Abel. "And you still brought his ass up here?"

Felix walked over to hug Jack then teased. "Yeah, what's this world coming to? If that had been me back in the days I'd be spending the weekend scrubbing floors at the gym not snowboarding." He pulled back smiling at Jack. "You gettin' soft old man?"

"Nah," Jack waved his hand in the air. "He got in a fight. But he had good reason. I've always told all of you. Fighting is not the answer to everything but sometimes it can't be helped. In this case I probably would have been more pissed if he hadn't fought the asshole."

"I'd say kicked his ass is more accurate," Hector smirked, leaning against the car. "But I guess you could call it a fight."

Gio laughed going from Hector's amused face to Abel who shook his head. "Why? What happened?"

Hector shrugged. "I've been listening to the drama go on all week from this chick whose locker is right next to mine. She wasn't telling me but she and her friends stand there talking so much it's hard not to overhear things. Her ex-boyfriend posted some crap on his Facebook about her. Stupid shit. And," he put his hand up looking at Abel, "I couldn't care less. I don't get involved. But his stupid ass came up to her yesterday and started talking shit to her in front of everyone making her cry. Even then, I kept my cool. Trying to stay out of it. But he took it too far getting in her face like she was a dude, all big man and shit, calling her a skank."

"Oh, hell no," Gio said.

"Yeah," Hector nodded. "So I slammed his face into the lockers."

"Luckily, the narcs stepped in quickly," Abel added. "But he still broke the guy's nose. We're waiting to hear if we're gonna have to pay for any medical bills."

"I hate fucking pussies like that." Felix reached out and shook Hector's hand. "Good for you, man. I would've cracked him too." He turned and pointed at Abel. "Let me know if you need help with that. I'll donate to the cause. We'll call it 'Cracking Down on Future Fucking Douchebag Wife Beaters of the World.' Can't think of a better charity."

Laughing and catching up about everything, they made their way into the cabin after Jack announced he was freezing his ass off. As expected they were all blown away by the cabin and the rest of the compound.

Lunch went well. Noah and Roni arrived an hour after Abel and the others had. Bianca got there right around the same time. With the distraction of everyone there, Gio and Bianca managed to keep their stares and stolen private smiles to a minimum. It helped that Nellie came along with Noah and Roni. Gio knew those two women were on to him and Bianca. He worked extra hard to not be so obvious. He had yet to ask Noah if he'd confirmed to them that they'd been right. But he had a feeling that more than likely Noah had.

They all went back to the cabin after lunch to get geared up for boarding. Since Roni wouldn't be participating, Bianca said she would stay back with Roni and Nellie at the outdoor bar in the resort. Then later Toni would be joining them. They could all watch the guys show off from there and chat while having a few drinks. All except Roni but she didn't seem to mind. She practically glowed any time her pregnancy was brought up.

What he hadn't prepared for is that since Bianca wasn't going snowboarding and they *were* going out to a bar she dressed up for the occasion. It was bad enough that she'd done her hair differently today in a sort of loose wispy braid across the top that pulled the front of hair away from her face bringing even more attention to her big beautiful eyes. The rest of her hair was still down with more tiny little braids here and there accentuating the sexy new style. He'd already been breathless when she first returned from the salon.

Roni was the first to notice what she called an adorable outfit. "That is so cute," she said, bringing everyone's attention to Bianca when she walked in the room.

Her long brown wool coat doubled as a dress because it went snug at her waist then skirted down to just above her knees. The black boots she wore came up to her knees and Gio could only assume she wore a dress or a skirt underneath because save for black leggings her knees were bare.

Gio gulped as Bianca thanked Roni then turned back to him casually. If she was looking for his approval she would've had it if it weren't for the fact that she'd just changed into that *adorable* outfit in the same bedroom with Felix. There's no way Gio could've watched her change into that and not attack her and he doubted that Felix hadn't either. He took a deep breath trying not to think about that. She said she wouldn't be sleeping with him anymore. He'd never wanted to believe something so much in his life.

To make things worse, not only did Felix come up to her from behind and wrap his arms around her, they held hands all the way to the resort. They hadn't done much of either lately. Gio knew because he'd been watching. Just what had happened in that bedroom?

Gio caught the way Noah watched him guardedly. Abel and Hector fumbled around trying to walk on their boards. Felix took extra time helping Jack who had to be practically dragged out there. The moment Noah realized he was alone with Gio he started in on him. "Dude, maybe it's just me because I know, but you're being pretty fucking obvious."

"Am I?" Gio turned, his jaw clenching as he glanced in the direction where the girls sat watching them.

"Yeah, you are. Hell, I thought you were gonna say something when he hugged her back at the cabin."

"It's just 'cause you know. I've been dealing with this shit for weeks now. I doubt anyone else has noticed."

Noah turned back to where Felix still had his hands full with Jack. "Did you forget Roni and Nellie noticed from day one? And I wasn't the only one that caught the way you all but froze today when she walked in from wherever she'd gone." Noah lowered his voice. "You gotta be cool, G. *He's* her boyfriend, not you. Did you ever talk to him about that? Is he real serious about her?"

"Nah, I started to but…" Gio wouldn't get into how he couldn't even stomach hearing him call her *his girl*. "I don't know. Somehow the subject changed to something else. But…" He stopped, wondering now if he should tell Noah. It sounded so absurd now that he was thinking of saying it out loud.

"But what?"

Gio peered at Noah for a second. If he could tell anyone, it was Noah. "She told me she's not sleeping with him anymore." Noah's eyebrows flew up. Gio knew he'd be surprised, if not disbelieving, and he was ready for it. "She promised actually."

"And you're buying this shit?" He turned back to Felix and lowered his voice again. "She's been staying at his cabin for two months. He's her boyfriend. Aren't they sleeping in the same bed?"

Hearing it put this way made Gio sound like an idiot. But Noah couldn't possibly understand what he felt when he was with her. She was the most genuine in-your-face person he'd ever met. He would've never guessed that Bianca had stopped sleeping with Felix but he'd seen the change. Seen how she acted completely different around Felix now. Everything had changed since their day at the meadow—until today. But even today's show of affection had been minuscule compared to the way things were between her and Felix before. He just didn't understand why anything changed today. Had it been his text that morning? Had something changed in that bedroom?

"I'm assuming they do," he said. "I don't go in their room."

Gio glanced back at the girls, suspicion and doubt sinking in fast. He didn't want to be mad at Bianca. He knew how ridiculously unreasonable that was. But she was the one that voluntarily promised not to sleep with her own damn boyfriend. He would've never had the nerve to demand something like that but since she had he was holding her to it. He couldn't help but wonder now if when she'd said it, it was on a whim. That morning she'd responded immediately like she always did to his texts but stopped responding the moment he mentioned things couldn't go on like this much longer. Did she really expect him to continue this shit forever? Maybe Noah's theory was right after all.

"Look at me, G." Gio turned back to Noah then followed Noah's gaze. Jack and Felix were coming toward them but they were moving slow and Jack was really struggling. Still, Noah spoke fast. "Whether she's still sleeping with him or not is beside the point. He brought you here as a favor. You're my friend but what you're doing is a *huge* disrespect to him."

Gio dropped his head back exhaling through his mouth. Noah was right and Gio couldn't argue there, but he was too far gone to try and fight this thing, whatever it was, no matter how wrong he knew it was.

"I know you're not as close to him as you once were. But you're still his friend. Now I don't know what she's thinking," Noah continued adamantly as Jack stopped walking to take a breather. "But she's staying in his cabin—sleeping in his fucking bed. If this is really what she wants, then maybe she should move out. Have you two talked about that at all?"

"I haven't had a chance. We text when we can but since the last time he left I haven't had a moment long enough to talk to her about anything like that." Gio glanced around making sure Abel and Hector weren't within earshot either. "It's not like I've slept with her. I'm telling you it's not even about that. I don't know what it is about her but I can hardly think straight when I'm around her." He stopped, letting out a frustrated sigh. "You know me, man. I'd never do something like this to *any* of you guys."

Noah nodded. "Yeah, I know you wouldn't. That's why I'm still shocked that I'm standing here having this conversation with you in the first place." He turned back to the girls. Roni waved at him, blowing a kiss and he waved back. "And Bianca seems so damn innocent. Even now that she's older—so damn sweet."

"She is!" Gio insisted, leaving out the fact that she could also be sexy as shit when she wanted to be.

"All right, shut up," Noah said suddenly looking over Gio's shoulders and in the next instant, someone slammed into Gio nearly bowling him over.

"What the—" Gio said, barely able to keep his balance but he managing to stay on his feet.

"Sorry man," Hector laughed, holding onto Gio's arm. "I couldn't stop."

Abel came up behind him and laughed too. "I keep telling his ass to slow down."

After falling a few more times Jack said he'd had enough and was heading back to the bar with the girls. They teased him about quitting but weren't able to convince him to hang out longer. Jack headed to the bar and Gio and the rest of the guys headed to the lift.

Having to share a lift with both Noah and Hector Gio was spared any more lectures on the ride up but he did inwardly promise he wouldn't disrespect Felix in his own cabin. It wasn't just because of the cameras either. As much as he knew he simply didn't have it in him to fight his urge to touch — kiss — taste Bianca, he wasn't that big of an asshole. *Some* things were still sacred.

For the next couple of hours Gio focused on enjoying his time with his friends. It felt damn good to revert to the ways of the old days: the days when things were so much simpler. Each time he got caught up laughing and enjoying this day that was all on Felix — he'd paid for the season tickets, the snow gear, even the snowboards. Gio couldn't help feel the chafe of guilt grating away at his conscience.

By the time they hit the bottom of the mountain for the last time, they were all good and ready for drinks. Something Felix no doubt would be paying for all night. Even when Gio had tried to pay the last time they'd come to this very bar the waitresses had apparently been forewarned that they were not allowed to take any money from him and that it would all be put on Mr. Sanchez's tab. Great.

Felix insisted most of the time that Gio and all his

guest's drinks were on the house. The bars enjoyed the extra business just having him there brought in, but Gio couldn't help feeling like a freeloader.

There were so many heaters all around the outdoor bar that it was actually quite warm even outside. So warm Bianca had removed her coat. She wore a body-clinging knit dress, long sleeved and dark brown, like rich chocolate. It was simply cut but for the scooped neckline that nearly froze Gio in place. It wasn't *how* low it dipped. That would have been bad enough. It was the provocative way it laced, beginning mid-chest and ending at the upper curves of her breasts. Bianca had left the corded strings loose, making it even sexier than an open, plunging neckline would have been. Almost as if she'd planned it this way, she'd left little to the imagination.

She'd gone from adorable to crazy hot with the simple removal of her coat. Gripping the bottle of beer he now held, he almost wished she'd put the coat on so he wouldn't have to think about it. If she were Gio's girl he wouldn't mind her dressing this way, even in front of other guys, as long as he was there. He wanted to believe as doubtful as it was that she'd worn the dress to drive him crazy, but the fact remained she'd be going back to Felix's room tonight not Gio's.

They'd been at the bar drinking for a while though Gio had kept a slow steady pace compared to the rest of the guys. He felt even stupider now about telling Noah what she'd promised. Noah had to be thinking the same thing. Maybe something *had* changed today. Maybe his text this morning had snapped her into the realization that this *couldn't* go on anymore. That they had been incredibly delusional to have ever even considered getting into this situation in the first place.

The very idea that she'd changed her mind made him sick but with every shot Felix took, he was getting more and more touchy-feely and she was letting him. The last straw was when she'd walked back from the restroom toward the table with the rest of the girls and Gio's heightened senses followed her. His nose followed the lingering scent of her perfume. He fought the losing battle to keep his eyes off her only to watch Felix pull her to him as she'd nearly made it past him and kiss her, blatantly shoving his tongue in her mouth for an instant. She jerked away, obviously irritated by his drunken kiss, but it was enough to make Gio want to run out of there. "I'll be back," he said exchanging glances with a stern faced Noah. "I gotta make a phone call."

Without even glancing back in Felix and Bianca's direction, he took off to the inside bar area of the resort. He didn't care anymore about staying sober. Needing a shot but not about to stand and watch Felix and Bianca while he took one, maybe more, he headed straight to the bar. And he'd buy it with his own fucking money, too.

Irritated, he pushed the fact aside that even his own money was coming from Felix. Money he'd paid Gio to stick around and fall in love with his girlfriend. Gio nearly stopped walking. He'd known all along that she was different. That he felt things for her he'd never felt in his life. That he'd crossed a line he would've never considered crossing but he had only because it was her. She possessed the power to make him lose the capability to hold on to any reasonable thinking. But had he really fallen in love with her this quickly?

He fisted his hand as he continued to walk through the crowded bar. How the fuck could he be stupid enough to fall in love with someone so completely off-limits?

Just as he reached the bar, he thought he felt his phone go off in his pocket. In no mood to talk or even text anyone he almost didn't pull his phone out. The remote possibility that it might be Bianca made him reach for it. Surprised not only that it was Bianca's name on the screen but that it wasn't a text, she was calling.

He glanced back through the glass doors and saw the guys still drinking by the bar. They all held shots up in the air but Bianca was nowhere to be seen. Feeling a little hesitation, he answered anyway. Who the hell was he kidding? He was suddenly dying to hear her voice. "Hello?"

"Meet me out front in the parking lot," she whispered rapidly.

"What?" he asked, already headed for the front exit. His heart sped up with every long eager stride.

"Just do it," she urged.

"I'm on my way." He nearly broke into a sprint, her voice alone vanquishing all the negative thoughts he'd so recently been thinking.

Yep, there was no question about it. God help him. He was in love.

CHAPTER 21

Pushing through the front door Gio's eyes scanned the huge parking lot. His eyes zeroed in on Bianca waving at him over by a van. Gio skipped down the stairs in the front now in a full sprint to get to her. When he reached her he didn't even ask. They could talk later; the first thing he did was take her in his arms. He kissed her with a hunger he'd only experienced since the first time he tasted her mouth.

He hadn't even given her time to remove the mint and it was now in his mouth as he pulled away grinning and holding it between his front teeth, then pulled it back in his mouth and kissed her again. "I love you," he whispered against her lips, his eyes closed, afraid of what she'd say but more of what she wouldn't.

As usual, she surprised him. She pulled back and he opened his eyes. Her big eyes stared at him very determinedly. "Before I say this, I want you know that even though this may or may not matter to you, it's still important to me that you know. I care about Felix but I've never loved him. I know you heard me say it to him but I know now what it feels like to be utterly and completely in love. What I felt for Felix... feel for Felix doesn't even come close to what I feel for you. I don't know what you've done to me, Giovanni Bravo, but I love you so much it hurts."

He let out a slow breath and felt his heart start up again. "Jesus, Bianca. You scared the shit outta me for a moment there. I wasn't sure where you were going with that."

He slid his tongue in her mouth not caring that they stood in the middle of a parking lot where anyone could see them. None of that mattered anymore. He loved her and she loved him. Nothing would keep him from her now.

From the moment he first kissed her she'd kissed him back just as eagerly as she did now. She pulled away, licking her lips then glanced around before turning back to the van and sliding the door open. "Hurry up. Get in."

"Whose van is this?" Gio glanced around as he climbed into the small cargo van.

The back was completely empty, no seats at all and no cargo of any kind. He glanced back at her as she slid the door closed. Gio about to ask how the hell she scored this when she sat on her knees looking very serious. "It's Toni's boyfriend's," she said, the apprehension in her eyes as if he'd actually disapprove confused him. "Her car broke down," she said as she caressed his face now, staring in his eyes. "I just wanted a moment with you alone. I was desperate Gio. It's what you do to me."

Feeling the enormous relief of once again having confirmation that he wasn't in this alone — he wasn't the only one feeling this maniacal. She was too. He'd never seen anything so clear in another person's eyes.

He kissed her deeply wanting to assure her he understood completely stopping in between kisses only to tell her again how much he loved her. If there was any doubt about it earlier it was completely gone now.

With that certainty another unrelenting urge had begun to surface. The need to claim her — make him his but it couldn't happen here.

He pressed against her as she moaned into his mouth. "I want you like I've never wanted anything in my life," she whispered barely able to catch her breath. The flavor of her mint had been pretty strong but it didn't entirely conceal the taste of wine in her mouth. He had to wonder if this was the alcohol talking.

"I want you, too." She sucked his neck, making him nearly lose it. Breathlessly, he asked the question that begged for an answer *now*. "But here?"

She stopped kissing him, staring at him the emotion in her eyes so real, so indisputable no way could there be any truth to Noah's theory. She was as afraid as he was that this thing between them could never be.

"Do you have protection?" her hushed words fell on him like precious water droplets in the mouth of a man dying of thirst.

"I do, but this is not how I wanted our first time to be. Not in a van. You deserve better, Bianca. You—"

Her fingers touched his lips as her tongue swept over her own lips. "I've never done anything like this. It would be a first for me."

Gio stared at her swallowing hard. The thought of being her first *anything* had him fighting the urge to rip off her dress. Even with everything her eyes were saying to him, that she loved him just as desperately as he loved her and that she wanted her first reckless sexual experience to be with him, something still nagged at him. He had to know. "Just tell me this. Has anything changed? You didn't respond to my last text this morning."

She brought her hands to her mouth her eyes widening. "Oh my God. I did respond but I accidentally sent it to Felix instead."

Gio sat up. "What?"

She shook her head quickly, placing her hands on his chest. Tracing his lips with calming kisses, she spoke quickly. "It was nothing bad. All I said was that I could hardly wait but he called me on it because it still made no sense to him. I was able to cover up saying I meant to send it to my mom."

Gio hadn't paid much attention to anything she said after hearing what her response to his text had been. His mind was back on the condom in his wallet. This was too big of a risk. Someone was bound to notice the two of them had conveniently disappeared at the same time. But just like all the other times his ability to reason sensibly was shot to hell. All he could think of now was getting her down on the floor of that van and doing what he'd been fantasizing about obsessively for too long.

Still feeling what he'd always felt from her regardless of the impossibility of it all, he knew in his heart he'd stop at nothing to get what he wanted and they'd have plenty of time to make up for this later. For now his need to have her, make her his beat out every sensible thought that dare cross his mind. He kissed her pulling her down with him.

He had more than enough experience with the fast and dirty. Fast and dirty was not what he wanted with Bianca but at the moment they had no other choice. Gio already knew Noah must know or have some idea what they'd be up to. It was only a matter of time before Felix noticed their absence.

Nearly losing it when he slipped his hand up between her legs and realized she was more than ready for him, he stopped his ravenous kissing to look at her. "Are you absolutely sure about this?"

She smiled, her eyes ablaze with desire. "Yes," she

gasped.

He devoured her mouth again moving her panties out of the way, and sinking a finger in her. Fearing her moan just like he'd imagined after seeing all those orgasmic expressions of hers. His own desire uncontainable now he moved fast to get the condom out, pull his pants down as he got on his knees and slipped it on.

He looked down at her now, her dress lifted to her waist, exposing places he'd only dreamed of seeing, touching, licking. With her legs spread even as she still wore her long boots, it made this already unbelievable moment even sexier than some of his wildest dreams about her and he'd had some *wild* ones. It was all he could do to not plunge right in but he had to get one thing straight. He leaned over again and stared deeply into those beautiful eyes that now held the key to his heart. "After this there's no going back."

With her eyes locked onto his like they had been so many times in weeks leading up to this, she nodded.

"I need to be sure you understand this, Bianca. After this if you change your mind and you and him..." He squeezed his eyes shut not able to even say it—think it.

"Gio, I told you I love you. I won't. Ever. I swear."

Opening his eyes slowly, looking intensely into her eyes again, Gio believed her. He couldn't explain it but there was something in those eyes. He saw it deep in them. Even though she was betraying Felix, she'd never do it to him.

Knowing this had to be fast, he placed his thumb on that perfectly wet, already pulsating, spot—right where he knew it would drive her crazy and began the gentle circular strokes as he slowly slid into her. Arching her back with a tremble in reaction to his touch Bianca let out a gasp.

Never once, did he take his eyes off hers and he watched as her expression changed dramatically doing that thing she did when she felt the fireplace against her back, tasted the hot chocolate for the first time. That alone nearly did him in but he held on sliding in and out, moving faster as he began to feel that familiar tremble and he knew she was close.

She moaned loudly, lifting her hips up to him and he sped up, slammed in harder now, feeling his own build-up ready to erupt. Just as she cried out he buried himself deep in her letting out all the tension he'd built up in the past weeks—the anger and blood boiling jealousy he'd felt earlier. He came so hard and so much for a moment he worried the condom must've burst.

A few minutes later, they still lay there as the reality of what had just happened sunk in. Gio turned to Bianca lifting himself to his elbow and caressing her cheek with his finger. The connection he felt to her at that very moment was mind-boggling. "No regrets," he whispered.

It was more of a statement than a question but she responded with a smile, shook her head and repeated the two words he'd spoken with as much conviction as he felt. "No regrets."

That only furthered his faith that as wrong as what they were doing to his friend felt, there was no going back. They were no longer *doing* it. It was done. This had sealed it. Bianca was more his now than she was Felix's. As far as Gio was concerned her relationship with Felix was a thing of the past. Though it would still have to be dealt with delicately. For now they'd remain discreet until they could figure out how to move this forward as painlessly as possible because this changed everything. Gio wasn't about to take even one step backward now. If it meant they'd both move out of Felix's place a lot sooner than they'd planned, so be it.

That was inevitable anyway because if he'd had a hard enough time concealing his feelings for Bianca before tonight, it would be near impossible now. It was just a matter of time before he'd have to man up and accept the consequences of his actions. He was ready to do that now, but he knew now was not the time.

Bianca sat up. "We should get back before they notice we've been gone together."

They cleaned up, fixed their clothes and started out but not before Gio pulled Bianca back to him kissing her one last time—making sure she understood things would be different from here on. "Just so we're clear," he whispered against her lips. "This was not our only chance. This was just the beginning. All right?"

"All right." Bianca nodded. With a look of pure elation, she threw her arms around his neck nearly knocking him back down.

"I love you, Bianca," he said the words he knew now he'd never get tired of saying.

"I love you, Gio," she whispered back.

They were both feeling the excitement of what lay ahead. "Let's go," he said straightening back up.

They decided to go in through separate entrances. Bianca would walk in through the front of the resort while Gio would go around the back way. Giving her a few minutes so they wouldn't arrive back together, he slowed his stride as it really sunk in. This was actually happening and she wanted it as much as he did.

Noah's words from that first conversation Gio had with him over the phone about this came to him. *No matter what, this won't end well. You know that right?* Gio had thought about this many times—about the possibility that somehow he could pull this off.

Maybe once she broke things off with him and after some time passed, if Felix was in another relationship even, maybe then Bianca and Gio could reveal their relationship. Maybe then, it wouldn't be so bad. Those were a bunch of big maybes, because in the meantime, Gio would have to deal with the situation as it stood. Gio had barely been able to hold it together earlier when he watched Felix kiss her. The way he felt now, seeing Bianca engage in *any* physical contact with Felix might blow everything out into the open.

*

Bianca did her best to appear as casual as possible as she made her way back to the table with the rest of the girls. One glance over at the guys by the bar had her heart racing. Felix eyed her and he didn't look happy. Could it be possible he knew what she'd been up to? The idea that he may have had one of his security guys follow her, even as a security precaution, didn't even dawn on her until she was on her way back but now it was major cause of worry.

Felix started toward her as she got closer. She slowed not wanting to be too close to the girls now if they were going to argue. Starting to smile as he stepped in front of her, Bianca's smile went flat seeing the fiery contempt in his eyes. "Where've you been?"

Assaulted by the stench of tequila, followed by his slurred speech Bianca realized he was drunker than she'd ever seen him. "To the ladies' room. I got caught up on my way back when I ran into someone from school."

His eyebrow jerked up at that. "A guy?"

"No," she tried not to sound too defensive. Obviously, his reaction was fueled by the alcohol because he'd never once been angry with her and now his body language and the obstinate glare almost frightened her. He was more than angry, he was furious. "A girl I have class with."

"You sure?"

Bianca swallowed hard. What did he know? "Of course I'm sure."

"You think I haven't noticed, Bianca?" He spoke through his teeth, now lowering his voice but stepping closer to her, speaking right in her face. "Suddenly I'm not allowed to touch you but I have to watch while you smile and giggle at all your fucking little texts. Texts you say are all from your mom?" He took another menacing step forward as she took a cautious one back. People around them started to take notice. His eyebrow arched again sharply, as a sardonic smirk spread across his lips. "Oh, you thought I hadn't noticed did you? How stupid do you think I am? You were probably on the phone with him now, weren't you?" When she didn't respond he raised his voice. "Weren't you?"

What happened next was a giant blur. Gio jumped in Felix's face. "Calm your ass down, man."

Noah and the others followed as Felix continued to bark at Bianca to answer his questions.

"He's drunk," Noah attempted to downplay Felix's erupted temper.

Felix suspected she was cheating but apparently had no idea with who because his anger was all directed at her. The girls all stood as one of the bodyguards informed them it was time to go while the guys continued to try to calm a now completely unreasonable and belligerent, Felix.

The last words she heard fly out of his mouth were "Fucking whore!" That's when Gio's fist flew into Felix's mouth. Bianca's stomach fell and chaos ensued.

Between Felix's bodyguards, Noah, the rest of the guys, and the bar security trying to get control of the situation the place was a mess. Toni tugged at her hand. "Let's go," she urged.

Bianca didn't understand the urgency until she saw the cameras. First it was just a couple of people with their phones snapping pictures but then she saw what appeared to be paparazzi. They'd been there the whole night and she hadn't even considered the possibility that she might be seen by them earlier.

Toni and Bianca rushed out the back but even then cameras flashed in their faces. Hurrying to the van, Toni searched in her purse for her keys.

"I have them," Bianca said, handing them to her as Toni's eyes widened.

"Why do you have my keys?"

Her heart still pounding and feelings of guilt mounting by the minute, Bianca was beginning to feel like she might throw up. "I'll explain later; let's just hurry and get out of here."

Bianca had asked to borrow Toni's compact after watching Gio bolt out of there obviously upset about seeing Felix kiss her. Having told Bianca about the van situation earlier that day, Bianca had acted on a panicked whim and took the keys without Toni's knowledge. Then she'd rushed out saying she had to use the ladies' room and called Gio. The guilt was coming in from every direction—even this one. Toni hadn't been thrilled about the predicament Bianca had gotten herself into. Just like Bianca knew her mother and Nana would think, while Toni did think it exciting, she also thought it was dangerous. Tonight had proved exactly why. Things could escalate quickly and unexpectedly. Hearing Felix call her a whore still burned in her ears, and here he didn't even know the whole truth.

As they drove away in stunned silence, Bianca thought of Gio's words. *No regrets.* She still didn't have any — even after tonight's disaster — but she did regret that she hadn't decided to leave Felix's place sooner. She wouldn't be going back to his cabin. After tonight, she couldn't. Not just because of the way he'd behaved or because it was plain wrong to continue to stay at his place while completely betraying him, but because tonight she'd seen firsthand how a guy she thought she knew, could turn into someone completely different when angry. Felix didn't even know what was really going on. She cringed to think what might happen if he did.

"You think you'll be able to go get my things from Felix's place sometime this week?"

Toni turned to her and pulled off the road into a gas station. She stopped then turned off the engine. "Of course I will." She smiled. "First let me just say, holy shit Gio and his friends are *hot.* But Gio's eyes, my God! I can see why you'd be so tempted. But can you explain why you had my keys and..." Toni squeezed her eyes shut crinkling her nose. "Bianca, tell me you didn't. I noticed you and Gio were gone for sometime and I figured you might be doing something sneaky but..." She turned to look at the back of the van and Bianca saw the flicker of horror in her eyes the moment Toni spotted it — the condom wrapper. "Oh my God, you did!"

Bianca covered her face with her hands. "I didn't

plan it. I swear." She turned back to Toni and spoke rapidly, hoping she'd understand. "I mean, it's insane, Toni. I don't even know how to explain it but with Gio I just think differently. I do things I would've never done in a million years. I did hope to get a moment alone with him tonight, but the whole van idea didn't come to me until Felix kissed me right in front of Gio and I saw that crazed look in Gio's eye.

"I just kept thinking of how I would feel if it were the other way around. I probably would've been in tears and I'd seen the way he was looking at me earlier. I knew he was questioning my behavior with Felix." She shook her head, glancing out at the falling snow. It reminded her that she'd left her coat at the resort. "Since all his friends were there tonight, I didn't want to be so blatant about continually rejecting Felix's putting his hands on me. So I was a little more accommodating with the holding hands and allowing his embraces and I was dead right, Gio did think something had changed."

Her phone beeped in her hand making her flinch. It was a text from Gio. She glanced at Toni and couldn't help but smile. "It's him." It amazed her that the world could be falling apart around her and just knowing she was about to read his words made everything better. She clicked on the envelope.

Where are you? Are you okay?

She texted back quickly, her insides warming at his obvious concern.

I'm fine. I'm with Toni. She's taking me home. I'm not going back to Felix's cabin anymore. I can't.

She sent it and turned back to Toni. "So what now?" Toni asked.

"I don't know. But after tonight I just can't go back

there."

"You shouldn't," Toni agreed immediately. "But maybe you and Gio should cool it just a little until all this blows over. No telling what kind of stuff will be all over the TV and internet by tonight."

Bianca thought about that, chewing the corner of her lip for a second. The thought of being separated from Gio, even for a short period, was one she didn't want to entertain.

Her phone beeped again. His message made her gasp and she was instantly near tears.

I'm not either. Well I will tonight only because he's already passed out and Noah and the guys are insisting I do, but I'm going back to LA first thing tomorrow morning. Hopefully before he even wakes.

Obviously noticing her sudden change in mood, Toni asked if something was wrong.

"Yes," was all she managed to whisper as she rushed to text Gio back. She'd long ago decided she wouldn't hold anything back. She always said what she wanted and asked what she needed with Gio and she wasn't holding back now that it mattered most. So she sent her text, needy as it might sound.

Why? What about us? When will I see you again?

Bianca knew the answer to her first question. She'd just hoped maybe he stick around a little longer. She wasn't ready for him to be gone so soon.

I promise you. There is more of an us now than ever before. But I can't be there anymore. It was wrong from the moment I realized I was falling for you but it was worth the guilt to be around you. After tonight I just can't justify it without feeling like a total dick even if you're not there anymore.

The second she read it she began responding, feeling an enormous relief.

Okay but you didn't answer my third question. When will I see you again?

His responses came as fast as hers did and she was eternally grateful for that because her heart was still at her throat. Even though he was promising everything would be okay between them she had no idea when she'd see him again—be in his arms—feel his lips on hers again.

Bianca was no longer embarrassed to admit she felt addicted to him. Forget the embarrassment, this scared her. She clicked on his text the moment it came through.

Soon. I promise. I miss you already. We just got to his cabin. I'll call you tomorrow.

That calmed her a little and she glanced up realizing Toni had been watching her and waiting patiently. "I'm sorry, Toni. I didn't mean to ignore you but he's telling me he's going back to LA tomorrow and it just freaked me out a little."

She texted back. Her final text mimicked what he'd once texted her:

I miss you, too. SO MUCH.

She began telling Toni about what Gio had said when another text came through and she stopped to read it.

Love you! Goodnight.

Toni laughed as Bianca quickly responded saying she loved him too. That made Bianca look away from the text and at her friend; just then realizing she was smiling hugely. "What?" She hit send feeling all fuzzy inside.

"Girl, I've never seen such a display of emotions like the one you just put on for me. In a matter of what?

Five minutes? You went from mortified, to excited. Then giddy, then suddenly panicked and teary-eyed to giddy all over again." She shook her head. "You weren't kidding when you said this guy has you all tied up in knots."

Now Bianca was a little embarrassed but she wouldn't deny it. "I don't know what it is, Toni." She glanced out the window at the falling snow, remembering the first day he kissed her. "I'm beginning to wonder if maybe I should be a little worried about how addictive this feels. Just like what we did tonight, I feel like I'd do anything, take any risk." She glanced back at Toni knowing she'd be looking at her disapprovingly like she had earlier that day when Bianca had said something similar. "Within reason, of course. I wouldn't risk my life for him or anything like that." She didn't feel entirely sure about the sincerity of that last statement but she'd leave it at that.

"You may not believe this but you already have." Toni started up the car. "That boy back there was furious. And he doesn't even know the half of it. Things happen in the heat of passion *all* the time, Bianca. All I'm gonna say is I'm so glad you're not going back."

Bianca thought about that. Until tonight Felix had never even raised his voice at her and she admitted he had spooked her a little when she thought for a moment that he knew she'd just had sex with his friend out in the parking lot. She was thinking earlier when she decided she wouldn't be going back to his cabin that she'd finally come clean with Nana and her mother about what was going on. Maybe now she'd keep it to herself and just tell them it didn't work out.

CHAPTER 22

Gio walked out of the bathroom fully dressed. The room was still dark. He'd set his alarm so he could get out of there early. Knowing Felix he'd be feeling like shit about what happened last night. His suspicions about Bianca had nothing to do with Gio—yet.

If Gio didn't hurry to miss him this morning Felix would probably be all apologetic about his behavior last night. Although it hadn't happened in a long time, this wouldn't be the first time one of them got drunk and stupid and had to be held back or dragged out of a party or club. Whoever it was always felt stupid the next day. Gio wasn't about to stick around and have Felix apologize to him.

Sure, Gio had swung at him and landed a good one but it was justified. All the other guys agreed. Although they all might've just given Felix a good shove in the chest to shut him up and maybe told him to have some respect. Felix's anger and unreasonable fit of jealousy seemed to stem from him overdoing the shots and nothing more, so his calling Bianca a whore was seen as way out of line by everyone. That meant Gio's infuriated punch didn't raise any eyebrows, except Noah's, of course.

He'd packed his bag the night before and wrote Felix a short note thanking him for everything and telling him he'd call to explain why he had to leave. That wasn't something he wanted to cowardly write in a note or a text. Besides everyone was here to witness what would probably get very ugly. Most importantly, Gio had done enough damage. He didn't want to embarrass Felix in front of all their friends. As angry and betrayed as he'd probably feel, his ego and pride would likely be taking a hit. Gio wanted to spare him any possible humiliation and do it in private.

Noah rushed in the room. "Hurry up, let's get you out of here."

"What?" Gio was surprised Noah was even up. Abel had agreed to get up early and take him home but Gio didn't know anyone else was leaving so early. "You don't have to leave so early, Noah. And why you rushing?"

"I'm not leaving but you're dumb ass needs to get out of here *now*." Noah grabbed Gio's bags and started shoving Gio toward the door.

Gio tried taking the bags from him. "Give me those. I can carry them."

Noah gave him one but kept the other. "Just hurry, will you?"

Not wanting to argue, Gio hurried out of the bedroom. A very concerned looking Roni was already in the kitchen as he walked by. "What's going on?" he asked, glancing back at Noah.

"You fucked up. That's what," Noah said, picking up his pace as they walked to the front door. Noah turned to him just as they walked out the front door, his voice lower now. "Really, dude? In a fucking van? On a night when he took us all out? " Noah shook his head, hurrying down the stairs toward a very sleepy looking Abel, leaning against his car with the trunk open. "You couldn't wait?"

Hector was already in the car. Jack would be driving back with Noah later. Both brothers seemed unaware of the news that Noah had obviously gotten so early in the morning.

"It's all over the Internet, G," Noah said as he slammed the suitcase in the trunk.

Gio lifted the other suitcase in as well. "I didn't plan for that to happen." But he wasn't about to throw Bianca under the bus either. "It just happened."

"Leaving so early?"

Both Gio and Noah turned at the sound of Felix's voice. He stood at the front door still in yesterday's jeans and a t-shirt but wearing snow boots. Obviously, he planned to come all the way out and confront him. He held up his cell phone as he walked down the stairs "Or do you wanna stick around and explain to me about all these pictures everyone is sending me? My agent, my publicist, even my mother. Photos of you and my fucking girlfriend.

"Get in the car," Noah said, coming around and standing in front of Gio.

"No," Gio said, moving over and standing next to Noah.

Gio knew what Noah was thinking. Felix was the welterweight champion of the *world* for good reason. His fists were lethal. But last night he'd taken a punch from Gio and hadn't swung back—didn't because he knew he deserved it. Now Gio, too, would stand here and take like a man whatever he had coming to him.

"I'm sorry, Felix. You didn't deserve this but—"

"Did you fuck her in my house, too, asshole?" Felix spat the words loudly as he stalked toward Gio.

"No. I never touched her in your house. I swear. And I didn't *fuck* her, okay. I love her."

Gio saw it coming but, unlike in the ring, he didn't attempt to dodge or even block it. Felix landed a solid hook right on Gio's eye knocking Gio on his ass. Abel and Noah were immediately on Felix and Hector jumped out of the car. "What the hell?"

Gio's hand was on his eye, shaking his head to rid him of the stars he was now seeing. Ever grateful for his friends or Felix might've beat the shit out of him and Gio would've let him. Doing what he had with Bianca, wrong as it may've been, was totally worth the well-deserved ass kicking.

He grabbed a handful of snow and brought it to his already swelling eye. Felix sure as hell could pack a punch. Gio would probably be sporting a shiner for at least a week, maybe longer. Of course Felix's fat lip would probably be around for just as long. Gio was surprised he hadn't knocked a tooth out with as much force as he'd hit him last night.

"You're fucked up, Gio!" Felix yelled, still being held back by Abel and Noah. "To come here to my place and fucking do this. I'd never do something like this to you."

"I know you think you wouldn't. I didn't think I ever would either." Gio frowned as Hector helped him up, still feeling a little woozy. He spoke again, hoping somehow they all could understand. "I didn't do this to you, man. It just happened."

"Fuck you!" Felix pushed Abel and Noah away, looking completely disgusted. "Did you guys know about this?"

"No!" Gio yelled before Noah dared implicate himself. "Nobody knew."

Felix stared at him, still utterly disgusted. "Get this piece of shit off my property." He turned back to Gio just before heading back up the stairs. "Don't ever call or even text me again. You hear me? You're dead to me now." He stopped and turned to face him again. "And tell that whore there are plenty more boxers at 5th Street. She can work her way down the line."

Gio jumped, ready to go at him but Hector stopped him. Abel and Noah readied themselves to stop Felix if they had to. Gio pointed at him infuriated. "Say whatever you want about me, dude, but leave her out of this."

Felix scoffed. "Yeah, I have so much respect for that bitch now. I wouldn't dare say shit about her." He threw his hand in the air. "Get the fuck outta here!"

Gio wanted to yell back that he had a lot of nerve calling anyone a whore — wanted to push Hector aside and charge at Felix for even implying the nasty things he had about Bianca. She may've betrayed him but Gio knew she wasn't *that* kind of girl. She was as much of that kind of girl as Gio was the kind of guy who would betray a friend like he had Felix. This whole thing was something completely unexpected that had just happened to the both of them. But Gio knew it was pointless. Regardless of why or how it happened Felix had every right to be angry — hurt. He'd trusted them both completely and they'd both stabbed him in the back.

So, he didn't spew out all the angry words he had for Felix for disrespecting Bianca even though he'd do anything for her now. He leaned against Abel's car and said what he really meant from the bottom of his heart. "I'm sorry, Felix. I really am."

Felix's only response, without so much as turning around, before walking back into his cabin was an outstretched arm and his middle finger up in the air.

Gio exhaled loudly and glanced at Noah who shook his head. "All right, I get why you didn't block his punch but goddamn, Gio. You better make sure you buy an icepack before you start down the hill. That shit is gonna swell shut before you even make it out this driveway."

Noah examined his eye. Both Abel and Hector stared at him like they didn't know him. Gio could only imagine what they were thinking. He knew he had to explain to them on the way home. He didn't want them thinking he was just an asshole who'd screwed a friend over—a friend who could've just as easily been one of them.

They drove silently until they reached the drug store where they bought the ice pack and some aspirin . When they got back in the car Gio, who sat shot gun, rested his head back, holding the ice pack to his swollen shut eye.

"Look guys," he began. "I know what I did seems despicable but I didn't just decide to go after his girl. We fell in love. Both of us, not just me. I tried to fight it. I—"

"You should've left," Abel said staring straight ahead as he drove.

Gio lifted his head and glanced at Abel's unsympathetic almost angry, expression. He reclined his head back again and closed his only good eye. "Yeah, I should've." He had no choice but to agree. "I fucked up but it couldn't be helped."

He didn't expect them to understand because if one them had done what he'd done to one of their closest friends before this ever happened to him, he'd be just as disgusted.

"So what?" Hector sat up leaning against the back of the front bench seat. "You and her are together now? Isn't that gonna be weird?"

Gio shrugged. "It's not like we'll ever be around

him anymore. You heard him. He never wants to hear from me again."

"Yeah, but what about when he comes into 5th Street?"

Abel turned back to Hector. "He probably won't anymore."

Gio opened his eye. "He wouldn't do that—block you guys out and Jack—because of me."

Abel lifted a shoulder. "He might. Maybe he thinks we were all in on this. We all decided to come up here and enjoy the weekend while you screwed around with his girl."

Something tightened in Gio's stomach and he sat up straight. "We weren't screwing around."

"Call it whatever you want, G. Bottom line is you betrayed your friend for a girl. A friend who was doing you a favor by bringing you up here in the first place." Abel tightened his jaw. "That's not cool."

Hector sat back now that the conversation had taken a turn for the uncomfortable. Gio laid his head back again. It was beginning to throb and he hoped the aspirins would kick in soon. "I know it isn't. I don't know what else to tell you, man. You can't fight love. Trust me. I tried."

Nobody said another word about it the rest of the way home. They stopped and grabbed breakfast sandwiches which they ate in the car but other than that made no stops.

Gio thanked Abel for dropping him off and went inside, glad no one was home. He wasn't in the mood to answer all the questions he knew would be coming from his mom and sisters. He was sure by now they'd heard something. He plunked down on the sofa in the front room and did what he'd been thinking about doing since last night—called Bianca.

"Hey you. Are you home now?"

Just hearing her voice made him feel better already and he smiled despite his rough morning. "Yeah, just walked in."

"So did you tell him or did he find out on his own?"

Gio sat up slowly. "He found out. Why? What did he say to you?"

"I just got a couple of harshly worded texts."

Already he could feel the anger bubbling in him. "Harshly worded? Like what?"

"He's mad, Gio and hurt. He's doing and saying the expected."

Gio sat at the edge of the sofa now. "*Doing?* What's he doing?"

She sighed. "Nothing bad really. He set me up with a laptop so we could video chat and was paying for the internet service on it so I could have the fastest service available up here. This morning Toni called to tell me about the photos going viral all over the internet. When I tried to log on the service was already disconnected. It's no big deal. I didn't expect him to keep paying for it. I'll just get it under my name when I get paid again. It's kind of blessing actually. Maybe it's best that I don't read all the stuff being posted about me."

Gio stood up, glad that money didn't buy every-thing otherwise Bianca might still be with Felix instead of him. "And what did he say?"

"Gio, what do you think? I betrayed him with his best friend."

"Noah's my best friend," he reminded her. "And I don't give a shit if he's pissed, Bianca. I don't want him harassing you. Maybe you should block his ass.."

He got that Felix was pissed. But Felix hadn't exactly been an angel himself. Gio thought about the jazz singer he'd brought with him to the gym the day he invited Gio to train with him. According to Bianca, they'd been exclusive since last summer. So the chick in Chicago probably wasn't the only one he'd been screwing while in a relationship with Bianca. As mad as he was now he had a lot of fucking nerve saying *anything* harsh to her. Like it or not, Bianca was Gio's girl now and he'd be damned if he would put up with Felix or anyone disrespecting or harassing her.

"It was just two texts early this morning," she said. "Basically to let me know he knew and had thrown you out, though I already knew you were leaving. And of course to tell me he wanted nothing to do with me ever again."

"Yeah," Gio turned when he heard the front door open. "He said that to me, too."

His mother walked in the room. "Giovanni? Oh my God, your eye! What happened?"

"Nothing, Ma." He covered the mouthpiece on the phone not wanting to get into the whole thing right now. "One of Felix's jabs slipped during training, that's all."

"Your eye?" Bianca asked. "What's wrong with your eye?"

Gio moved the phone to his other ear as his mother moved in to examine his eye closer. "I'm taking you to the emergency room. This looks terrible!"

"I'm fine, Ma, really."

"Emergency room?" Bianca's voice got louder. "Did you two fight over this?"

Great, he had two hysterical women on his hands now. "Bianca, let me call you back."

"No. Answer the question. Was there a fight?"

Gio sighed turning his back to his mom. "Something like that. I'll tell you about it a little later, okay? I'll call you back soon. I promise."

His mother walked around to face him, as adamant about taking care of his eye as he knew she'd be. Bianca finally agreed to wait for him to call her back and he hung up.

After finally convincing his mother there was no need for a trip to the emergency room, he was able to take a moment and log onto the internet. Bianca's friend Toni and Noah were right. The pictures and story were everywhere. He frowned at some of the headlines.

Sanchez's two-timing girlfriend caught red-handed in the arms of his best friend.

But the comments from readers were even worse. Some made him slam his fist against the table. They were making comments like the one Felix had made about Bianca doing the rest of 5th Street.

The only good thing was that apparently whoever took the photos took only two of them together that night. It must've been on a phone camera because the quality was very poor but they were clear enough that there was no denying what was going on. One was of them against the van kissing and another as they climbed in it. The rest of the photos going viral were taken at the bar. They had the story all wrong too. Most said Felix caught them and that's what the scuffle at the bar had been about.

Clicking on link after link other photos of the two of them began to surface. Stills of them on the slopes and even a couple of them leaving her grandmother's shop. He'd searched online before for stories about Bianca and Felix and he'd never seen any of these. Whoever took them obviously didn't think them newsworthy until now. Now they could add their captions and create a story. All of the photos were innocent enough but the captions told stories of how they'd been betraying Felix for months and how these photos captured their "growing affair." As if any of these people knew what the fuck they were talking about.

For a moment Gio understood the frustration Felix talked about when he said he hated having to explain the stories about him with other girls to Bianca over and over.

Worried Bianca might have seen these already and that she might be upset he called her but it went to voicemail. He left a message and took another aspirin. Logging off the internet he swore he wouldn't read even one more story about it. Everyone could just screw themselves. The stories would die down soon enough and the tabloids would move on to the next celebrity scandal. The only thing that mattered was that no matter what anyone felt or said about it, he and Bianca were free to be together now. Nothing and no one could keep them apart.

CHAPTER 23

It'd been days since the scandal broke — days since Bianca had last seen Gio and an eternity since she'd last kissed his lips. She hadn't even been able to say goodbye properly. What was worse was that this could go on for much longer.

Both Bianca and Gio had assumed that the story would die down soon enough. Not only had it not calmed down, they were turning it into a full-blown soap opera. The paparazzi were relentless in their pursuit of a statement from any of the three parties involved in the, now internationally talked about, love triangle. Because they were all Hispanic, even the Spanish tabloids had gotten in on it.

Bianca dropped the only class she'd taken on campus that spring because the once respectful photographers and sleazy journalists were on her now, as Nana so nicely put it, 'like flies on shit.'

Gio had been fined for flinging one photographer's camera across the 5th Street gym parking lot. They were forced to lay low for now. The media wanted nothing more than to get more of the story that had everyone talking. At first, Bianca didn't understand why it was such a huge deal, then she remembered Andy. Felix's publicist always said any publicity was good publicity. Felix's fight was just weeks away and Andy was probably loving the media circus surrounding Felix. If she didn't know any better he was probably working around the clock to keep refueling the story himself. If she was right, this wouldn't die down at least until after Felix's fight two weeks from today. Bianca groaned at the thought that it might be that long until they could be together again.

Nana and her mother who'd, as expected, been upset about the dangerous situation she'd put herself in, were over it now. She knew they'd understand that she would've never even considered doing something like this unless she was crazy in love. Her mother even offered up her theory on why this had happened. It was simply meant to be. Bianca thought about that a lot. It made perfect sense. All the unlikely circumstances that led them to one another.

As usual, Nana had managed to shock her into silence when she told her she'd seen the twinkle in that boy's eyes way back when he'd first been in the shop. Nana said that was the reason she made her comment about Felix being a fool to leave Bianca alone with such a good looking boy. Needless to say, neither her mom nor her grandmother were too surprised about how things turned out.

Having already been forced to drop her only class that semester, and most infuriatingly being forced to stay away from Gio, Bianca refused to let the media frenzy dictate any other part of her life. So when Nana suggested she take some time off and stay home so she wouldn't have to be hounded as much, Bianca adamantly refused.

She drove up the street toward the shop. Her grandmother had since made sure the paparazzi knew they weren't welcome anywhere near her property, which included the parking lot, but they knew the law. As long as they stayed out of the parking lot they could still stake out the place from the street.

On top of the usual photographers' parked cars she'd become familiar with, there was a news van today. A reporter stood facing the camera, speaking into the microphone as if she were covering some important news story. "Oh, give me a break," Bianca muttered as she drove past the reporter and into the shop's parking lot.

Both she and Gio had agreed to stop reading or watching any of the ridiculous tabloids. Each day they came up with another twist to the story that as far as she was concerned was over. She wasn't even able to see him now. How could there be any more to add? She'd made Toni promise again to keep anything new she heard to herself. Bianca didn't need to know even one more stupid unfounded detail of what they were saying.

She heard the cameras as the photographers stood in the street blatantly snapping away. Why the hell they wanted more photos of her walking into her grandmother's shop was beyond her. Like she had all week, and unlike Gio, she refrained from flipping them off.

To her complete surprise, Felix was waiting for her inside. The last time she'd heard from him was the morning he found out. He'd obviously been furious because both texts were utter filth—the F bomb among other outrageous accusations. And when Toni had gone to pick up Bianca's things from Felix's place she hadn't even been allowed on the property. Felix had one of the drivers meet her at the gate with a trunk full of Bianca's belongings. The media had a field day posting pictures of the very van from the incriminating 'caught red-handed' photos driving up to Felix's gate.

She stared at him speechless. No words. None at all

came to mind. She hadn't bothered to prepare anything to say to him if she ever spoke to him again because she honestly thought she never would.

"Can we talk?"

Bianca glanced at her mother and Nana who stood behind the counter. He'd obviously already spoken to them because they didn't seem to have an issue with walking into the back room and leaving her alone with him in the otherwise empty shop.

Curious about what he could possibly have to say to her Bianca nodded. She walked around behind the counter and waited.

"I wanted to apologize to you."

Bianca kept her jaw from dropping open as she stared into Felix's genuinely remorseful eyes. She shook her head unable to find the words.

"I was mad when I found out—real mad. And hurt like hell, but I shouldn't have said those things to you. I'm just glad I was too proud to call you. I didn't want you to hear the hurt in my voice. I probably wouldn't have even made it through the call the way I was feeling. You probably think I'm the biggest hypocrite in the world now. I should be..." He took a deep breath and glanced away. "I should be the last person on earth who'd buy into the media crap and maybe it's just wishful thinking but I have to know. Is there any truth to what they're saying?"

Bianca blinked, not understanding exactly what he was asking. "What they're saying? They're saying a lot of things, Felix. Most of it is all made up or assumptions but those pictures..." she gulped back the wave of guilt that threatened to drown her. *No regrets.* "The pictures were not doctored or anything if that's what you're asking me."

"No, I know that. But I know I wasn't completely honest with you before about Shelley and now that she did the interview I got to thinking maybe there is some truth to it. Maybe you did already know and that's what drove you to —"

"What are you talking about? Because just so you know I haven't watched or read any of it for days."

His eyes went wide for a second before he recovered and stepped forward. "So you don't know?"

Now she was getting annoyed. She'd gone out of her way to avoid hearing anymore of the madness and now here was Felix, of all people, forcing her to hear what the latest stupid story was. But she had to admit she was curious. It was big enough to have him come see her. "No, I have no idea what you're talking about."

"Shelley." He scratched his head. "When I told you about having seen her again even after me and you had become exclusive, I didn't tell you everything. You were so mad already, I was afraid to."

Just like he had the day he confessed the first time his eyes bounced all over the room before coming to rest on her. A few customers walked in forcing them to pause their conversation.

Bianca smiled at them. "Someone will be right with you."

Having heard the bells on the door Nana was already out from the back. The customers stared at Felix, obviously recognizing him and then their wide-eyed stares were on Bianca. Bianca motioned for Felix to follow her in the back. "Where did you park? I didn't see any of your cars out front."

"I came in through the back. They still saw me but didn't have as good an angle as they would've had if I came in through the front."

Bianca walked through the small storage room all the way to the back door and stuck her head out. If there were any photographers out there they hid well because she didn't see any. But then there'd been plenty of photos of her where she'd clearly been oblivious to the photographers because she didn't remember seeing any of them when those particular photos were taken. Those were the ones that crept her out the most.

She turned back to Felix. "You think any of them are out here?"

"If they are, don't worry. My bodyguard is out there. They already know him. He does the same thing I saw Gio do to one of their cameras."

Bianca had to laugh as she stepped outside remembering the image Gio had downloaded and texted her of him hurling the guy's camera clear across the parking lot. That was one of the last times either of them had checked or read any of the stories.

She turned back to Felix ready to hear the rest of his story. It was odd that they both stood there smiling even if for just a fleeting moment. She crossed her arms ready to finish this and cleared her throat. "So, you were saying?"

His wandering eyes started up again, wearing her patience thin. She didn't want to be out here all day. "Shelley's pregnant—with my kid." Again Bianca held her jaw up but it was harder this time. "I didn't tell her she should have an abortion. I just said at that time in my life I wasn't ready for a kid. But that's what the headlines everywhere are saying. And the only reason I didn't tell her about you was because by the time I found out she was pregnant I'd already fallen for you *hard*. I was afraid she'd keep the baby just to spite me and I treated her pretty badly. Said some really nasty shit to her in hopes that she wouldn't wanna have my kid because I was scared to death of losing you. I broke it off completely, Bianca I swear to you. You changed everything. You changed me. Everything was different with you —"

Bianca raised her hand. She'd heard enough. "Okay, you can spare me all the bullshit, Felix. None of that matters anymore, now does it? I honestly don't care if you've changed or not. Just explain to me why you felt the need to come here and tell me all this now."

He looked down at his feet and moved the snow around with the tip of his boot. Just another way to keep his eyes off hers. "You really didn't know any of that?"

Bianca crossed her arms again and shook her head exasperated. "No, I didn't Felix. What difference does it make now anyway?"

"Well, now that Shelley sold her story to the tabloids, they're saying maybe you did this to get back at me. That maybe that's why you and him aren't even together anymore, you just wanted to hurt me like I hurt you."

"What?" she gasped.

"And, and..." he added quickly, his previously wandering eyes now fixed on hers. "If that's true, then I deserve it, Bianca. I understand why you did it. It makes sense now why you stopped sleeping with me. I suspected you might know — even suspected you might be having some kind of flirtation with someone because of it but I never imagined that you and Gio —"

"That is not why I did it," she huffed. "Believe it or not, Felix, I never set out to deliberately hurt you. I can't believe you would even think such a thing. It just happened."

"Okay, okay." Now *he* held out his hands. "Maybe it was just karma then. Maybe I just deserved to be hurt. Which is what I was really thinking this whole time. I was a total dick with Shelley but now that's all out in the open." He tilted his head. "And now that we're even, maybe we can still work something out." His eyes went all sad on her and Bianca could barely believe what she was hearing. "I know after what I just told you, you probably don't believe this anymore but I really am in love with you. I would've never even considered trying to work something out with any other girl after something like this but I'm telling you, with you, it's different."

The sincerity mixed with alarm made her nervous. And then he let out a breath and frowned."Andy wanted me to threaten her. Threaten to go after her with everything I had. Dig up any skeletons she might have and threaten to go public with them. All for the sake of intimidating her into having the abortion." He looked away and Bianca sensed he couldn't look at her anymore. She was almost afraid to hear more. "I might've done it if this had happened before I met you. I actually considered it then I thought what if it was you. What if this had happened when I first ran into you again, before I really got to know you and I'd done this to you. I didn't know much about her either but I kept thinking she could be just another sweet and special girl like you, who I'd be screwing with just to cover my own ass—I couldn't do it. That's when I realized I'm not the same guy I used to be and it's because of you. I'm giving her whatever she needs and I plan on being there for my kid but there's nothing else going on between me and her. So I guess..." His eyes looked deep into hers for a moment then looked away again. "I guess I was hoping this was just your way of giving me a taste of what I deserved but maybe now that you had you might consider giving me a second chance."

Bianca stared at him flabbergasted, for a moment before shaking her head and speaking. "Felix, I'm sorry that I hurt you. I really am. But let me assure you I *am not* that type of person. I would never play those kinds of games just for the sake of revenge. I wish that I could explain to you why I did it. Why it happened but I don't even understand it yet myself." She brought up her hand and waved it over her head. "And this. All this craziness with the media is why Gio and I haven't been together lately. Not because we've stopped seeing each other but because I don't want to give them any-more to write about. I want it to just go away already so that seeing him won't be such a circus."

The disappointment in his eyes made her feel guilt-ier and at that moment she knew everything he'd said about how he'd changed after falling for her was true. Unfortunately, it was too little, too late. "I believe you, Felix. I believe you've changed and that's good for you. But my heart is in another place now. I can't do any-thing about that... I don't want to."

They spoke for a little longer before he apologized again and actually wished her happiness with Gio and she hugged him goodbye. Just like she'd known from the very beginning, Felix did have a good heart. It just took him a while to figure out his heart could be happy in only one place.

*

Gio walked into the gym office ready to pack up his stuff, just as Jack stood from the desk where he and Hector had been playing chess. "He beat you again Jack?"

"Yeah, damn it. I'll get him one of these days."

Hector laughed. "Not likely. It's been a long *long* time since anyone's beat me."

"Abel's right, you smart ass," Gio said throwing the paperwork for the new youth boxing classes he was trying to get going into his backpack. "You should join the chess club at school. There's gotta be some kind of scholarship you can pick up as good as you are."

Hector rolled his eyes. "Don't get him riled up on that again. I walked in there once and walked right out. Nothing but nerds and don't get me started on the chicks in there." His face soured.

Gio glanced at Jack who was over by the wall heater fiddling with it. "Well, you're not there to pick up, ass. You're there for the possible scholarship." He turned back to Jack. "I thought you had that fixed."

"I did," Jack said without turning away from the heater. "But it stopped working a few days ago."

That thing was so ancient Gio didn't know why Jack bothered with it. It didn't even heat much either when it did work and it always stunk like gas. Gio had warned Jack a few times about getting it checked again.

His phone rang just as he finished zipping up his backpack. He pulled it out of the backpack's front pocket and saw it was Noah so he answered. "What's up?"

"So what happened?"

"With what? The paperwork?" Noah was going to be helping him get the classes going.

"No, with you and Bianca. You ain't seeing her

anymore?"

Gio pinched his brows together. "No. I am."

Noah was quiet for a moment. "They're saying she's back with Felix. Roni saw pictures. She'd told me earlier this week that's what the rumor was since you two haven't been seen together. I told her it was bullshit until she showed me the pictures of the two of them just today. She's laughing in some and then in another one they're hugging. They're calling the whole thing with you and her a publicity stunt for his fight. You haven't heard about this?"

As much as Gio knew the media was full of shit and how ninety percent of everything they printed was completely made up he hated that his heart was already beginning to beat a little harder. This had to be some kind of bullshit story. "I don't read or watch that shit anymore. I'm sick of it. So no, I hadn't heard anything about this but just like the rest of the crap they write it isn't true either. She's still with me and those photos are probably old."

"The stories are probably a lie but the pictures aren't old." Noah said very matter of fact. "They were taken today. Did she tell you about seeing him today?"

"I haven't talked to her. I was just now gonna check my messages and texts but my phone rang. I'll call her right now."

Anxious to get this straight now, Gio was off the line with Noah in seconds. He did have a text from her and he clicked on it.

Call me when you can. We need to talk.

No x's and o's or smiley faces like she usually added to her texts. Gio gulped hitting speed dial. He wasn't jumping to any conclusions. The damn paparazzi had done enough already by keeping them apart this long. He wasn't about to let them mess with his head. He'd get this shit straight right now. Thoughts about how the last two times he offered to drive up to see her and she discouraged it popped in his head. She had perfectly good reasons for it. It'd been a media frenzy up there ever since the story broke about them. His showing up now would only make it worse. Not once had it even entered his mind that she might be blowing him off.

When it went to voicemail he sat down in front of the computer on Jack's desk and set the phone down. He logged onto the internet and googled Bianca Rubio. Immediately all the endless articles about the scandal came up. He scrolled through the newer ones. The ones he hadn't seen or heard anything about.

Boxer's love triangle all a publicity stunt to hype fight. Exclusive first photos of Sanchez and Rubio back together again.

He clicked on the link and froze. The pictures of Bianca and Felix were dated today. Like Noah said, these weren't old. In them, they were engaged in what seemed like a happy conversation, since in some of them they were not only smiling but laughing. Then there was the one of them hugging, Felix's arm tightly around her waist, her arms around his neck, face resting against his chest, eyes closed — today.

His phone rang just as the thrumming in his ears started up. With his heart in a near panic he glanced at the caller ID. It was her.

"It smells like gas in here." Hector's words barely registered as Gio answered his phone, still staring at the picture on the screen.

"Bianca?"

"I have to make this quick, Gio. I'm rushing back to

my car right now. I tried to make a stop at the market. Bad idea. This is getting out of control."

Gio clicked on more of the headlines.

Love triangle ploy to boost publicity of Sanchez/Bautista fight. Couple happily back together.

"Were you with Felix today?" His own words sounded odd. Like he was hearing someone else say them.

Bianca sighed on the other end just as Jack banged the heater making Gio look up.

"Yes, that's what I wanted to talk to you about."

Gio straightened out in his chair, feeling a bolt of something almost electric sear through him. "So these pictures were really taken today?"

"Pictures?"

"Yeah, Bianca," he stood up unable to sit anymore. "Pictures of you and him together laughing—hugging—his fucking arms around your waist."

"Oh my God," she whispered. "They have pictures of that already?"

It all sunk in at once. The realization that the photos weren't fake. They weren't old. She'd really been with Felix today. Her sudden declining *need* to be with him. Noah's theory. The pungent smell of gas in his nose as he looked up to watch Jack take that last hit at the heater with a screwdriver that caused a small spark.

The explosion was massive, sending Jack flying across the room. Gio's body was lifted into the wall behind him whipping his head back violently. The desk, with everything on it, flew right into his face and everything went silent.

CHAPTER 24

It'd been over an hour since the line between Bianca and Gio went dead. She tried to convince herself that he hadn't hung up on her. There had to be a reasonable explanation for why they'd been cut off and he was now not answering any of her calls or returning her texts. Even with the pictures he couldn't possibly believe the stories about her and Felix being back together.

Toni had called her about a half hour after her call with Gio to warn her about the new stories. The new photos of her and Felix coupled with the stories the media was circulating were pretty damning. She suggested Bianca give Gio a head's up. The media sure had a way of making even the most innocent of photos seem like some kind of deep moment between them.

The more time that passed without her hearing from Gio, the more anxious she felt that he might actually be buying into the hype. He couldn't possibly, could he? But it was late already. They usually talked in the evening until bedtime.

The television was on low as she walked into Nana's house. Having to be sneaky just to run her errands after she got off work tonight had made her get home later than usual.

Everyone was home now, including their neighbor Jerry, a widowed man her mother's age that often came over to have coffee and chat with them. They were all in the front room as she walked in through the kitchen door from the driveway.

Her mother was the first one to turn to her, the expression on her face alone was alarming. "What is it?"

"You haven't heard?" Nana asked, picking up the remote.

"Heard what?"

"I'll rewind it. It's been on the news for the past hour."

Bianca began to roll her eyes. The pictures—the rumors—she was so sick of it all. Her mother and Nana couldn't be falling for this, too, could they?

She took a few steps through the dining room. They all sat staring at the television as Nana rewound it. All set to hear more about her and Felix's 'publicity stunt', Bianca crossed her arms and leaned against the door frame that separated the dining room from the spacious front room.

Nana stood and started toward Bianca as she hit play. The reporter's first sentence sent a heart stopping chill down Bianca's spine rendering her literally unable to breathe.

"We are live on the scene where an explosion at the 5th Street gym in East Los Angeles has left one dead and several critically injured. It is unclear what caused the explosion but authorities believe it may have been a gas leak. The name of the deceased is being withheld at this time pending notification of next of kin.

"According to witnesses, the explosion took place just after eight this evening when most members are usually gone but we have no confirmation yet if the deceased or the injured were employees or members of the club. The fire that destroyed more than seventy percent of the old building is now completely out but the investigation will continue into the night."

"Bianca," Nana's words came through a tunnel. "Bianca, breathe."

Gio hadn't responded to her calls or texts because he couldn't. "He's dead?"

Nana caught Bianca before she went down. "Bianca!"

Somehow Bianca managed to latch her arms around her grandmother's shoulders. Her mother and Jerry were already by her side helping her grandmother get her onto a chair. "Honey, they don't know anything. He could just be one of the injured. You haven't talked to him at all?"

"No!" The reporter had said an hour ago. That's how long it had been since she'd last talked to him. When the phone went dead. That's when it must've... "Oh my God!"

She tried standing, wanting to bolt out of the room and drive to LA but they held her down. "Bianca, you're hysterical! Sit down, sweetie. Calm yourself!"

They managed to keep her there but each passing minute was torture. Nana tried giving her a pill to calm her but Bianca refused. She didn't want anything blurring her state of mind. She needed it clear in case she managed to escape out of there and drive to Gio's side.

After watching more of the news broadcast, which didn't seem to have anything new to report other than more small details of the possible cause and more witnesses giving their accounts of the event, Bianca finally gave in and called Felix.

"Do you know anything?" she cried into the phone. "Is Gio dead?"

Just saying it made it hard for her to breathe. Her mother stood next to her stroking her hair and back.

"No, but he was one of the ones rushed to the hospital. That's all I know about him. I'm getting ready to leave now. I'm flying down. Jack..." He paused and Bianca heard him take a trembling breath. "Jack didn't make it."

The intense relief of hearing Gio was alive was replaced with bone numbing sorrow. Sorrow for Felix — sorrow for Gio — for all of them. Jack was their father and what Bianca had done to Felix and Gio struck her like lightning now. She hadn't just come between two friends. These two were like brothers. "I'm so sorry," her words were barely audible as the invisible fist that squeezed her windpipe didn't allow for more.

He didn't speak for a few moments but she heard his trembling breaths. He was crying. And more than likely he was all alone. Alone in his huge cabin. Bianca wanted nothing more at that moment than to be there to comfort him.

"I gotta go," he finally said but he was clearly broken up.

Bianca knew it was too much to ask. A blatantly shameful request given the circumstances but even now like all the times she'd been helpless to fight her feelings for Gio, she couldn't hold back. She'd beg if she had to. "Take me with you," she whispered. "Please."

To her surprise his response was immediate. "I'll pick you up in a few minutes."

The moment she was off the phone she rushed off to her room to pack a bag, her mother and Nana right behind her. She explained to them quickly through tears about Gio and Jack. The emotions utterly consumed her. The grief of their loss was overwhelming but at the same time Gio was injured. She didn't want to think the worst but if Jack had been killed, how bad were Gio's injuries? Were they life threatening? Was it something he would bounce back from or was it something that would alter his life forever?

And 5th Street—it was all of their livelihoods and it had been virtually destroyed. Noah had a child on the way. A family to think of now. All these things bounced around Bianca's frazzled mind as she signed rapidly to her worried mother that she'd be fine. She was just processing it all, she wasn't hysterical, even though she felt the incredible urge to let out a blood curdling scream.

She ran out the front door as soon as she saw Felix's car arrive. Bianca promised Nana and her mother she'd stay in touch, and stay calm no matter what, even though she knew that latter was doubtful.

The paparazzi had followed Felix and were already snapping photos as she reached his car.

"Are you moving back in with him now?" one of the photographers yelled just as he snapped the photo of Felix's driver taking her overnight bag from her.

"Is it true it was all for publicity?" a different one asked now. "Or did you really screw his friend to get back at him about Shelley?"

Bianca had been patient enough with these vultures and they had said the wrong thing at absolutely the wrong time. She didn't care anymore if they got this on camera; she was so sick of them. With her middle finger in the air she yelled what she'd been wanting to say to them all week. "Go fuck yourselves, you bunch of blood sucking assholes!"

Bianca actually felt a tiny bit better as she got in the car until she saw Felix's grief stricken face. She hugged him hard feeling the incredible anguish she'd felt when he first told her about Jack all over again as he cried unabashed against her shoulder.

*

Gio stared at the news reports numbly, switching from one channel to another as they went to commercial, ashamed to admit the stories and images of Felix and Bianca hurt just as much as the coverage of the fire.

His second home, 5th Street had been destroyed. Jack was gone and Gio still had room to mourn for Bianca. He watched the latest reports that showed her getting into Felix's car with her luggage and flipping off the photographers. They were now said to be on their way here—together.

Gio had never felt so stupid in his life. He'd hardly said two words since he came to, over an hour ago, and the doctors advised him that the pain he was feeling was from his body being slammed against the wall. He'd been bruised and scraped up pretty bad from all the flying debris but otherwise the worst injury he'd suffered was a concussion. They didn't think it was too bad but they did warn the pain would probably worsen in the coming days when the whiplash and soreness really set in.

Even that had him thinking of Bianca. Memories of the day they'd gone snowboarding for the first time and the days after when he'd barely been able to walk but it had been worth every single ache.

Then they let Noah and Abel in. Both looked wretched and he knew something was very wrong. When they told him Jack hadn't made it he'd gone mute. Not even his mom or sisters could get him to talk until he said the only thing to them he'd said at all: "Can I be alone?"

The only other thing he'd been sure to say after flipping through the channels on the television for nearly an hour was to Noah. "Whatever you do. *Do not* let Bianca in my room. I don't even wanna see her."

He knew it was stupid to continue to obsess over the reports on TV but even when Trinidad died it was the only thing that numbed him. Staring at the television put him almost in a trance. After a while he wasn't even listening anymore just staring and watching the images.

Images of the charred remains of 5th Street. Then images of Felix and Bianca laughing and hugging — getting in his car together — and now the latest of the two of them arriving at LAX hand in hand rushing past the paparazzi to his car.

He switched the channel again and froze. The most painful image he'd seen all night was on the screen. Jack's smiling face with his birth date and today's date across the bottom of the image. They'd just released the name and photo of the person who'd died in the fire and the agonizing reality really hit home. Jarring memories of his own father's death assaulted him and his body shook violently.

Dropping the remote he brought his hands to his face and let the massive buildup of sorrow out, crying like he hadn't cried since he was a kid — since his father's death.

*

Even knowing her last conversation with Gio had ended the way it had and Toni warning her that the stories were damning, nothing could've prepared Bianca for the cold reception she received at the hospital.

Nor did it prepare her for what Noah informed her almost as soon as she arrived.

All eyes were on them as they rushed into the waiting room. Noah quickly met them near the entrance.

After hugging Felix tightly and explaining what he knew about the gas leak, he turned to Bianca. Felix walked away to talk to Abel. Noah's eyes were red and swollen from all the crying he'd obviously been doing. They also held a mixture of determination and sympathy.

"Gio's okay," he said immediately, giving her what she needed to hear to keep herself from breaking down, too.

On her way there, she'd held it together for Felix's sake. He was so inconsolable. "When can I see him?"

"You can't."

That panicked her. "Why? You said he's okay. Is there something you're not telling me?"

"No." He nodded. "He has a concussion but the docs say he's gonna be all right. He just..." He took a deep breath and glanced away.

"He just what?" Bianca's heart couldn't take anymore. "What is it?"

"It's not a good time right now. C'mere." He placed a gentle hand on her arm and walked her further away from where everyone else was crowded in the small waiting room and lowered his voice. "He's real upset about Jack. We all are. He just suffered a concussion and well that may cause him to be even more upset than the norm. He's hardly spoken since he came to and we told him about Jack." He turned around and glanced at where Felix stood with Abel. "This is isn't the time or place for this. Gio is gonna need time. It's none of my business what's going on with you two, but whatever it is, I'm asking, as a favor to me and the rest of everyone who's grieving, respect Gio's wishes for now."

"His wishes? What wishes?"

"He doesn't want to see you right now." Noah said firmly. "The last thing we need right now is any emotional outbursts or arguments. He's real broken up right now about *everything*. This next week is gonna be real rough for everyone. Maybe you should just hold off until after all the services to try and talk to him."

He doesn't want to see you right now.

The words stung like nothing Bianca had ever felt in her life. He actually believed it. All the bullshit they were saying on television. The stupid pictures. She didn't care how damning they were. She could not believe he'd bought into it. Believed them without so much as giving her a chance to explain.

Barely able to see through the tears, Bianca's breathing began to accelerate. She glanced back taking in the desolate crowd. Even Roni kept dabbing tears away. It took everything she had to hold it together because Noah was absolutely right. This was not the time or place for it.

"Can you tell me which direction the restrooms are?"

Clearly relieved that she didn't push, he walked her out into the hallway and pointed. Bianca rushed away without another word. She barely made it into the restroom; glad that it was a single restroom because she burst out crying as soon as she closed the door behind her.

Waves of painfully anguished sobs came again and again. Everything she was forced to hold in when her grandmother and mother begged her to calm down.

The entire trip down when she refused to add to Felix's grief by letting out her own incredible fear that Gio could be seriously injured. Then the slap in the face that Gio didn't want to see her. It all came out now as she curled up in the corner of the cold little room and cried until she thought she couldn't cry anymore.

CHAPTER 25

Glad that Noah hadn't walked in ten minutes earlier and seen him break down like he had, Gio looked up at him. Noah had news for him and from the looks of it, like when he'd walked in there hours ago to tell him about Jack not making it, this wasn't good.

"Abel said Hector's fine. He is, right?"

"Hector's fine," Noah nodded. "Just a broken arm and lots of bruises and scrapes."

"Then what is it?"

"Felix and Bianca were here." Gio turned away with a gulp, glad now that it was past tense, meaning they were gone or he might be tempted to tell Noah to forget his earlier request. Even with everything he'd heard on the stupid TV his heart yearned to see her now. "You told her I didn't wanna see her?"

"I did."

Gio glanced back when Noah didn't say more. "What did she say?"

"Nothing. She bolted to the restroom. She was upset but she didn't say anything even when she came back to wait for Felix."

"Wait for him?" Gio squeezed the sheet, and clenched his teeth, the jealousy eating him up.

"Yeah, they got here together so they left together."

Gio almost didn't want to ask but he figured he may as well get it over with now. "Did he say anything?" Noah didn't answer immediately so Gio glared at him, his patience running real thin. Whatever it was

Noah should just spit it out. "Did he?"

"I didn't ask him anything but Abel did—asked him if he was seriously taking Bianca back after all the bullshit. Felix said this wasn't the place to talk about it but he did add that we wouldn't understand anyway."

"Understand what?" There was no way he could hide the utter disgust he felt. Felt because he hadn't seen this coming—because he'd been stupid enough to get caught up in a situation like this.

"He didn't say. But he did say they were staying at the Royal Towers for the next few days before heading back up to Big Bear." This was the final blow to his already devastated heart. "He also said he'd pay for Jack's services. He wants to make sure Jack gets the services he deserved."

Gio stared at Noah. Noah didn't say it. He didn't have to. This was his way of reminding Gio of what a loyal, selfless guy Felix had always been. That if it was true, that they were back together again, Gio should stay away this time.

Noah didn't have to worry. The last thing Gio wanted now was to be anywhere near her. Be tortured by her eyes—her laugh. His heart wouldn't be able to take it. Gio thought about that numb dark place he'd sunk into after killing Trinidad. How hard it had been to climb out of that place. It had ultimately been Bianca who had helped him leave it behind him and even when he began feeling like he might sink back in how easily she'd brought him out. He could feel it already. He was sinking fast. If this was true he had no idea how he'd ever make it out now. This was so much worse.

Looking away from Noah he stared at the muted television still running the story of the explosion. As hard as this was to take in he noted how his heart was still thinking in terms of *if*. That frail hope was still holding out that his worst nightmare hadn't actually come true. Three words were keeping it alive. *She was upset.*

Why the hell would she be upset? *If* this was all true then she should've expected for Gio to not want to see her. But she hadn't said anything. This confused the hell out of him. All he could do now was wait it out — and pray.

*

The light from the television illuminated the garage. On top of everything Gio had dealt with in the last week, he now had to deal with shame. Shame that he should be in mourning for Jack and all he could do was drown in despair over Bianca's betrayal.

Through the services, through filing the insurance claims for the place he'd called his second home that was now destroyed, through it all, she'd been front row center squeezing the life out of his aching heart.

Deciding his heart had been in denial in the hospital Gio gave up hoping this was not happening. Instead he focused on the shame. As hard as it was, it was easier to deal with. Shame that because of him and the fact that 5th Street was now in his name only, Felix hadn't even mentioned his promise — a promise he'd made to Jack not Gio — that he'd help renovate the gym.

No one said it but they were all thinking it. The money he'd be getting from the insurance wouldn't be enough to rebuild. The whole thing would have to be knocked down and built back up from the ground. There was no way they could afford to do that. At best,

Gio might be able to rent another place out of the area and buy some equipment for it but it wouldn't be the same.

5th Street had practically been a landmark of East Los Angeles—the pride and joy of the local community. The only chance they'd have of rebuilding it now was if someone with Felix's kind of money would help them. Gio had ruined that chance for *everyone*. And for what? He hadn't even gotten the girl—the girl he'd thought worthy of risking it all.

Mercifully, Felix hadn't brought her to any of the services but the reports of them being back together were still going strong and Gio would sooner die than ask Felix straight out about it. The night she'd flown out with him they were photographed going into their hotel together. Gio still obsessed about the smallest things. They hadn't held hands as they walked into the hotel but they had at the airport when they arrived. She had to know, especially after how their phone call had ended that day, that he'd be watching now and still she'd held Felix's hand in clear view of the photographers. There was no *if* anymore.

Gio had since replaced his phone with a new one but blocked her number. He wouldn't even be able to stomach an apology from her. The worst part was he couldn't say he blamed her. There was no way he'd ever come close to offering her everything Felix could, especially now. He didn't even have a job.

"How dare you!"

Forgetting about his still injured neck Gio jerked his head at the sound of Bianca's voice, regretting it instantly as the pain burned through his neck muscles. She charged toward him tears streaking down her cheeks. Gio stood up cautiously, his body still sore all over.

"How dare you shut me out just like that!" Gio had seen many sides of Bianca but this batshit crazy side was a new one. "Apparently, the words of the gossip reporters and tabloid shows mean more to you than anything I've ever said to you, right? Because you were so quick to believe the bullshit about me and Felix getting back together."

"Bullshit? You've been hanging out with him! You stayed in the same hotel!"

She pushed him hard with both hands in the chest and he fell back into his beanbag. "We had separate rooms!" She was screaming now. "How can you believe them? How could you do this to me? Do you have any idea what I've been going through this week? Do you know what it was like to be told at the hospital that you didn't want to see me? To know this whole time you'd believe that I would do something like this? Why? Why would you believe it? I told you I love *you*."

The pent up anger and hurt he'd felt all week kicked in and he stood up suddenly making her take a step back. "Yeah, well, you said the same thing to him and then you cheated on him with me, remember?"

Her mouth fell open and she stared at him for a moment, her big stunned eyes searching his face for something. With her chest still heaving she shook her head blinking a couple of times. More tears leaked out of her eyes and down her cheeks before she turned around and walked away without saying another word.

Drawing a blank about what to do or say to her now, he watched her walk away. As much as his heart begged him to go after her, he knew there was nothing more to say. He stood there immobile as the minutes passed. He wasn't even sure how long he'd been stand-ing there but it was long enough to rewind everything he'd been through with Bianca since the day he'd first gone up to Felix's cabin.

Relentless hope flew out from the grave, suddenly pounding questions in his head. Why would she come down here just to lie to him? Why would she be so hys-terical about it? He'd let his clobbered ego strangle those two questions down when she'd stood there be-fore him and unleashed what the blinding anger would only let him believe. What he'd obsessed about all week — she'd had regrets.

The only thing that kept the whispering hope from increasing into a roar was Felix. Gio hadn't been able to hold back from hearing Abel's version of Felix's an-swer to his inquiry at the hospital. Gio had expected nothing less from Abel. He'd been far less careful about hurting Gio's feeling; telling him straight out, it sure as shit appeared that they were back together and to him Felix had confirmed it.

Gio wasn't dead yet but he may as well be because that's how he felt. Hope beat out pride and he pulled out his phone. Plopping down into his beanbag he scrolled down his contacts. He could hardly believe what he was about to do but he hit send.

It rang a couple of times before Felix answered. "Hey, G."

Felix's tone worried Gio. He sounded too laid back for someone who'd been so mad at him just a few weeks ago. Sure, he'd been civil at the services but that was to be expected. His tone now sounded almost pleasant. Gio didn't even know where to begin.

"Felix, I uh—"

"I'm glad you called," Felix interrupted him. "I was

just waiting for all this laying Jack to rest business to be over. I don't want you or anyone to think that because of the beef between me and you I'm turning my back on 5th Street. Now more than ever I want that place to represent what Jack always dreamed it would: hope for the troubled youth of East LA. It's what he lived for. I don't want the dream dying with him. I promised him I'd help. I wanted to be part of that dream to give back to him what he gave to me — to all of us."

Gio was getting choked up thinking about Jack. The reason for this call now felt so selfish, so petty. "Thanks man. I don't even know what to say. We couldn't do it without you that's for sure."

"It's my pleasure broth —"

The line went silent for a moment and Gio squeezed his eyes shut, feeling like the biggest dick on the planet.

Felix cleared his throat and continued. "It's my pleasure, G. It's the least I could do for a place that did so much for me."

"Well, it will be extremely appreciated by so many for years to come. I can guarantee you that." Gio took a deep breath. "You're a good guy, Felix. I only hope some day you can forgive me for what happened."

"That's another thing I wanted to talk to you a-bout."

Gio's breath caught. Was this it? A final warning that he stay away from Bianca? This would definitely be the nail in the coffin because no matter how much he loved her there was no way he'd be that selfish to ruin this second chance for the rest of the guys.

"It sucks the way everything went down." Felix spoke with a little less conviction than when he spoke about Jack. "But I got to thinking long and hard. I knew there was something different about Bianca from the moment I ran into her again last summer—different than any other girl I'd ever met." Gio brought his hand over his eyes. God he didn't want to hear this, Felix didn't have to tell him how special Bianca was. "I just didn't figure it out soon enough. She deserved better than how I treated her, than what I did to her and it cost me in the end."

The end? Gio's hand came down slowly from his face and he sat up a little straighter. He dare not interrupt.

Felix continued. "The night we left the hospital Bianca nearly had a panic attack in the car. At first she didn't want to admit to me, of all people, that it was you she was so upset about. She did admit it later when she was calmer but said she'd be okay."

Felix paused, prompting Gio to ask what he'd been dying to know all week. "What did you mean when you told Abel at the hospital it was complicated and they wouldn't understand?"

He heard Felix sigh. "Even though I knew it was ultimately my own fault I'd lost her, that I was going to lose her anyway once the truth about Shelley came out, I was still hurt about how it all went down. I wanted them to think there might still be a chance for me and her. I knew it'd get back to you and with all the shit on TV I knew you'd believe. I was still pissed at that point. Hell, I still am, only not so much at you as I am myself." Felix let out an exasperated breath. "I ran into Evelyn just a few days after you left. She told me about you blowing her off. I know you wouldn't blow off someone like Evelyn, especially after she said to you what she told me she did. I could only assume you and Bianca were already..." He stopped for a moment before continuing without ending that last statement.

"You were loyal to Bianca even though she had someone else and I'd bet my savings account that you still
haven't even thought about another girl, right?"

Gio didn't answer. He didn't have to. Of course he
hadn't thought of another girl. He could barely think
about *anything* else much less moving on to someone
else.

"You know what I did that night, G? I made Evelyn's little dangerous fantasy a reality." Felix sounded
disgusted with himself. "I think we both know who is
more deserving of Bianca. And she deserves someone
who can truly appreciate her. Except for the stuff about
that girl being pregnant with my kid, none of that other
shit they're saying is true, G. It's what those fucking
tabloids do. Create a story where there's not one. But
even I wanted to believe there might be."

Felix told him about how he'd swallowed his pride
and went down to see her the day the press got all the
pictures of them "back together." Only what the press
didn't know was she'd turned him down flat.

Gio stood up in alarm. Bianca had been all but hysterical when she'd walked in. "I gotta go."

"What?"

Obviously Felix was stunned that Gio would cut
him off mid heartfelt speech. But Gio didn't have time
to explain. He'd never forgive himself if Bianca had
some kind of panic attack while driving or something
because of his dumb ass.

"Listen, Felix thanks for this. We'll talk some more
soon," he said pushing the garage door open as he
stormed out. "I'll explain later but I gotta go!"

He hung up and dialed Bianca, already sprinting to
his bike.

CHAPTER 26

Nearly hyperventilating for the third time this week, Bianca pulled over and got out of her car. She leaned her arm against the hood as the dry heaves kicked in. If her mother and Nana knew she was driving in that condition they'd be furious.

The anger but mostly immense hurt nearly suffocated her. Gio's beautiful eyes had never looked at her the way they had tonight. They were so cold and full of revulsion. She was convinced whatever love he'd felt for her was completely gone now.

As the dry heaves slowly calmed, Bianca's breathing began to go back to normal. Her lip began to quiver as it had so much this week. She was out of options now. All week she'd tried one thing after another. Trying hard to do as Noah said and respect Gio's wishes, she'd held out this long and for what?

Her efforts to reach him had been in vain. Even after she stopped getting the "not in service" message. Now when she tried calling the new message was even worse. *This number has restrictions which prevent the completion of this call.* And she knew he'd blocked her number.

Bianca figured everyone had felt heartache at some point in their lives. She knew people went through divorces and breakups all the time. But much like what she felt for Gio during their happier times, the intensity of her heartache had been unbearable. She didn't think she'd get over it—still didn't.

She'd meant to walk in and calmly assure him that the stories were all lies. That she hadn't and would never go back to Felix. She'd never be happy with *anyone* else but Gio. Just like all her other emotions when it came to him, she'd lost it when she saw him. The questions she'd wanted to ask him all week came blasting out.

She still didn't understand — couldn't fathom how he could possibly believe it after everything they'd gone through. After he'd seen, *felt* all the love she couldn't hide from him even if she tried.

Toni suggested that perhaps Felix had said something to him to further his belief that the stories were true. Bianca had been so close to calling him to ask but each time she'd stopped when she remembered how inconsolable he'd been about Jack. She'd already felt horrible about the way she'd completely broken down in the car on their way to the hospital. There was no way she'd force Felix to further witness her heartache over his friend — the guy she cheated on him with.

Bianca had all but forgotten she had Roni's number and after calling her and explaining to her as she sobbed, Roni made her promise she wouldn't tell a soul that she'd been the one to tell Bianca about Gio sulking in his garage. Even as she drove down there she still held out hope that if he didn't believe her she could, eventually, once a little time passed, beg Felix to help her get Gio to believe. She knew she was completely undeserving of any help from Felix, especially when it came to this but she'd been willing to plead with him if she had to.

Now even that last resort was out the door. Her biggest fear was confirmed tonight. Since she'd cheated on Felix with Gio, he now believed her to be *that* kind of girl. Not a girl who'd made a once-in-a-lifetime exception for that once-in-a-lifetime guy that she really was. She saw it in his eyes. He was convinced of this and *that's* why he'd been so easily manipulated by all the lies.

No one. Not even Felix vouching for her would convince him if that's what he truly believed. Just like the rest of the week the pain was a physical one. Her mother and Nana had said it was in her head but it wasn't just her heart that ached. Everything inside her ached. Toni said it was normal to hurt this bad. But this couldn't possibly be normal.

She walked back to the side of the car. Her phone rang in the passenger seat. It'd been ringing. She heard it earlier but she ignored it. As she picked it up it stopped ringing. She had three missed calls. All from Gio.

Her heart had just calmed from her near panic attack and it was going again. About to hit the voicemail key to listen to his messages it rang again.

Not sure what to think and almost terrified of what he might have to say to her, she answered anyway. "Hello?"

"Where are you?" his worried words demanded.

Confused, she glanced around. She hadn't even noticed where she pulled over. "I don't know, on Evergreen somewhere."

"Pull over and lock the doors." He spoke quickly — firmly. "Evergreen and what?"

"I am pulled over." His tone was making her nervous. "Why? What's going on?"

"I'll tell you when I get there." She heard his motorcycle rev up. "Evergreen and what?"

Glancing around, then behind her she saw the cross

street was Third Street. She was almost embarrassed to tell him she'd only gotten a few blocks before having to pull over.

"Third," she said, as it sunk in that he'd be there with her soon.

"Stay there, Bianca. *Please*. I'll be there in less than five."

"Okay," she said nodding, already looking around for him as the line clicked.

As soon as she saw the bike turn the corner and come toward her she got out of the car and came around to the sidewalk. She leaned against her car, her heart now pounding full throttle, the knot in her throat already unbearable. Regardless of what he had to say to her, just being close to him would have her in tears. She hated it but she was already sucking back the tears now and he hadn't even gotten off his bike.

She watched as he pulled off his helmet, hung it on the handlebar and jumped off his bike. With a few long fast strides he was standing in front of her in seconds.

"I'm an idiot," he said breathlessly as his big hands cradled her face and she could no longer hold back the tears. They poured out as she squeezed her eyes shut then felt his lips on them, kissing her eyelids softly. "I talked to Felix. He confirmed what a fucking idiot I've been. Please forgive me," his voice broke as he pleaded. "Please. I should've never doubted you. I'm *so* sorry."

Not even for a second did she consider not forgiving him. In hindsight maybe she should've been a little angrier at him for the hell he'd put her through. But that week alone had been enough to show her she could barely breathe without him. She forgave him instantly throwing her arms around him and hugged him tightly.

For once holding back the words that would've normally just flown out, she felt slightly empowered. Then he surprised her by saying the very thing she held back. "Stay here. Not just tonight but for good. We can get a room tonight and I'll figure something else out later but I can't be this far from you anymore. My heart can't take it."

Her heart doubled over and she could hardly believe just minutes ago it had been agonized by the very person who now made it flutter with joy.

Before the explosion she'd already begun to talk to her mom about the possibility of moving back down. Being away from Gio for days, maybe weeks, at a time just wasn't going to work. Because her mother knew Bianca would finish school faster if she went back to Cal State LA, where she'd been attending before her father died, her mother had been all for it.

Bianca had no idea how this was going to work. No idea how an unemployed girl with no place to live and who still wanted to finish school with a boyfriend whose place of employment had just burned down was going to make it down here. But she nodded, already excited about the prospect of being with Gio every day. One way or another they'd figure it out.

Gio kissed her softly leaning his weight against her. "I love you," he whispered again and again between kisses.

She laughed after the eighth or ninth time and he stopped to look in her eyes. "There's my happy girl."

Bianca had stopped fighting the pull he had on her long ago and fell happily into his deep gaze, taking a very deep and satisfied breath. "I'm never happier than when I'm with you."

He smiled making her sigh. "Good, because I plan on having you with me all the time."

"All the time?" she teased, noticing that since he got there that her tense body was finally relaxing.

"Yes, all the time." He kissed her again, biting her lower lip when he was done. "Starting right now." He pulled away. "Follow me back to my house. I want you to meet my mother and sisters."

Her eyes flew open wide assuming that like the rest of the world his family must've been thinking the worst about her with all the news casts about her supposed publicity stunt.

His soothing smile immediately calmed her. "Don't worry. They're gonna love you." He kissed her one last time softly before adding, "My mom doesn't buy any of that shit on the tabloid shows." He smiled. "I promise."

Bianca stared at him as he walked back to his motorcycle. Was this really happening? Did everything actually get worked out? Was she really going to be moving down here and see him every day?

He climbed onto his bike, grabbing his helmet off the handlebars. Then he looked up at and smiled at her so tenderly it took her breath away.

*

Gently patting the warm soapy sponge over Gio's big strong shoulders and then down his chest, Bianca examined all the bruises and scrapes that were still very visible. As the water from the shower rinsed away the soap she kissed the bruises gently. She worked the sponge down to his hips as Gio brought his hand around her behind and squeezed a handful of her wet behind. He'd been hard from the moment she'd begun to undress him in the small hotel bathroom. Now he pressed against her, taking her mouth in his and kissing her with that need she loved feeling from him. As the warm water splashed down against their faces she kissed him back, with just as much need, moaning into his mouth.

Gio brought his hand around the front spreading her legs. If she let him and gave into her own yearning she'd spin around and bend over letting him take her right there but she was determined. Determined to not allow him to over exert himself—take care of him like she hadn't been able to this whole past week.

She pulled back breathlessly just as his fingers entered her. "No," She managed in a very strained whisper, his fingers still playing inside her. "Let's go to the bed."

Gio sucked her bottom lip, then brought his playful fingers up for her to suck—taste herself and she did, staring straight into his flaming eyes. "We could do this here," he whispered, grabbing a fistful of her hair and tugging her head back a bit roughly, he dove into her neck sucking and nipping with his teeth.

The sensation was one she'd never felt. Felix had always been so gentle with her but it excited her like she never would've imagined. Still, she remembered his badly beaten body.

Barely able to catch her breath to get the words out she caressed his hard back. "Let's go to the bed, Gio. I promise I'll take care of you."

His head lifted and their eyes met for a moment before the corner of his lip rose. Without another word he reached over and turned off the water. They walked out and toweled off, then walked over to the bed dropping the towels and climbed in bed.

Before Gio could take the lead and climb atop her Bianca took charge. "Lie very still," she whispered then kissed his lips softly.

Gio was supposed to be still getting a lot of bed rest. But according to his mother he'd spent most of the week sulking in the garage. He now lay completely naked on the bed and Bianca began what she promised to do now and forever: "take care of him."

She kissed the bruise on his collar bone and worked her way down past his sore ribs and hip bones. He wasn't kidding when he told her just about every inch of his body had been bruised or scraped in one way or another.

Bianca glanced down at the one part of his body that seemed to be in perfect working order, erect and ready to go, then kissed it as Gio's body went taut. She looked up at him staring at her. "Relax," she ordered with a smile.

With their eyes still locked she began licking the shaft. Trying very hard to not make it obvious this was her first time doing this ever, she continued to keep the eye contact going. Bianca had read enough steamy romance novels and how-to articles in women's magazines. She was pretty sure she could wing it. She just hadn't expected him to be so big. In the van it'd been too dark to really appreciate it at all but now she'd appreciate every inch.

Gio's body shifted slightly carnal moans escaping him as she continued to lick up and down and then took him in completely. His hips moved with her and she moved up and down his length, amazed at how much she was enjoying doing this to him.

Then she swiped her tongue on the salty tip like a

windshield wiper over and over just like it said in Cosmo and was thrilled at his reaction. This really worked. His entire body arched and she heard him gasp. "Baby, that's it," he urged. "I think I need to take over before it's too late."

"Oh no, you don't." She smiled, feeling sexier than she'd ever felt in her life. She was enjoying being in charge. She pointed at his wallet on the nightstand. "Condom," she said simply and he complied immediately, even opened the packet and pulled it out before handing it to her.

This would be a first also. She'd never actually put one of these things on anyone. Smiling because she knew this was just one of the many firsts to come with Gio she slowly and very carefully rolled it on. "No over exerting yourself, remember?" She sunk her teeth into her bottom lip as their eyes met and she was suddenly locked into those striking green eyes. "You ready?"

He nodded his heavy lashes blinking over his eyes almost in slow motion. Bianca climbed over him carefully, afraid to hurt him. She brought her hips down over him trembling as she slid onto him slowly, still locked in his eyes, until he was all the way in.

Gio held his hands out to her and she took them, not moving for a few seconds just enjoying the fullness she felt with him deep in her. Again, careful not to hurt him, she lifted herself up and began to ride him slowly, gently as he squeezed her hands.

Unable to help herself she picked up speed, the sensation building with every wet slide. "You sure you're okay?" she asked through her teeth.

"God, yes!" he said bringing his hands around her waist and lifting her, slamming her back down on him even harder.

Now even he lifted himself with each thrust as she slammed back on to him again and again. Feeling her eyes roll back she ran both hands through her own hair and began to moan, knowing she'd be climaxing in a big way in just a few more seconds.

Gio slammed into her one last time, holding his pelvis up against her with a groan triggering Bianca's orgasm and she cried out, her heart pounding with every wave of pleasure that ran through her body.

She stayed on him even after it was all over, her heart still banging away as her breathing finally came under control. Grabbing the towel she'd put on the bed in preparation for this, she climbed off him gently, cleaned up and came to rest next to him.

Gio kissed the top of her head. "I'm not that handicapped, you know."

Bianca smiled. "Your mom says you've been stubborn so I'm taking over now. No arguing. You need to take it easy."

He brought his big arm around her and squeezed her to him. "If this is how you take over then I ain't arguing."

She giggled now, making herself comfortable against his warm hard body. Still clueless as to how things would work out for them, unbelievably she felt even more sure about what she'd told her mother and grandmother over the phone earlier. As long as she was with Gio she'd be fine.

This day had started so horribly bad and now she could hardly believe how perfect everything had turned out.

*

Calling Felix had been the best decision of Gio's life. Not only was Bianca back in his life for *good*, they'd start with the demolition of what was left of the old gym as soon as the investigation was over and rebuild from the ground up.

The guys couldn't have been happier but none more so than Gio. Gio told them he'd get all their names on the title as soon as possible. Felix was going to do everything he could to get this thing going fast and have them back in business in no time. Felix might be relationship-challenged but he truly was loyal to 5th Street and always had been.

As promised, he figured something out and while their new set up wasn't nearly as glamorous as something Felix could offer Bianca they were happy. That's all that mattered. He was already working on bigger and better but for now this worked out for everyone and would have to do.

"What do you think?" Gio clicked the remote turning off the TV in their bedroom as Bianca walked in wearing a bathrobe and a towel on her head.

She closed the door behind her. "One bathroom for four people is going to be interesting but I think we'll manage."

Gio pulled her to him as soon as she was close enough and she dropped the clothes she carried onto the bed. "Noah and Roni said we're welcome to live here as long as we need to, but I promise you it's only until 5th Street is up and running again."

With Noah out of a paycheck until 5th Street got going again, Gio would use some of the insurance money to pay rent and help him and Roni with the utilities. Noah had assured him he and Roni would be okay with her pay and what they had in their savings. He'd refused to take any money from Gio at first but Gio insisted.

He slid his hand under her robe, immediately aroused by her soft and warm nakedness. "The only thing you have to promise me," Bianca had her sexy siren eyes stare going and Gio loved it, "is wherever I end up, it'll always be with you."

Gio laid back on the bed bringing her with him. She laughed outright as she toppled over him.

"I promise," he whispered, slipping his tongue in her mouth, already pulling her robe open. "You're with me for good now." Boy, did he mean that. He didn't think he could go a day without her now. "I love you, Bianca."

"I love you, too, Gio." She sucked his tongue before pulling back and looking deep in his eyes. "God, I love you."

EPILOGUE

It's not that Bianca didn't want to live with Roni and Noah anymore but the other spare room was their office now. Even though Roni assured her that for the first few months the baby would sleep in their master bedroom in a cradle, Bianca knew Roni must be anxious to start decorating the nursery.

So she was thrilled when Gio's mom told her about the apartment above her friend's garage being available and very affordable.

She stood at the top of the stairs as the guys hauled the last of their furniture up the stairs. Glancing back into the small apartment she knew this was a far cry from the glamorous life she would've lived if she had stayed with Felix. But even as humble as her life would be for now Bianca couldn't imagine feeling happier than she was now.

Gio assured her things would get better once things really got going with the new gym but Bianca didn't even care. Already with the money he was making she could afford to not have to work and go to school full time. She'd soon be a teacher for the hearing impaired. Something she'd wanted to be since she was a little girl and most importantly she was with Gio every day. Her life couldn't be more perfect.

She walked back into the apartment where Nellie and Roni were helping her unpack the few boxes she and Gio had brought back from her grandma's place just last week. In the few months she and Gio had lived

with Noah and Roni, Bianca had become very close to
them both. It was hard to believe these two were eight
years older than her. She felt more in sync with them
than any of the girlfriends she had in high school.

"Where do you want this, babe?"

Bianca turned to Gio and Abel who held the wood-
en table her dad had built when she was kid. It was
supposed to be a desk but it was so big and sturdy Bianca thought it'd make a perfect kitchen table. Their
eating area was just big enough.

"Over there," she pointed to the kitchen area where
Roni and Nellie stood.

Hector and Noah walked in carrying the last of the
boxes. Hector put his down on the floor looking into it
then turned back to Bianca. "You play chess?"

"It's been a while but I used to be pretty good."

"You should play Hector sometime," Gio said,
wrapping his arms around her waist from behind. "But
I gotta warn you." He stopped to kiss the side of her
face. "Unless you're at like genius level, he'll probably
beat you." Gio tsked. "Total waste."

"Yeah, yeah." Hector rolled his eyes. "Let me know
if you ever wanna play. If anything I could show you a
few tricks." He turned his attention back to Gio. "We
done here?"

"Why?" Abel asked. "You got a date or something?"

Hector bounced his brows with a sexy grin so remi-
niscent of his older brother's. They both looked so
much alike it was uncanny.

Gio laughed. "Yeah, thanks for helping out, man.
We're done here."

One by one they were all thanked as they made
their exit. Bianca closed the door after the last ones,

Roni and Noah, left. When she turned around, Gio pinned her against the door and kissed her softly then pulled away. "Now that we have our own place, what do you say we go to Vegas and get hitched."

Bianca's mouth fell open and she stared at him. "Oh my God. Your mother said you'd do this. She *does* know you like the back of her hand."

Gio's head fell back. "She got to you first, huh? Damn it. I should've known." He lifted an eyebrow. "Let me guess. She made you promise we wouldn't elope."

Bianca tilted her head to the side. "It's not really what I'd want to do." His expression fell making her cup his face and kiss him. "I do wanna get married. I just don't want to elope. I want my mom and grandma there. And I don't need a big reception but I would like a little something. Don't you want all your friends there?"

Gio smiled that smile that made his green eyes so vibrant they almost sparkled. "If that's a yes — you'll marry me, then we can do it anyway you want."

"Yes," she whispered, amazed how the butterflies never stopped anymore when she was around him.

He picked her up so suddenly she squeaked and they both laughed. She wrapped her legs around his waist kissing him wildly like she almost only ever did in private. "Let's go break in our new bedroom."

Bianca smiled inwardly as Gio began walking. Gio had this thing about how innocent she seemed compared to most girls. She agreed, but that didn't mean she didn't have it in her to be risky as long as Gio was okay with it. And so far he had been.

This wouldn't be the first time they'd do it in this apartment. Just days ago when they started moving in the smaller things, they'd known the guys would be there any minute and the front door was unlocked. They'd broken in the kitchen counter. It wasn't as risky as a men's public restroom but it'd been just as hot. Bianca could hardly wait to break in the rest of the apartment, including the stairs outside.

Acknowledgments

I do it every time but I must *must* thank my wonderful husband Mark and my two teens Mark and Megan. Without you none of this could be possible. There is no way I could write as fast as I do if you guys weren't here doing *everything*. You all run the show now here at the house and I'm so grateful for your understanding and support! I'm so very blessed to have you and I love you!!!

I also feel so blessed for the critique partners and new friends I've met along this journey. So I *have* to thank my two wonderful critique partners Tammara Webber and my newest partner, and I swear I'm still so fan girled out about this, Abbi Glines. Thank you two so much for your input, and suggestions. Your comments and honest but very constructive criticism is always spot on and very much appreciated. Not only do I have these two exceptionally talented writers helping me make my stories even better I get to read their stories before they're ever published! Somebody pinch me!!!

Beta readers are so incredibly important and invaluable to a story. It is because of them that some things get toned down greatly, much needed description is added and some scenes get thrown out all together. I'm extremely lucky to have 3 betas now that are speed reading demons. They get my MS and in hours I'm already getting feedback! You three, Judy DeVries, Dawn Winter and my newest addition Theresa (eagle eyes) Wegand are enormous help to me and I thank you from the bottom of my heart!

Thank you to my editor Stephanie Lott aka Bibliophile for all the hard work and effort you put into my stories. As fast as I pound them out I know they are very rough when they get into your hands. I always feel a little bad when I get the edit back and the highlights are endless. LOL =/ You're very much appreciated!

Finally but certainly not least as usual I'd like to thank my readers many who are also bloggers for all the support and enthusiasm about my books. You are why I get up every morning and log onto my computer with a smile. Thank you for your continued loyalty and wonderful emails, PM's comments, posts and tweets! Keep 'em coming! I love hearing from you! <3

About the Author

Elizabeth Reyes is also the author of the best selling Moreno Brothers romance series. For more on her other works and upcoming books visit her website at www.ElizabethReyes.com You can also like her official Facebook fan page at www.facebook.com/TheMorenoBrothers You can follow her on Twitter @AuthorElizabeth and follow her reviews on GoodReads. Feel free to reach out she loves hearing from every single one of you!

A short answer to inevitable question: What's next? I'll be taking a little break from 5th Street to get back to the Moreno world — Vince & Rose's story. I already have the cover and I'll be announcing the name of the series, title of their book, and cover reveal in the coming months! Very excited about getting back to the Morenos. I've missed them! Although I've yet to announce the title of reveal the cover you can add Vince's book to your "To read" shelf on GoodReads here now. Stay tuned for more announcements!

Made in the USA
Charleston, SC
08 August 2012